Penny for your thoughts

An ordinary woman
on an extraordinary journey
to find herself

Patricia Wynne

Penny for your thoughts: An ordinary woman on an extraordinary journey to find herself

© 2021 Patricia Wynne

The moral rights of the author have been asserted.

This novel is entirely a work of fiction. The names, characters and incidents portrayed in it are the work of the author's imagination. Any resemblance to actual persons, living or dead, events or localities is entirely coincidental.

Set in Crimson with Dancing Script and Princes Sofia as display fonts. Made with Reedsy Book Editor. Printed by KDP, An Amazon Company

ISBN 978-1-7397676-0-0

HERBARYBOOKS

Published by Herbary Books
Caernarfon, Wales

www.herbarybooks.com

contact@herbarybooks.com

Contents

Dedication

To my family, whose love and encouragement have always kept me going through the trials and tribulations of life...

Prologue

London... 1959

T he young girl wakes to see bright light seeping through the crack in the curtains. She turns towards her sleeping lover. Smiling, she slips out of bed. If she wakes him, he'll want more, let him sleep. Her lover... that she's been sleeping with for the last three nights... her first ever lover... at nineteen... her body trembles with suppressed joy. And she needs to pee. Naked, she hastily slips on her bra and panties to go to the bathroom shared by the other three rooms on this floor, hoping it will be free. Teeth brushed, a quick wash; a lick and a promise is what her mother would call it, and a quick return to the bedsit before anyone might see her on the landing.

The room is small and sparsely furnished. A bed takes up half the space, leaving room for a chest of drawers and a small table and two chairs in the window. She fills a kettle in the bathroom to set it on a gas ring in the fireplace while dressing in a simple blouse and skirt. The kettle boiling, she makes a cup of Camp coffee to have with a slice of bread and butter. She

1

glances at her watch, then bending over her still sleeping lover, she kisses him lightly on the forehead and whispers... going to work now my love... see you at lunchtime.

A bright October morning, the pale sun shining through mists rising from Parks and Gardens as the stream of commuters and shoppers pour from the Underground. Buses, vans and cars filling the streets with business as usual. She steps out of the door onto Oxford Street into the cold air and pulls her jacket closer, crossing through traffic to disappear down a side road on her way to work.

Just another working day in London.

Chapter 1

London 2009. Week 1: Day 1... Tuesday... Sylvie

S ylvana Crosby was there. She saw it all, as she explained to her older sister Kay later that evening on the phone.

"I'd been shopping in Selfridges for your Birthday present and dying for a coffee and a bite to eat."

"You got my Birthday pressie already?" Kay interjected.

"Well no, I couldn't decide! Don't interrupt or you won't hear all the story! So, as I say, I was coming out of Selfridges and turned left to go to that nice little Bistro in the next street. Anyway, I was on the corner before crossing over and a man on a bike just missed me, I mean he was going so fast down the street he cannoned straight into a woman just near the Bistro. She went flying into the lamp post and I couldn't believe it; he just carried on round the next corner. Well, that's what we worked out. It wasn't an accident; he'd grabbed her shoulder bag, one arm through the strap, talk about expert, it happened so fast I couldn't move for a moment. Then of course, as soon as I caught my breath, I ran over to this woman lying on the ground."

"What? Are you serious? I can't believe it!"

Sylvie ignores her, anxious to continue her story.

"Well, I thought she'd been knocked out, but by the time I got there she's struggling to get up and I said *"Can I help you? Are you hurt?"* Silly question. She was worried about her knees. Well, that's when Robbie came out of the Bistro. You remember young Roberto? Old Italian family, been there for years! So he helped get her up and sat down in the café and Robbie brought her a glass of water. I picked up her travel bag before someone walked off with that too!

Naturally, she was in shock, who wouldn't be? Holding her head, which must have hit the lamp post. No blood or anything. Didn't seem to have any broken bones. She kept muttering... *'What happened?'* She could barely speak. I explained what I'd seen and Rob was furious... "That's modern-day mugging for you. You hear about these things, but that's the first time I've seen it happen." He said he'd phoned the Police; they'd be along in a little while, but I wouldn't hold your breath. There's so much crime going on round here they don't have the time to attend to minor incidents! He's such a sweet boy.

She was looking round for her bag... I tried to comfort her; but she's not likely to see that again! I was really feeling for her. Can you imagine? A woman's bag is her lifeline. Makeup and mirror, and all the things one needs these days; money, credit cards, identification, diary, mobile phone and keys, at the very least! A woman without her bag is like Mona Lisa without a smile, a car without an engine, a story without a plot; a disaster! I mean, losing one's bag; what a nightmare! If that was me, I'd be going crazy! I wonder how anyone can live without a bag. If I ever see a woman without a bag, without any doubt there will be a man right behind her, to supply her every need."

She stops as she hears Kay laughing at the other end of the line.

"Shut up Kay, it's no laughing matter. I asked her what she might have on her that wasn't in the bag; is there anything in her coat pockets? No, there's nothing but gloves, old tissues and a lip salve. She was saying… *'I have no money'*… she looked absolutely shocked!

I pulled the case round to show her… *at least your travel case is still here.* She gives me a funny look; like she's puzzled. She said… *'That's not mine, I've never seen it before.'* Well, I know it is, I have the image in my mind. She was definitely pulling it along when the bike hit her. You know, I have a feeling that something's not quite right… I'm beginning to think this woman may be older that she appears, a grandmother even. She might have dementia. I think of our own Grammy, you know, she's been gone a few years now, but she was my protector and I still miss her."

"Yes, I know, I do too. Poor lady. Go on, what happened next?"

"Well, I tell her I'm Sylvie, and ask for her name and she crumples up all teary, but she doesn't answer. She's looking so upset, I put an arm around her shoulders and she starts sobbing."

"You are such a soft touch sis. This sounds like another scam! Did she ask for money?"

"No, of course not. This is serious! She calmed down eventually, but she just couldn't say who she is! Only that she's on her way to work! It's funny though, I thought that if she's on her way to work she might know where we are. So I ask her. She says she's not sure but she usually has lunch at this little Italian place… with candles in Chianti bottles and red checked tablecloths and she usually had Spaghetti Bolognese with chips for 2/6d. Then… you'll never believe it, but Rob's grandfather Giuseppe comes over, all excited. He was behind the bar and he's overheard what she said. He sits down and tells us that, what she's described, was just like that when he was young in the 50's and 60's, but of course it's changed over the years, and it's bigger because they took over next door as well."

"Oh my god! You could win the Booker Prize with this story! Sorry, go on."

"I looked at her and she'd gone even paler if that were possible. Looked as though she's going to faint and kept saying... *'I don't understand'!* All I could do is tell her to take deep breaths, then Giuseppe brought some brandy, bless him."

"What about the Police?"

"Well... eventually a young Policewoman arrived and asked for all the details. I told her everything I'd seen, but, of course, this woman didn't remember anything. But she did know everything about her bag and what was in it... she knew exactly! A tan leather bag with a fringe, small purse containing about £5.00, a small notebook and pencil and a diary. Well, we were all curious. I mean, £5.00 isn't much in London these days! And no Credit cards... no keys... no makeup... and then... no phone! She just shook her head and looked bewildered at all these questions. Well, the Policewoman was asking her name and she mumbled something... the Policewoman seemed to hear Ida Knowles and wrote that down. I'm not so sure... I don't think she remembers her name! But when she was asked for her address she looked really upset. So out of the blue, without really thinking, I said that she's staying with me and gave my own details."

"I don't believe it! You didn't? Yes, OK, you would. Mad or what?"

"You know I just kept thinking of how Grammy might have needed help from a stranger. A Police message came through and this Policewoman said they'd let us know if anything turns up, but usually nothing does. After a while, Ida, if that's her name, calmed down a bit as she finished the brandy. Then she said, *'I must find Davy.'* Naturally I asked *Who's Davy* and she says he's her boyfriend."

"Whoa! A boyfriend? At her age?"

"That was my reaction too! Ok... so I told her we'll find the boyfriend, but I'm not letting her out of my sight. I didn't think she'd be safe on her own. She started to protest, but hey, I can see she's in need of protection and I'm determined to help this woman. So I ask where are we going to find him. She says it's only round the corner in Oxford Street, he has a flat there. Well, I'm impressed. Anyone with a flat in Oxford Street had to be someone rich and important. I asked Rob to hold onto the suitcase. She led me across Oxford Street and towards Bond Street to a door between shops with the name *Gilbert Court* on a brass plate at the side, above a panel of bell pushes. She looked confused, as if she was not sure... she had no key, of course. Then a door opened with a man leaving and he held the door open for us when she said she'd lost her key. I followed her up the stairs to the second floor. She was breathing heavily and I took her hand and I asked her what's wrong. Then she said she doesn't recognise any of it. Where's the door to number 4? She's panicking... saying... *'Everything's different! Where's Davy?'* I have to help her back down the stairs. Then I'm trying to get her back to the Café to work this all out."

"*This is turning into a Soap Opera! OK, go on.*"

"Well, she thought if she could go back to her place of employment in the next street then everything might fall into place, so we walked around a couple of blocks but she couldn't recognise anywhere familiar. *'It should be right here'* she kept saying... *'A Photography Studio in a big old building on that side of the square.'* All we can see is a big block of flats. By now she was almost in a state of collapse so I got her back into the Bistro. I ordered coffee and cakes. I was determined to get the whole story, but that wasn't so easy. I said to her I can see she has a problem and I want to help if I can. She said she's very grateful, but she's obviously very confused and doesn't know what's happening, and she's getting tearful again.

I asked about the boyfriend. Who is he and where does he work? That gets her started. His name is Davy and he plays the double-bass.

That's all she remembers. My ears perk up; naturally, as a singer I know all the clubs in London, so I could know him. She says he's currently at the Café de Paris, very upmarket! So we should be able to find him there, by the weekend anyway."

"So the mystery woman could be sorted soon then?"

"Well, I hope so... I felt sort of responsible for her now... I told her she's coming home with me... and she tried to protest but she looked relieved and kept thanking me. But honestly, we can't have another homeless woman on the streets! So I retrieved the trolley case from Rob and took her arm."

"Oh my dear sister!"

"Whatever possessed me I have no idea, except that I knew that's what Grammy would have done. You know she was kindness itself and wouldn't see anyone in trouble without trying to help. Remember how she used to say, *"That's what we did in the war. We'd all help each other out; cuppa tea, food, whatever we had, bed for the night. Shows how human you are, during hard times."* The way she took us in, both of us, whenever Mum couldn't cope with us and decided to go travelling again. She was a real good soul, our Grammy. I find it hard to pass by any homeless person on the street, but I can't help everyone. This one is different, I feel I know her."

"Sylvie, my dearest sister, I might have known you can never resist a hard luck story. But I do understand. You are a brick! And you tell a good story! What can I do to help?"

"I'll let you know. Tune in tomorrow for the next episode! Goodnight Sis. Love you."

Maybe I am mad... she thought.

Week 1: Day 1... Tuesday... Penny

I'm so confused. How could I forget my own name? But try as I might, there's nothing in my mind except Davy. What did he call me? *Baby... my love... darling...* That's not a name. What's wrong with my memory? What do they call me at work? *Here, I've got some more printing for you.* Don't I have a name? The tea lady calls me *Love... or Duckie...* but that's what she calls everyone! What did Mummy call me? *Darling... good girl... Freckles...* Yes, that's what they called me! Freckles! And that's not a name.

This woman, Sylvie, that's her name, is determined to take me home with her and I am very grateful, as I don't know what else I could do. It isn't far by bus to Paddington and Sylvie's chatting, saying how she'd inherited it from her Grandmother; that's how lucky she is. The front door to the small terraced house opens into a cosy living room full of interesting objects, shelves crammed with books and walls covered in pictures. "Welcome to my home." she says. "Meet Barney! I hope you're not allergic to cats...", she adds as a beautiful black and white cat uncurls itself on a comfy chair. I stroke its lovely smooth coat. I've never had a cat, because Mum always said animals are unhygienic.

Sylvie helps me up the stairs to a small bedroom, bringing up the case and laying it on the bed. "This bed's very comfy, I used to sleep here, but it's had a new mattress, and the bathroom's just here, very handy in the night. Why don't you freshen up while I go down to put the kettle on. I'll get a towel for you. Take your clothes out of the case and hang them up."

I'm so grateful for a chance to sit down quietly and think about all that's happened. My mind is in such a turmoil and nothing makes any sense, and my heart's beating hard and fast. I'm feeling so lost, cold and fragile. Everything seems to be different; people look strange, the speed of passing traffic, even the look of the buildings is unfamiliar, as though I'm lost in a dream and can't wake up.

Looking at the case that Sylvie insists belongs to me, it doesn't look familiar. I would have expected to see the large leather Gladstone bag that's really heavy to carry, but examining this, I decide that wheels on a case are a great idea! It opens with an all-round zip and I carefully inspect the contents. Lovely clothes, though nothing looks familiar and I'm sure they won't fit me; being far too big and baggy. Three tops, a cardigan, one skirt and a pair of trousers to go on hangers. Sensible underwear, pyjamas, cotton dressing gown and a bag of toiletries. In the bottom are a pair of sandals and slippers. In a zip pocket I find a new notebook, with nothing written in it, and a small framed picture of four smiling faces. Still, there's not a flicker of recognition. I think this case can't possibly be mine, but whoever it belongs to, I'm grateful for its contents. Hopefully, whoever has my case will be just as thankful.

I go onto the landing to find the compact bathroom and I'm surprised to see a shower, having only seen them at the swimming baths. Then, as I wash my face and look into the mirror, I come face to face with my own mother. I peer at the reflection in shock with panic rising… *This isn't me! What's happened? Who am I?*

Sylvie knocks on the door. "Here's a towel for you."

I just stand there… I don't know what to say… but she must see the look on my face and she comes to me and holds my shoulders. I can hardly breathe. All I can say is… *"I'm old. I look like my mother."* Sylvie leads me into the bedroom and we sit down on the bed. "It appears you've lost your memory, that's all."

"I don't even know my name… How can this be?" I'm aware of rising hysteria in my voice. *"I'm an old woman… what year is it?"*

"It's 2009. What year should it be?"

It takes a few moments before I can speak, thoughts racing round my mind in ever decreasing circles. I can hear my voice shaking as I whisper... *"1959 and I'm 19."*

"Hang on... that's 50 years ago! And that means you're now 69..." Sylvie looks at me in disbelief.

I'm speechless for some time, trying to catch my breath. *"I can't believe what's happening. "How can it be? What happened to the last 50 years? How can I lose 50 years?"*

Sylvie gives me a hug and I can't help myself... I burst into tears. Sylvie's so kind...

"Don't worry, I'm here for you. Life can be very confusing sometimes. We just have to trust that it will sort itself out in time. Just give it time." I really don't understand why this woman I've only just met is helping me. I only know how grateful I am for her kindness.

"I don't know what I'd have done if you weren't there. I'm fine, thanks to you. "

"That's it! Put a brave face on, pull yourself together, get a grip, and pull your socks up while you're at it. Except you're not wearing any." Sylvie's laughing and the cold fear in my heart begins to drain away, as if the sun has just come out.

"I'm making supper; we've got soup, then quiche and salad, if that's ok? Ready for a glass of wine?" Sylvie rises to go back downstairs. *"Yes, thank you."* I'm not sure what quiche might be, but think that whatever Sylvie makes will be very nice. But wine? I've only ever had wine at a posh dinner I was once invited to.

The glass of red wine warms me through and quiche turns out to be cheese and onion pie, only better. I'm feeling so tired and as I relax into the comfortable chair, I'm lost in thought. What could have happened? Who am I? Then I'm dozing off.

* * *

"Penny for your thoughts?" Sylvie's speaking to me.

"*Penny...?*" I query, wondering what she means.

"Could that be your name, I wonder?" Sylvie looks at me quizzically.

"*Penny...*" I'm trying it out and it feels familiar. A name suddenly comes to me. "*Penny Lane...*" I say, without really knowing why.

"Ok, Penny Lane... that will do!" I'm not sure if Sylvie believes me and I'm not sure I do either, but that will suffice for now.

I can hear music playing in the background while we relax in the cosy sitting room, gentle jazz that sounds familiar. Sylvie's encouraging me to talk and I find myself telling her about how I'd met Davy while working as a Photographer in a hotel on Guernsey. How he'd asked me to take pictures of him while he played Vibraphone in his posh white jacket, and how we'd had fallen in love during the long, sunny, glorious summer on that beautiful island.

The music relaxes me so, or is it the wine? I can barely recall Sylvie helping me up the stairs, falling asleep as soon as my head hit the pillow.

A song buzzing around in my head... 'I didn't know what time it was... till there was you'... I don't hear the door, but here is Davy, his cold face nuzzling into my warmth as I wrap my arms around his coat that he hasn't even taken off yet. I can feel the texture of the fabric, wet from the rain. As he takes off his wet clothes, hardly pausing between kisses, I feel such longing for his touch, his loving arms, his being, bathing in a sea of warm, rapturous bliss. I'm home.

'Oh... what a lovely time it was... so sublime it was too...'

Chapter 2

Week 1: Day 2… Wednesday… Penny

Sunlight streaming between the window curtains wakes me, slowly bringing life back into stiff limbs. Opening my bleary eyes, I don't recognise the room at first, before memory comes flooding back. At last, memory of the previous day gradually returns. I can hear Sylvie singing in the bathroom. Yet I'd been with Davy during the night and the feeling was so intense, I'd expected to wake up next to him. I don't want to wake up here; I want to be back with him.

"Are you awake?" Sylvie pops her head around the door. "Just going down to put the kettle on, come and get a cuppa. Then you can have a bath or shower, whatever you like, before you get dressed. OK?"

As I slip my legs out of bed they feel heavy and unfamiliar, but then, so does everything. The slippers and dressing gown fit and I'm suitably attired to go downstairs.

"Tea or Coffee?" Sylvie asks.

"I don't mind thanks, anything going."

"Well, I like coffee in the morning. Filter coffee suit you?"

I smell the aroma. *"We always have Camp coffee, out of a bottle."*

"I think Grammy used to have that!" Sylvie laughs.

I enjoy the coffee with a spoonful of sugar and a little milk.

"Hope you slept ok?" Sylvie asks. I nod. I don't know whether to tell Sylvie that I'd expected to wake up with Davy. Not yet anyway.

"Well, I think we should start getting you sorted out. You must have family somewhere? And we need to go to the Bank and get you another Bank card. What Bank are you with?"

I just can't think.

"You don't remember?"

"I don't have a Bank."

"Everyone has a Bank. Can't live without one! And you'll be drawing a Pension by now."

I don't know what to say. I can't remember ever having a Bank Account or a Pension. It's all too much to think about.

"Never mind, all in good time. You go up now for a bath or shower before you get dressed while I make us breakfast."

I obediently go upstairs and decide to run a bath as I can't work out how to use the shower. While it's running I take a look at the jewellery I'd taken off the night before; a fancy gold chain necklace, pearl earrings and several rings, not knowing where they'd come from. They look expensive. A single gold band would seem to be a wedding ring, and three others are set with sparkling and glowing stones. Diamonds? Rubies? I can't remember having any jewellery, except maybe a couple of pairs of cheap clip-on earrings and some beads.

As I undress, I suddenly catch sight of my naked self in the mirror. I'm shocked at the unfamiliar image. What are these rolls of fat and sagging belly, this wrinkled skin? Whose body is this? What happened to my young slim figure? I can't believe what I'm seeing and stifle a sob, not wanting Sylvie to hear me crying again. Looking at the clothes again, I begin to realise how they are designed to camouflage this old body.

The bath is so warm and relaxing I could stay in it much longer, but I don't want to keep Sylvie waiting. I can hear her singing in the kitchen below. She reminds me of my mother; always singing when she was busy.

It's such a lovely sunny day. I choose the skirt and a loose flowery top, nothing like the buttoned blouse that I'd normally wear. And sandals. The clothes I'd been wearing the day before are more practical; trousers and a plain cotton top that slips over the head, no buttons, with a loose jacket and comfortable shoes. Nothing feels familiar.

Sylvie has made a good healthy breakfast. Scrambled eggs and mushrooms with toast. And more coffee. A good start to the day.

I'm determined to get one thing straight and lay the jewellery on the table. *"I'll need money and these must be worth something. Perhaps I could take them to a jeweller or pawnshop, so I can pay my way."*

Sylvie touches my hand. "Please don't even think about it. I can afford to look after you till we've found out who you are. You'll probably turn out to be filthy rich and then you can reward me handsomely! Look… this is a wedding ring… you've certainly been married! And I bet your family are frantically trying to find you anyway. I could search for Missing Persons online. Why didn't I think of that before? You just put your fancy jewellery on madam, they're yours."

I'm baffled, but indebted to this new friend who is able to cope with this modern life.

"I've been thinking." Sylvie looks serious. "My sister Kay is a Psychotherapist. She's very good… has a thriving practice in Slough. I've phoned her and she's very interested in seeing you, if you think that would help."

I have no idea what that means, but I'm ready to trust Sylvie's judgement.

"I think she may be able to help; you know, release your memories. Practises Hypnotherapy, that's the sort of thing she does."

That sounds interesting and I start to feel a frisson of excitement, rather than fear. *"Hypnosis? I've heard about that. Must have read about it somewhere. Maybe in a magazine."*

"Good. She's suggested we go over tomorrow. It's usually her free day, so she's invited us for lunch. How does that sound?"

I want to know more about Kay, and Sylvie is glad to sing her sister's praises.

Kay is her elder sister by seven years. Their mother was married to her father Henry for only a few years before she left him to join the hippie movement. What's that exactly? Anyway, Kay is the clever one of the family and did well at University, then married James who is something important in the Civil service. They live in a beautiful house in the country with two dogs and have two children doing well at University. The perfect life!

I'm impressed. I begin to wonder what I've actually done in the fifty years I can't recall. Have I done well? Did I marry Davy? Was he successful and did we have lovely children? Or did I marry someone else? I must be married, I'm wearing a wedding ring. Have I done all the things I'd dreamed of; to be a great Photographer, to travel the world, to write of my adventures? Who am I anyway?

My mind is a turmoil of indistinct impressions. Although I'm feeling so alone in the world, maybe I'm not. Where is my family, if I have one? I must have a life, somewhere. What happened to make my memories disappear? So many questions crowd in on me.

As Sylvie has things to get on with, I decide to go out for a walk to clear my head. I have to convince Sylvie that I do know my way around London, so she finds a bag for me to use and a purse with some cash. She's so concerned that I might get lost, she writes down her name, address and telephone number, with strict instructions to get a taxi back if I can't remember the way. "Here's the spare key. If I'm not here when you get back, just let yourself in. OK? And help yourself to something from the fridge when you're hungry. While I'm out, I'll get you a cheap mobile so we can keep in touch."

Again, I have no idea what she's talking about. "It's a phone that you can use anywhere" Sylvie explains. Sounds like science fiction. So much has changed in fifty years.

"Just a minute, don't hang that bag on one shoulder, that makes it too easy for a passing thief, if you remember! Keep the bag slung across your body, so there's no chance of losing it. And I've got a street map for you. Look, this is where we are, I'll mark it for you. Where do you think you'll go?"

"I need some fresh air. I think I can find Kensington Gardens."

" Well, have fun and don't get lost. Once I've been online, I may have news for you," she calls as I leave the house. 'Online' is another mystery that I can't fathom, but that can wait.

The noise and smells of the busy roads feel overpowering... big, shiny cars with darkened windows sail past... and people look different to how I remember... I notice Arabs in flowing, white gowns and headdresses and dark glasses! But I find my way along the Bayswater Road until I reach the tranquillity of Kensington Gardens and slowly meander along the leafy paths I loved to explore with Davy. The trees are already starting to lose their glorious gold and red foliage and decaying leaves strew the ground. I pick up a newly fallen leaf and marvel at its beauty, the symmetry of shape, the strength of the veins holding it together in still vibrant colours. Kicking through the crisp leaves like a little kid... a memory of walks with my parents down country lanes when I was very young, Dad in his Air Force blue uniform and Mum in a flowery dress holding my hands. They would tell me the names of all the trees. I wish I could remember. I collect more leaves as I walk along, all different. A bouquet of colour to take home to Sylvie. Home? Where is home? Why can't I remember?

The late summer sun is warm and I find a bench away from the path where I can sit quietly and reflect on my situation. It seems that all I know about myself is from fifty years ago. It's as if I've been transmuted into another body, another person that I know nothing about. Am I who I think I am? Or am I someone else? I can't stop hearing the lines of a song... so melancholic... *'The Shadow of your Smile... when you are gone'*... yet it's lovely.

I'm so tired after all that's happened. Sitting quietly in the sun, relaxing my mind and body, I'm melding with the drone of insects all around and foliage rustling in the gentle breeze, as if I were part of nature, and nothing else matters.

* * *

I feel the texture of coarse sand between my fingers; lying on a warm beach. As I turn over, there is Davy, bronzed and beautiful, beside me. It's so hot and the cool blue water beckons. As I rise to my feet, he looks up at me. 'Race you,' I beckon and run down the beach into the gentle waves lapping the shore, relishing the weightlessness of my body as I swim out to deeper water. He comes up right beside me and I swim away, teasing him to chase me, right out of the sea and back up the beach where we collapse onto our beach towels, bodies entwined. I pull away. "Not in public!" I caution, looking around at the families nearby, but they are all busy packing up their things. We were never so intimate as at the beach, near naked bodies touching, arousing my senses, but it's not done to be too familiar in public.

Davy fishes his watch out of his jacket pocket. "Time we were heading back, if we're to catch the last boat" he grins, "Unless you want to be marooned on this desert island with me!"

"Yes please..." I laugh.

Walking back across the island, holding hands, through honeysuckle scented lanes, I feel as though I'm in heaven. We don't have much to say, savouring our closeness on the short boat trip back to the mainland.

* * *

As I open my eyes and find myself back in the Park, I feel a sudden surge of panic again. Have I been dreaming? Was it simply a memory of being with Davy? Maybe this is a dream and I'll wake up back with Davy again. It feels so real while I'm with him. I'm near to tears again, but wipe my eyes, take a deep breath and resolve to be strong. I can adapt to this brave new world.

* * *

The sound of music slowly permeates my thoughts. The gentle chords of a guitar nearby beckons. A soft Irish melody. *'She stepped away from me and she moved through the fair... and fondly I watched her move here and move there... and she made her way homeward with one star awake... as a swan in the evening moves over the lake.'* I'm singing the words softly as I leave my seat to investigate. There, under a tree, I see a young man playing a guitar, oblivious to passers-by. He's obviously practising in the peaceful tranquillity of the Park.

As I stop to listen, he looks up and smiles in a warm friendly way. "You know this song? I love those old Irish tunes." He must have heard me.

"I'm sorry, I didn't mean to intrude," I apologise.

"Not at all, it's nice to see you again."

Now I'm startled. "I didn't know we'd met."

"Well, not exactly, but I'd like to thank you for your kind contribution yesterday."

19

I look around for someone that he may be talking to behind me.

"You don't remember? I was busking in Leicester Square when you dropped £10 in my hat! That's very generous. Thank you."

I'm shocked. £10 sounds more than generous. More than I've ever earned in a day, or even a week, more like a month, as far as I can remember.

"Your performance must have been incredible," is all I can say, thinking that a very special concert wouldn't cost that much. What had I been thinking? Then I recall that was fifty years ago and how so much has changed. I'm beginning to feel weak and lightheaded.

"Hey, you don't look well. Come, sit down here." He gets up and leads me to a convenient seat. "Are you alright?"

"I'll be fine, thank you, just a little faint…" feeling grateful for his support. "I've had a bit of a shock, that's all."

"You can tell me all about it if you like… or not. I don't want to be nosey. Not true, I'm really nosey! I'm a writer when I'm not busking and always listening out for interesting stories. I'm Dylan, by the way. Pleased to meet you…", proffering his hand.

I can't help but warm to this young man, who seems genuinely interested, and shake his hand.

"I'm going to get a coffee, why don't I buy you one? I owe you. The Café's not far, right by the lake." He picks up his guitar and backpack and leads the way.

Over tea and cake conversation comes easily. I'm taking in his dark good looks… not very tall, but tanned and fit-looking, with dark curly hair and deep dark eyes. I comment that he looks almost Mediterranean, though I don't know why I said that. "Italian grandfather…" he grinned. "Prisoner of war, working on my grandmother's family farm. He never went back!"

He tells me about his life, how he lives on a boat on the Canal with his girlfriend, among other boat people, mostly musicians and artists of some kind. I'm intrigued and when he extends an invitation to meet his friends at an open-air exhibition of their work the following weekend at Little Venice, which sounds exciting, I ask him to write down the details, sure Sylvie would love to go as well.

Dylan asks about me, but I'm reluctant to tell too much before I even know who he is. So I keep it simple.

"I seem to have lost fifty years of my memory. So I don't know where I belong, or who I am."

Of course, as a writer, he's intrigued and begins to ply me with questions. But it's all too much.

"That's all I can say, until I know you better. I have a friend helping me. It only happened yesterday. I was knocked down and had my handbag stolen, so I have no identification. I'm still very confused..." feeling tearful again.

"Wow! That must be pretty traumatic. But I would like to know more, if you wouldn't mind a humble writer getting involved? What a fascinating story! I'd love to help you find yourself."

He's so enthusiastic I have to smile. I think that anyone else would back off so as not to get involved with a strange old woman's problems. But I like this young man who, although a stranger, feels somehow familiar.

Dylan walks with me as far as Lancaster Gate, as he's on his way home to Little Venice, chatting all the way. I have to assure him that I know where I am and continue to the end of Kensington Gardens, finding my way back to Sylvie's house without any difficulty.

Having lost track of time, though it must be mid-afternoon, I'm glad to let myself in and go upstairs. A cool breeze stirs the window curtains and I lay back on the bed trying to recall everything that happened, before and after I'd been mugged. That's what they call it, *being mugged*. Which makes me a prize mug, I suppose. Not funny!

Dylan had said something about Time Travel. He said my story reminded him of a film he'd seen. He was fascinated with the idea of Time Travel. I'm drifting off...

* * *

Davy is saying "See you at lunch. Love you". He's still half asleep, but I'm ready to go to work, only a short walk to the Photography Studio, where I work in the darkroom. I kiss him goodbye and leave the flat. When I say flat, that's a slight exaggeration; it's only one room. Actually, this is Davy's place. I'm supposed to be living at the Women's Hostel in Bloomsbury, but I only go there now to collect my post. This is my secret, so far.

As I step onto Oxford Street in the autumn sunshine, I feel so happy I could skip to work. He loves me, I love him. 'When I fall in Love... it will be Forever...' I'd heard it on the radio last night... Nat King Cole. I turn left and cross Oxford Street then into the side street leading to the Studio.

Then... someone is helping me up off the pavement near the Italian Café. Go back... go back... I must go back...

I awake in a lather of perspiration, my body thrashing about, full of fear and anguish, wet with tears, sobbing...

I've lost him... my love, my love. Did I call out loud?

* * *

It's late afternoon when Sylvie comes back and as she reaches the foot of the stairs she thinks she hears sobbing. She wonders if she should go up to see if Penny is alright, or maybe give her a few minutes? Instead she goes into the kitchen to put the kettle on, making as much noise as she can and singing, listening out for her. Then she calls upstairs. "Penny, are you there? Just making a cup of tea." Going upstairs she taps on her door. "Are you alright?" and opens the door a fraction. Penny rises from the bed unsteadily and comes towards her.

Sylvie puts her hand out to comfort her that turns into a hug as Penny stumbles against her.

"I was dreaming," she sobs. She holds her for a few moments as her sobs subside.

"Well, there now," Sylvie's talking like her Grammy did when she'd been upset. "Just a dream, eh?"

"I'm so sorry. Don't know what came over me."

"Nothing to be sorry about. You have every reason to be upset. I'd be worried if you weren't. Here dry your eyes. There's a cup of tea in the kitchen and I've got cake!"

Tea and cake; the ultimate panacea of the phlegmatic British. Grammy used to say that during the Blitz, even after a bomb had blasted your home and loved ones out of existence, someone would offer a cup of tea, as if that made everything alright.

As Penny relaxes, she recounts her walk in Kensington Gardens and meeting this busker Dylan in the Park. That worries Sylvie a bit; who knows what his motives might be.

"Did you get his name, apart from Dylan?" Penny shakes her head.

"If he's a writer we should be able to look him up, unless he's not been published. Anyone can say they're a writer. I suppose I'm a bit paranoid about strangers these days. I've been taken for a ride more than once. I have a chequered history, as Kay puts it! Anyway, it will be interesting to meet him at Little Venice on Saturday. I'm so used to being with people who live an alternative lifestyle and I did consider living on the canals at one time, so I should feel at home. It was only when Grammy died and I inherited the house, that I had to choose between selling it or living here permanently and decided to live here as it was my only security. I'm so glad I did, not only because it's worth so much more now, but also my refuge against the world."

After supper Penny has recovered her composure, and wants to know more about Sylvie, who is happy to explain all her family's various relationships. This seems to help her temporarily put aside her own predicament. Sylvie tells her about Grammy and how she practically brought up her and her sister when their mother was on the road. She'd spent most of her childhood with mum and her hippie friends, especially in the summer when she wasn't at school. Until she was nine, most of her schooling had been with other travelling children, learning about so much more than the three R's from the other travellers, most of whom had such fascinating knowledge and ideas. Sometimes Carlos, her Papi was there with them and sometimes they'd go out to Spain to be with him in his cabana by the sea, though his usual home was in Barcelona, where his work was centred.

Penny seems much better when they retire to bed early, as the following day would be the trip to Slough. Sylvie doesn't tell her that she's checked with the Café de Paris, who have no knowledge of any Bass player called Davy, which doesn't surprise her, or that she's looked online at the Missing Persons Register and found no description of anyone who might be her. She doesn't want to upset her even more. She phones her sister to tell her about the progress with her newfound friend.

"I've realised that Penny... if that's her real name... Penny Lane she told me.. yes that's right... she hasn't just lost her memory. She's lost fifty years of memory!"

Kay is suitably shocked. "Don't you think you should have let the police deal with her? Maybe she should have been taken to hospital!"

"Really Kay... wash my hands of an inconvenient problem? She's not ill or injured. And what then? What would they do with her if nobody claims her? Let her rot in an institution? Or put her out on the street? I don't know... really... I just feel responsible for her... and I want to try to help find her identity. I'm hoping you'll be able to do something about that. What do you think?"

"Of course I'll do what I can to help... but I do think the authorities have more resources to deal with a situation like this. Can't you at least let them know?"

"You know what I think about authorities, don't you? I'd hate for her to fall into their hands! Are you with me on this? Because I think we need to support her... financially as well... and I know you can afford to help there Sis!"

Kay agrees that she'll do whatever she can to help Penny recall her identity. It will be quite a challenge. Yes... now she's looking forward to doing some research before meeting them tomorrow at the station.

Chapter 3

~~~❧~~~

Week 1: Day 3… Thursday… Visit to Stoke Poges

Another sunny day dawns. The days are drawing in, but the Indian Summer is a blessing of warmth and vibrant colour before winter sets in.

A good breakfast sets them up for the day and the journey by train goes smoothly enough. Kay meets them at Slough station to drive them to her palatial home. "Well, it's palatial to me," Sylvie had told Penny on the way… "though Kay seems to take it all for granted, as though it's her birth right. Of course, Henry, her Father, comes from a wealthy family and is himself not only a Barrister, but also a QC. He has a very spacious property in London, where he lives alone, with no-one but a housekeeper. Allegedly! I do wonder about him; no women, no scandal! Or maybe the faithful housekeeper provides for all his needs!" which amused them both.

Leaving the main road, they follow a narrow country lane bordered with lush hedges, snaking between sun-warmed fields of harvested crops strewn about with hay bales and copses of trees dotted about the landscape; a picture of the English countryside at its best. They pass a few scattered houses, picturesque old cottages and others proclaiming ostentatious wealth, before turning into a drive that winds around a sloping lawn to approach the house on a small rise. *The Beeches* on a fancy sign. Built in the thirties in a much-loved colonial-style, the house sits gracefully in its privileged position overlooking a small hamlet below. With is long front veranda and tall chimneys, this house encapsulates the graciousness of English country living. For the well-heeled anyway.

They are greeted by the dogs. A little cocker spaniel bounds up to be petted and a big old yellow Labrador ambles up more sedately. As an old friend, he nuzzles into Sylvie as she crouches down to stroke his head affectionately. "Hey Buster. How are you, old feller?" He's been part of the family for years and always knows her in spite of infrequent visits. The younger dog, Patch, is excitable and eager to investigate these new arrivals.

As Penny looks around, she's impressed. "It's lovely. How wonderful to have a home like this," her eyes shining with admiration.

Kay is delighted to show them around. "This is James' family home. He bought it from his parents when they wanted to downsize and I have to say, I feel privileged to be living here."

She leads the way into the large conservatory, a later addition at the back, that looks onto more sun dappled gardens and orchard, with a vegetable garden round one side. Kay has prepared a delicious lunch ready for them in the shade, with a cool breeze coming through the open doors and conversation flows easily between the 'Oohs' and 'Ahhs' of appreciation.

As they clear away, Kay suggests that Sylvie take the dogs for a walk while she talks with Penny, which she's glad to do.

* * *

Sylvie follows the dogs through the garden, reflecting on how much she misses the country while in London, although she sometimes manages to escape to visit Angie in Wales. Her mother lives in a small cottage in the hills, which she loves, with friends like her; single women who thrive in their rural setting, sustained by their meagre pensions and making art and handicrafts to sell at local fairs. Although she used to go abroad a lot, helping out in third world countries or attending conferences on Civil Rights and Women's Aid she hardly goes anywhere these days. She used to visit Spain quite a lot, to see Carlos, and he may have been to her cottage more than a few times. They still seem to be passionately in love, although they can't seem to live together for long. Sylvie thinks about how she loves them both dearly and would like to be with them both more, but it doesn't happen often enough.

Taking the lane leading away from the house, dogs obedient on leads, they soon reach the common where they can run free. *Gypsy Lane* it's called, though there are no gypsies around these days. She imagines they used to camp here on the common, with their grubby children and dogs around a camp fire. Not allowed now, of course. Health and Safety! So sad. Sometimes she thinks that she'd love to go back to the old days, when life seemed more simple, but maybe not. Who's she kidding?

The common leads into a wood and Sylvie and the dogs wander beneath old trees, scuffling through leaves which are beginning to fall in glorious autumnal colours. Feeling soothed and refreshed... she should do this more often. Her visits here are rare these days, except for Birthday celebrations and an occasional Christmas. Kay is usually so busy with her Therapy Clinic and maybe she herself just doesn't make the time.

She begins to think about how often they even phone each other, just to say, *how are you* and *what are you up to?* Not often enough. Imagine what would happen if she'd been mugged and lost her memory. How long would it be before anyone missed her? Would anyone help her? Would the Police help? Why hadn't she told the Policewoman? Right, she hadn't realised then about Penny's lost memory.

She's stopped in her tracks, suddenly overwhelmed with sadness.

How stupid can she be? All this time she's been treating Penny as though she's a senile old woman and now she's beginning to feel the way she must be feeling; panic-stricken, desperate, lost!

'I'm supposed to be an actor, for goodness sake. Why haven't I taken the trouble to feel into her state of mind before now? I hope Kay has more sense than me; after all she is a trained Counsellor and Psychotherapist. I hope for Penny's sake she can understand what I've missed.'

* * *

Sylvie returns to the house with confused feelings and lets herself in. Kay and Penny are already in the kitchen, brewing tea and cutting cake; enough to make them all feel better! Kay is her usual bright and breezy self, while Penny looks a little downcast.

She gives Kay a quizzical look as if to ask, how did it go? Kay shakes her head very slightly, as a sign not to ask. So Sylvie gives a colourful description of her walk, describing the antics of the dogs, watching Penny's reaction as she starts to look more cheerful.

Kay says that she'd like to see Penny again but she won't have any free time till next week. "I'd like you to stay here for a few days, so we can work in more depth, if that's alright with you Penny. We seem to have made a good start anyway." Penny nods.

Sylvie's glad Kay will be taking her on, as she doesn't know what else she could do.

"Not a problem, I have work next week, so that would be better from my point of view anyway." Kay's asking about this work. "A small part in a new soap… might lead to something permanent." She tries to sound enthusiastic, though the prospect of getting up early every morning to go to the studios for the foreseeable future is somewhat daunting. "And we have an Art Exhibition to go to on Saturday… with the Water Gypsies in Little Venice," she adds.

"How lovely, wish I could join you." Kay sounds enthusiastic but Sylvie knows she won't come. Her sister only comes to London if it's something really important; shopping or a Conference would be important enough. Whenever she does come, they always meet up for coffee or lunch, but she rarely comes to the house, saying it's too far out of the way. Sylvie wonders if her memories are too much; of Angie leaving her there when it suited her, especially coming up to teenage years. When she was twelve, she went to Boarding school at her Father's expense, getting top marks all round, which really helped her get to University. At that time Sylvie was happy to stay with Grammy, and Angie was happy to leave her there.

They decide that Sylvie will see Penny onto the train on Monday (though she protests she can get there on her own) and Kay will pick her up at the station.

Kay takes them back to the station before the rush hour, though it's busy enough and they get home in the dusk. Penny is very quiet and Sylvie lets her be, lost in her own thoughts.

After supper she thinks Penny might like to see a movie and finds a DVD of one she'd had a small part in. She seems to enjoy it and is moved to tears when Sylvie's character dies in a car crash. Maybe it's cathartic to have a good cry about something other than herself.

Sylvie makes them both a hot toddy and Penny gets quite chatty, asking about her acting career. "Such as it is!" says Sylvie. "I'd much rather be singing in small jazz clubs, although I have no illusions about making the Big Time. Once I auditioned for a part in a West End Musical and got to be understudy to a supporting character, but I only performed one night when she was ill." Penny says she loves singing too. She loves Ol' Blue Eyes... Frank Sinatra. They look through her pile of old records and play her favourites joining in a chorus of 'In the wee small hours'... Penny enjoying the whisky. She sleeps well.

Chapter 4

Week 1: Day 4... Friday... Penny

W aking to a new day I feel as though I've been sleeping for an eternity. I'm feeling disturbed, sure I was dreaming about something important, but all impressions fade as I open my eyes. Where am I? Recollection returns as I recognise Sylvie's bedroom.

Sitting on the loo, something comes back to me... *I'm angry... trying to slap someone... a man... too tall for me to reach his face... feeling this burning anger and frustration... as he holds me off... laughing at me... laughing as I try to slap his face.*

I still feel that frustration and anger. My face is hot and flushed. Cool down as I wash... wash it away... the heat... the rage. I sit on the side of my bed trembling. What's all that about? Is it a memory or a dream? And what are dreams anyway? Powerful, that's for sure.

Better get dressed and face the day. I hear Sylvie downstairs. Music on the wireless, the clattering of plates, means it must be time for breakfast.

I know Sylvie wants to hear about how I got on yesterday with Kay, but I'm not even sure myself. Over breakfast I told her how Kay had talked me into relaxation... *an altered state of consciousness,* she called it... and asked me questions... but I can't recall exactly what I'd said, and she hadn't commented. Maybe it will help to go further next week. Kay says I need to relax sufficiently to access my deepest memories, so that's hopeful. It will be lovely to stay in her beautiful home and the countryside will be a change from London. But I can't help feeling a little uneasy and I don't know why. Kay was warm and friendly, though very different to Sylvie, and I'm sure we'll get on fine. Kay had given me a small leaflet about Hypnotherapy to read, to put my mind at ease and I'm finding it very interesting.

I find myself humming along to a song on the wireless... or *radio* as Sylvie calls it. *'Isn't it rich? Are we a pair? Me here at last on the ground, You in mid-air...'* My favourite, Sinatra... I'm singing... *'Send in the Clowns'...*

"I know that!" Sylvie looks at me... surprised.

"You know that?"

"Yes, I love all his songs."

"You know he recorded that much later, when he was getting older?"

"No, I didn't know... Really?"

Sylvie looks quite excited... "I wonder how much music you remember from the last 50 years?" Now she wants to know if I remember each song that's playing, but there's so much that means nothing to me at all. Only an occasional song that I just know... and Sylvie tells me it came out in the 70s or 80s! Amazing! But no other memories come to me.

I notice Sylvie rummaging in the sideboard. "Here it is!" and she produces an attractive notebook and pen, suggesting that I might like to start writing down everything I can remember, so we can build up some kind of picture of who I might be. I can do that! But where do I start?

As it's another fine day, I decide a walk in the Park is just what I need and Sylvie has "things to do... people to meet." She fusses over me like a mother hen, making sure I have everything I might need, which is lovely, but I'm glad to get out and relax into my own thoughts as I walk.

Kensington Gardens, an oasis of calm and beauty within the great heaving metropolis of commerce. London wouldn't be nearly as attractive a city without its Great Parks, intimate Squares and Gardens. I'd paint these trees in all their brilliant autumn finery if I had the materials. Oh yes, I do love to paint! Another memory, but then I was always drawing and painting as a child.

Finding a bench with a lovely view, I relax gratefully. Runners pass me in their colourful attire and headbands; to stop sweat running into their eyes I suppose! Very practical. For school gym and sports, we just had aertex gym shirts and shorts or knickers, as far as I can remember. Bottle green... a colour I've avoided ever since! Strange how those memories of childhood are so strong and vivid... as though they were the times I was most alive. As though since then I've been in a dream of life... that I can't even recall. As so often I can't recall dreams as I wake in the morning, though they were so real while I slept.

My mind is buzzing as I surrender my eyes to the bright sunlight... with only the distant sounds of traffic... occasional voices passing by... seagulls wheeling and calling across the lake... disparate images flashing through my mind like a disjointed movie... thoughts slipping away...

Cycling through the shade of the pine trees... following Shelagh along the path to the sand hills... taking the picnic bag to find our favourite hollow... to lie in the hot sun in our sun suits... fingers intertwined... feeling so contented together...

I wake startled; a jolt to my body... as my heart lurched... and a hot flush... suddenly remembering my best friend's pixie face and impish smile, her straight bobbed hair, feeling the warm sensation of being with her; of wanting to be with her. Dear Shelagh... remembering how close we were... physically too... we'd cuddle up in bed when we had a sleepover... but nothing sexual... I think I'd remember that... or did we explore each other with sensual stroking? Is that a memory or a pubescent fantasy? Did we talk about sex, trying to imagine what it might be like? Was I attracted to girls rather than boys, or was it just that there were no boys around? How can I know what feelings I had for her? Was it love? I was devastated when she moved away. I wrote a poem for her. We were just adolescents... still growing up. We kept writing for a while... but finally lost touch. After she left, I had other friends, but I suppose I just didn't bother to keep in touch. I don't even know what happened to her. Feeling overwhelmed by sadness... of love lost... love forgotten... barely remembered.

I remain sitting for a while, until I hear the familiar sound of a guitar nearby. Dylan, practising again in his favourite corner. I rise to listen and see him not far away through the bushes. I don't mean to watch him so covertly, but entranced by the sound of his music I'm also, shockingly, absorbed by his attractiveness; dark locks spilling over the smooth contours of his face, the intensity of his eyes and determined mouth. Aware of his lithe brown body beneath jacket and jeans. I'd love to paint his portrait. But I can't help feeling something that's becoming more familiar the more I remember of my youth... the pain and joy of physical attraction... longing for the warmth of belonging to another human body... the anguish of love. Well, this is a love unattainable... only too aware that I'm old enough to be his grandmother.

I shake myself and follow the path around to be in full view, until he stops playing and looks up at me. "I thought I might see you here again..." and his warm smile melts my heart as he slings his guitar on his shoulder saying "Fancy a coffee? Come on then." Leading me through the trees till we reach the Café. That's alright then... friends we can be... so put those embarrassing feelings away girl!

He wants to know how I've been getting on and what more I can tell him of my predicament. "You don't mind, do you? I'm just fascinated by your story, and you've hardly begun to find out who you are! I do hope you'll allow me to write about your journey of discovery!"

How could I not agree? He's so agreeable. "You will be coming to Little Venice tomorrow? Should be a good day!"

Conversation comes easily... as though we're old friends catching up after some time... even though we've only just recently met. I seem to recall reading something about meeting people in this life who are reincarnated lovers, friends or relatives from a past life... or through many lives! Is this a past life relationship? I wonder. Walking together back to Bayswater Road, I have to resist the impulse to take his hand. It's not easy.

* * *

Sylvie's there when I return, wanting to hear what I've been doing. So I tell her about meeting Dylan again and how much he's looking forward to seeing us at Little Venice tomorrow. I don't mention my erotic feelings about him, out of embarrassment. I'm not even sure what these feelings are... except that I feel nineteen and not sixty nine!

Sylvie seems a bit preoccupied. Something's not quite right. I don't like to pry... after all we hardly know each other... but wonder what the problem could be. She hasn't even mentioned a boyfriend!

Over supper, I venture to ask how her day has been. She looks sheepish. "Well, if you must know, I met a guy a couple of weeks ago and he's been in touch. But I'm not sure about him... he's too gorgeous for his own good!"

This I know about. "Go for it," I say with authority...

"You'll soon find out!" If I could get to meet him I'm sure I could suss him out. How, I'm not so sure.

"Well, he's coming to this gig tonight in Stratford. Not Shakespeare's Stratford," she laughs... "It's in the East End. I'm not going till 7.00 pm so you can watch TV and go to bed whenever you like. Don't wait up for me... I'll be late!"

She was. I was going to the loo at some unearthly hour when I heard her downstairs, and hovered at the top of the stairs as she came up. "How did it go?" I was dying to know.

Her smile said it all. "Great... he brought me home and didn't expect to come in. That's a good start... I like some respect from a man."

"Good for you!" I was very glad to hear it. For her sake.

Chapter 5

⁓

Week1: Day 5... Saturday in Little Venice

"*A*nother lovely day..." Penny is in good spirits this morning. No dreams that she can remember... she's woken feeling quite refreshed.

As they share breakfast, Sylvie's happy to see Penny looking so much better. "A good day for Little Venice! Soon as we're ready then...," as Penny goes upstairs to dress.

It isn't far to walk and they soon join other people apparently going in the same direction. A loud booming bass announces the event before they can see the canal basin. The crowd grows with their approach and it's quite a jostle as they reach the quay. Plastic awnings give some shelter to the art exhibition as they wander along, admiring some of the pictures and pulling a face at others. "I wouldn't have that on my wall...," Penny mutters at one particularly dark and incomprehensible canvas. "Gives me the shivers!" Sylvie has to agree... it seems menacing to her too.

The canal boats are visible through the crowd and they wonder how they would know which one is Dylan's. Penny has forgotten the name of the boat that he'd told her, but they're moving with the crowd towards the source of the music, and she supposes that Dylan will be playing his guitar there. And so he is... making a great sound with the group of musicians... swinging! The people are loving it... tapping feet... swaying to the beat... the less inhibited dancing in open spaces... having a ball... and it's still morning!

Penny is awed... she thinks she's never experienced anything like it... all the people... not just English... but so many foreigners with darker skins... Chinese or Japanese young women... Indian women in beautiful flowing Saris... other women enveloped in long garments and scarves covering their heads, showing only bright eyes and happy smiles... and African women flaunting a kaleidoscope of bright colourful dresses and head scarves. As though they'd materialised from Hollywood films or pictures she'd seen in books and magazines into real people... talking and singing as they move through the crowd. "So many coloured people here!" she exclaimed.

Sylvie has to explain that they are not all 'foreign' as most of them have been born here... the children of Jamaicans who'd come over in the 50s and 60s to work in hospitals... and Chinese and Indians who'd came to open Restaurants and Takeaways... not to mention Africans who came here to study. "Don't call them coloured! Our colonial cousins are now our British brothers and sisters... and most of them live around here. You should see the Notting Hill Carnival...," she says. "It's so much more... you'd be amazed!"

It's too much to take in. Penny's overwhelmed! She'd seen an occasional Chinese face in Liverpool, and once a black man on a tram, very smart in a suit and so handsome she couldn't take her eyes off him, till her mother whispered it was very rude to stare.

And so much sound... coloured lights and bright colours everywhere.

She remembers the sedate dances she'd been to… pale in comparison to this surge of sound and light and emotional feeling. Different even to the jazz she loves. Something moves her, almost to tears.

Noticing her reaction, Sylvie takes her hand… inviting her to join in dancing… and Penny responds, smiling through her almost tears as she starts to sway and move her feet. She seems to know how to move… half-closing her eyes and surrendering to the rhythm of the music… as if she's done that before. But she's suddenly aware of what she's doing and feels so self-conscious she moves back into the crowd and watches Sylvie.

When the band takes a break, Dylan comes over with a big smile. "You must be Sylvie…," he greets her after he says hello to Penny, touching her arm briefly. "Great Band!" Sylvie smiles at him with appreciation. Dylan is modest… "Just a few mates… not in the big league… yet! But I hear you're a singer… strange we've never met!"

"Mostly Jazz… in small night clubs. Not so many of them these days. I suppose we move in different circles."

"Great… I'm beginning to appreciate jazz more as I get older… my Dad's a big fan and I heard a lot growing up… then I suppose I rebelled… as you do…," he laughed. "I don't suppose you'd care to join us in a number?" Sylvie demurrers… "I'm not sure…"

"We do quite a few jazzy numbers… come on… you'll fit in…"

Sylvie smiles. "Well if you insist…" She's actually delighted to be asked!

"Great… let's go over and see which numbers you'd like…" and they all move towards the stage where Sylvie finds a couple of songs she knows.

Dylan's set goes down well. Sylvie sings well with the band; 'I got Rhythm' in a very jazzy arrangement, and a seductive 'Summertime' seductively, Penny thinks as she mouths the words along with her. She does love Gershwin songs.

Penny experiences the day in a bright cloud of wonder... with various groups and solo artists taking over the stage, playing such a variety of music, from Irish fiddles and pipes to African drums... a Folk group harmonising... to black men with curious hair and colourful headgear (West Indians do their hair in dreadlocks, Sylvie explains) playing curious metal drums that sound like nothing else she's ever heard... originally made from oil drums, she's told.

At every turn, exotic odours entice her to sample small bowls of food... combinations of colourful vegetables of every kind which taste unbelievable, some very hot in her mouth. That's the chilli, Sylvie tells her... and more different breads and pastries than she could ever have imagined.

Dylan introduces his friends, including the folk who live here and there on canal boats. Jasmine, one of Gary's neighbours, invites her to come and see her home and leads her along the quay and past the crowds to a smaller Narrow Boat than the others they'd passed. Colourful painted designs adorn the outside and the roof is laden with a stack of firewood and bicycles. Inside is small and cramped, as she'd expected, but so ingenious and well- designed that it seems to have room for everything one might need in a home, with built-in furniture pulling down to reveal a table or seat, folding up to reveal storage spaces, the bed hidden somewhere, and embellishment everywhere, painted on cupboards and ceiling. Glass pendants and decorations hang in the windows. Woven designs like spider's webs hang from the ceiling... Dream-catchers, Sylvie explains. Bunches of herbs over the kitchen area with kitchen utensils. It's so warm and cosy. She says, she'd be happy in a place like this, and Jasmine hugs her.

"We love this life... don't want anything else! We can stay here or move on the canal as far as we like... not tied down here." Jasmine wears her hair in strange braids woven with beads and a long velvet skirt and long strings of beads over a loose top. Penny thinks she looks quite as exotic as the foreign ladies *'No, not foreign!'* she reminds herself. Over a cup of herbal tea, which is new to Penny, but quite delicious... Jasmine talks about her life with Rufus, her partner, who plays pipes and flute with Dylan's band.

"No, we're not married...," in reply to Penny's query. "What a mockery that is! But we've been together nine years, so I reckon we're doing alright."

"No children?" Penny asks. "No, we've chosen not to have kids... you know... the way the world is." Well actually, no, she doesn't know! Jasmine proceeds to expound on Women's Lib, the state of the world, destruction of nature and global warming to the astonished Penny. She's surprised, as the day darkens into night, how quickly the day had gone. And how much she's enjoying it all.

"How are you feeling?" Sylvie shouts over the noise. "Ready to go home yet?"

Penny is grateful for that. She thinks she's tired, though another part of her feels as though she could go on forever. They find Dylan to tell him they're ready to leave. He's about to go onstage again for their last set and looks disappointed. "It's just warming up...," he protests.

"I'm ok... let's stay for that...," Penny responds. She's really not ready for bed yet. Sylvie's glad to get another chance to join the band; she feels like singing all night.

The party is changing. As older people and families leave, younger people swell the crowd, some swigging beer from cans, making even more noise than before. Sylvie finds Penny a seat in a corner near the band. "Stay there...I'll get us a drink...," she tells her and is soon back with plastic cups of dark red liquid.

"I believe it's last year's elderberry," she laughs. "From Jasmine... enjoy!" Penny does... she can't help it. Soon she's swaying to the music again... self-consciousness gone... evaporated by the delicious wine... the warmth and beat of the music.

* * *

Penny wakes, aware that this isn't Sylvie's comfortable bed. Curtains are drawn across small windows and there's a hum of low voices nearby, and smoke, the glow of a fire and a strange smell. She sits up groggily and as her eyes became accustomed to the low light level, realises she's in a narrow boat. Not Jasmine's, she thought... missing all the decorations.

Sylvie rises from a group of people and brings her a glass of water. "You OK Penny? You were falling asleep so we brought you in here. This is Dylan's boat." Penny's glad of the water, then slides her legs off the bed and finds her shoes. She recognises the members of the band round the glowing stove with a couple of women she hasn't met. One of them rises to take her hand.

"I'm Grace... welcome to our home." So this is Dylan's partner... she's beautiful... with long flowing dark hair framing an elfin face and startling blue eyes... "Come where it's warm Penny... getting chilly now...," and sits her down beside her, draping a shawl over her shoulders. As she gets comfortable on a large cushion on the floor, she feels good, sitting there with other people she doesn't really know... feeling the warmth of the fire... chatting or staying quiet... it doesn't seem to matter. A cigarette is being passed around, but no ordinary cigarette from a packet... she watched one of the men making one. Penny had tried smoking once but didn't think it was worth the bother, so hadn't since. However, in the circumstances, she reckons it would be rude not to, so accepts it when passed to her, and not wanting to be seen as an amateur, takes a long drag... and another... before passing it on. Someone gives her a glass of wine... more elderberry... it's very nice. Another cigarette comes around to her and she takes another drag... feeling a strange companionship with all these people. She feels even more strange than when she got very drunk once at a party in Guernsey and made an exhibition of herself, but not sure how. That was before she'd met Davy... he wouldn't approve of that. She's crooning softly to herself... then what's happening? She just wants to lie down, so drags herself back to the bed and lays down, head spinning, feeling the world rocking from side to side... or is it the boat?

The next thing she knows, she's being helped into a car... then up the stairs of Sylvie's house into her bedroom... she's crooning softly... and without taking off her clothes... falls asleep.

Chapter 6

Week 1: Day 6… Sunday… The Tea Dance

Morning creeps in like a tardy schoolboy, grey, cold and wet. At some time in the night she'd got up to use the loo and drink some water, she was so thirsty, then changed into her pyjamas, snuggling back into the comfort of her warm bed.

Not surprisingly, they've both slept in and emerge like butterflies from a chrysalis for coffee in their dressing gowns. Sylvie is most apologetic… "I should have been looking after you," she keeps saying… "I'm so sorry, Penny." But Penny is totally unconcerned, insisting that she'd had a great time and would love to repeat the experience.

"Be careful what you wish for…," Sylvie laughs. "It's not always such a great experience! You have to be careful with these things." That confirms Penny's inkling that the cigarettes were not quite the usual sort… they'd certainly had a strange effect on her. She'd heard about the dangers of drugs, of course, without actually knowing what they are! Sex, Drugs and Rock'n'roll was a bit of a joke to her... that's what other people got into... not her.

Sylvie is already making breakfast and tells her to get dressed later... "I think we need to eat now!" and Penny realises how hungry she is, ready to tuck into a plateful of baked beans and sausage, mushrooms, tomatoes and poached egg, with plenty of fried bread... which she really appreciates, in spite of all the delicious food she'd eaten yesterday. She can't believe how much she's putting away. Sylvie chortles..."That's whacky baccy for you!" Well, that's a revelation!

Sylvie suggests a nice hot bath, as it's Sunday and they have no plans till the afternoon, and Penny's glad of the suggestion. What's happening this afternoon? she wonders. She still hasn't used the shower and really must ask Sylvie to explain its operation. A bath full of hot water with soapy bubbles is such a luxury after her own memories of economising with both water and heating. How can Sylvie afford it? She feels quite guilty, although Sylvie's explained that a gas-fired combi-boiler keeps her house warm and water hot and is very economical.

Freshly bathed and dressed and sitting in the kitchen with another coffee, Sylvie tells her they're going to a Tea Dance at a posh Hotel at 2 o'clock this afternoon, where Sylvie is booked to sing. "It's all 40s music... reminiscing the war years. Older people love this kind of thing. You'll enjoy it Penny!"

Sylvie asks if she's managed to write anything in her notebook. In fact, Penny has started a few times and got no further than...

My name is Penny Lane. Or is it?

Last Tuesday I was 19... but now I am 69.

What has happened in the last 50 years?

Have I travelled in Time? Am I a Time Traveller?

How can I get back to 1959?

Where is Davy? If I'm really 69, he'll be 75! He could be dead by now!

Sylvie is being matter-of-fact... "OK... that's not really getting us anywhere. Maybe write down the songs you remember... how about that? You might start to remember where you were and what you were doing when you hear them." Yes, that sounds like a good start. She'll take the notebook with her to make notes of the songs she knows.

* * *

They'd had such a good breakfast, neither of them want to eat again before they go to the Hotel. Sylvie sings here regularly at the Tea Dance and is greeted by everyone from the doorman to the band, and to the regulars who applaud her enthusiastically after every song. It's all so familiar to Penny... the songs, the clothes... nearly everyone dressed in 40s fashions as though they've been keeping their lovely dresses and shoes safe somewhere for the last sixty-odd years. Many of the dancers are not even old! They couldn't have been around during the war, but evidently love the music.

As she's sitting there, tapping her feet, a silver haired gentleman approaches and courteously asks her to dance. She hesitates and glances up at Sylvie on the stage, who's about to sing a Glen Miller number... *'Chattanooga Choo-choo'*... a foxtrot. Now Penny had taken dancing lessons when she was younger, but usually preferred to stay on the sidelines, taking photographs of other dancers... but Sylvie is waving to her... *Go on*... so she takes a deep breath and accepts his hand. As she's whirled away in his strong arms, trying to remember the steps, he simply takes over and she falls into the rhythm, which seems to work out ok, and they make it to the end.

He thanks her and she blurts out an apology, that she's out of practice. "You were divine...," he murmurs... "Let's make the next one a waltz, my dear...," and kisses her hand. Sure enough, a little later he returns, having danced with other partners, to claim her for *'Moon River.'* It's magical!

Sylvie insists she have tea and cake… after all, it is a Tea Dance… and she doesn't feel out of place, sitting there, with everyone enjoying themselves so much. It could have been one of the dances Davy used to play for, while she was taking pictures of everyone dancing and eating, but the thought makes her feel sad again.

She'd forgotten about making notes in her notebook, so takes it out of her bag to write down some of the numbers the band are playing that she knows.

They are home by 6 o'clock and Sylvie produces a bowl of pea and mint soup and a lovely salad with several different cheeses. They watch TV, but Penny's mind is elsewhere… back in 1959.

Wandering through the streets of St. Peter Port, hand in hand with Davy, down to the quay watching the big ferry boat coming in and all the small boats, yachts and motor boats, coming and going. One of her photographer friends saying 'Come on, give us your best smile' as they snap a picture. One that she'll treasure. Her and Davy looking so happy and in love.

Chapter 7

Week 1: Day 7... Monday... Kay - at 'The Beeches'

I'm usually up with the dawn. Early enough to spend up to an hour in meditation and Yoga exercise before I feed the chickens and walk the dogs. Kiss goodbye to James, my husband, who leaves early for work in Westminster. He's in the Civil Service, working for the Government; very important work that means he often has to work late when he stays overnight in the small flat in South Kensington that was our home before we moved here. He bought it in the eighties with help from his parents when it was a depressed area. Did it up gradually and it's worth a fortune now!

Then I dress according to what I'll be doing; smart for work or casual when at home. No breakfast except for a couple of coffees; black, no sugar, and I'm ready for the day ahead. I have to be organised in my life.

Sylvie thinks my life is too orderly, but it works for me. That's the difference between us. She's not as focussed as I am, which is why

49

she doesn't seem to achieve anything. Just muddling through life, but that's just who she is. I love her, but I couldn't live with her, she'd drive me mad! Anyway, I'm just happy that she's kept Grammy's house. She needs that security; as long as she can keep a roof over her head.

Sylvie can't resist helping. Anyone she thinks is in need of a meal, a bed for the night, or just a shoulder to cry on, she can't help herself. Very much like our Grammy, mum's mother, who always seemed to have an unwanted puppy or kitten to feed. She used to take us in too, when Angie, (that's mum, her name is Angela but for some reason she doesn't want to be called Mum or Mother) had dumped us and gone again. I'm named Kathleen after Grammy, but for some reason I've always been called Kay; I think my Father started it, maybe he didn't like Kathleen very much.

Well, I'm not much like her. I know some of my friends and even my family sometimes think I'm unfeeling, because I wouldn't take any waifs and strays in off the street. I mean, when you don't know anything about them, they could rob you blind! I suppose I just don't like being taken advantage of.

Having admitted that, I wouldn't be in the psychotherapy profession if I didn't care about people. Nothing gives me more pleasure than to be able to help a client overcome their issues and go on to lead a better life. That is my passion.

Anyway, maybe I can help with her new friend Penny Lane. Can that be her real name? Probably not. Why would she choose a Beatles song? What associations are there I wonder? Sylvie tells me she loves music and sings and seems to know more recent songs than 1960. I must say I'm looking forward to doing some hypnotherapy with her, see if we can unlock her memories. It's quite a challenge… not something I've ever dealt with before. Could be interesting!

Later today I'll be meeting Penny at the Station to bring her here for a few days, so in the meantime I'm researching what I can about amnesia and memory loss. The information is bewildering as every case seems to be different. A trauma, either physical or emotional, can trigger it and we think Penny was knocked out in the attack, when her head hit the lamp post. But she can only remember her life from fifty years ago, which seems to be unusual.

I make vegetable soup, which is enough for lunch and plenty left for another day. With bread and a little cheese, this breaks my fast, as I don't like to eat too much. Then I'm ready to drive into Slough to pick up Penny.

Chapter 8

Week 1: Day 7... Monday... Arrival at 'The Beeches'

It's a cold morning as Penny gets herself ready for her stay with Kay, dressing in warmer clothes and re-packing her suitcase. She's feeling a little apprehensive, though she doesn't know why. Maybe it's because she's got used to being with Sylvie's companionship in her warm cosy home for almost the past week, but it seems the sensible thing to do, as Sylvie will be out every day this week, getting into a small role in a TV soap, whatever that is!

Sylvie sees her off at the Station and the journey to Slough isn't very long. As soon as she leaves the platform, she's relieved to see Kay waiting to drive her back to the house. On their approach up the drive, she thinks she sees a shadow creep over the house, or maybe she only felt it as a little shiver. As there's no sun to cast a shadow, she must have imagined it.

Kay brings her case into the house. "I thought you'd like to settle in today. Then we can start therapy tomorrow, if that's alright with you. I hope you like your room." Penny really likes the room; quite large and beautifully decorated, with a double bed and what looks like antique Edwardian furniture. A polished mahogany chest of drawers and dressing table, with a huge wardrobe that opens to reveal more drawers and shelves as well as plenty of hanging space. The casement windows surrounded by elegant curtains overlook the garden with a comfortable armchair placed strategically for the best view. Kay opens another door to show her a small bathroom in gleaming white and chrome. "Your en-suite, madam." Luxury indeed, she thinks.

Kay gives her a tour of the other bedrooms. The master bedroom is beautiful; elegantly furnished in pastel colours with light oak furniture and a very large bed, with its own en-suite. Two other smaller attractive bedrooms, and a large bathroom with not only a bath but also a large shower. Then a small staircase leading up to a large attic. "Stuffed with old furniture and things stored for so long we don't know what's there!" Kay explained.

When Penny had unpacked, hanging her few clothes in the vast wardrobe and putting her toiletries in her en-suite, she hears Kay calling her to come down for tea. The wooden stairs creak as she descends. It isn't a very old house, but a lot older than she is, she reflects, and she creaks too!

Tea is laid out in the conservatory; a tray with pretty cups and saucers, sugar bowl, milk jug and teapot, just like her mother used to do in the guest house where she was brought up. That was a large old house too; the memory gradually returning like a scene from an old film.

She helps herself to a couple of dainty egg and cress sandwiches from a matching plate, while she tells Kay about it. Kay is delighted to hear it.

"I do love this old tea set. I don't know how it's all survived; could be Art Deco. It was James's mother's; she left it here for us. Said it goes with the house. She loved this house, but they needed to downsize when Alexander, her husband, retired. Poor Jane. She's nearly 80 now and has dementia; she's in a home now and Alexander died some time ago. The room you're in was Jane's bedroom. They each had their own rooms in those days…," she laughs. "Do have some cake; I made it especially for your visit."

Penny wants to hear more. "Was James brought up here?"

"Oh yes. His Grandfather had this house built. The family had money. Alexander took over his father's business and was very successful. I reckon I'm very lucky to have married James and we seem to suit each other." Penny thinks she detects a pensive tone in her voice, but dismisses the thought.

"This cake is delicious…," recalling the cakes her mother used to make when she was growing up. She was always cooking for the guests; everything was home-made in the guest house, which kept her mum constantly busy and Penny was expected to help as well, washing up, peeling vegetables, stirring gravy and serving plates of food at dinner time. Her mother was so busy she didn't have much time for her daughter, who spent most of her free time reading and drawing in her attic bedroom. Her parents' room was on the ground floor, which seemed an awfully long way when they first moved there, but she'd grown to relish the privacy and quiet of her little attic room, pinning her pictures of dogs and horses up on the walls. She'd always wanted a dog, but her mother said it would be unhygienic in the guesthouse, still her best friend had a lovely black Labrador that they used to go for walks together with.

The sun appears briefly and Penny says she'd like to see the garden. It looks so inviting as she takes a little path around the lawn and flower beds bordered by the big trees in their autumn colours. She thinks she sees a small boy running through the trees, and when she comes back to the kitchen she mentions it to Kay. "Really? Must be some local boy exploring. Though I've never seen anyone wandering in. There's no public footpath and we're well fenced in." Penny wonders if she'd imagined it.

Kay is saying… "Why don't you relax in the drawing room, while I prepare supper. We usually eat at 7.00 when James gets home. You'll find some good books in there, if you enjoy reading." She takes the tea tray back into the kitchen before showing Penny through into the large room leading off the hall. A spacious settee and armchairs are arranged around a coffee table facing the large television set and huge fireplace, one wall lined with bookshelves and a big picture window with views over the front garden and beyond, over the valley.

She looks over the books; all the classics, most of which look familiar, Dickens, Shakespeare and others she recognises. History and autobiographies of famous people, some of which she's never heard of. She pulls out one entitled 'The Lunar Men' and settles down in one of the chairs to investigate it. It turns out to be a fascinating account of the early inventors and industrialists of the 18th century. She's always loved history, which was one subject she'd excelled in at school, and is soon engrossed.

A shadow passes her… a tall man going through the door. She sees him walk into the kitchen towards the woman at the sink and put his arms around her. She hears a soft murmur as she turns to him… 'Peter… don't…' as they embrace passionately. She's puzzled. Who's Peter? she wonders. Is Kay having an affair? She's sure Sylvie had told her Peter was her son!

Penny is startled out of her sleep by Kay's face swimming before her. "Are you alright Penny?" Kay's bending over her looking concerned. "You were well away then."

"I thought I saw a man…" Penny tries to focus her eyes. "I must have been dreaming…," she doesn't continue, feeling very confused.

"Well, no-one's been here... must have been a dream...," Kay reassures her. "Dinner will be ready soon and James will be home any minute. You might want to go and freshen up while we're waiting. OK?"

Penny shakes herself as she rises to go upstairs. She can't understand why she'd dream something like that and is glad to have a little time to recover, to wash her face and brush her hair, hoping she'll look presentable by the time James gets home.

Dinner is very tasty; watercress soup, then vegetable lasagne with salad, with fruit and cheese to finish. She's grateful that Sylvie had told Kay she's vegetarian, as Sylvie is. She doesn't want to make an issue of it. How she knows she's vegetarian she isn't sure, but as far as she can remember, she's never liked to eat meat. When they've finished, Penny offers to wash up but Kay shakes her head. "No, I don't need any help... just putting them in the dishwasher."

Penny is intrigued by this unknown device that washes dishes. She's already been introduced to the washing machine that magically cleans clothes at Sylvie's. Her own memories of doing the laundry involved a gas boiler in the basement, a copper plunger to agitate the clothes and a pair of large wooden tongs to fish them out of the hot water and feed them through a large wooden mangle that threatened to mash the fingers of anyone foolish enough to get too close to the rollers. That was until Mum, overcome with all the work, started sending the sheets and towels to the laundry. So many things had changed since she was nineteen. Though frankly, she doesn't think washing dishes is such a big deal!

Later, as they sit in the drawing room, Penny notices a collection of framed photographs on a side table. "The family rogues gallery...," James laughs. "As if we need reminding!"

Conversation centres around the family and how the children are doing with their studies at University.

"Margaret is 19 and just started Uni. Seems to be enjoying it… Arts and Media. It's what she always wanted." Kay sounds enthusiastic.

James not so much… "Good looking girl… hope she marries well!"

Kay ignores this attitude to women, "Peter is doing very well anyway."

"What's he studying?" Penny queries.

"History and Archaeology," James replies, "though how that will make him a good living is beyond me!"

He grimaces. "Named after my eccentric uncle Peter, Dad's brother. He was never any good at making money either. Just living off the family as far as I can tell."

"Really, James, he was such a great storyteller and he did make a good living from publishing his stories. You all loved him!" Kay responds.

"Yes, well, he was such a big part of our lives as we were growing up, I thought he was my Dad when I was very young…," he laughs… "because Dad was away so much we hardly saw him! Yes, we did love having him around. I don't know what mum would have done without him, helping out with odd jobs and keeping us kids amused."

Penny wants to know what happened to him.

"Went off travelling on the proceeds of his books, after I went to Boarding school at ten… he used to send Mum postcards of all the places he'd been to. I expect they're still up in the attic somewhere, with all the old photographs and home movies. We hardly saw him for years, then he retired to Brighton or somewhere on the coast and died in the nineties. Mum was very sad. As was Dad, though he always said he was irresponsible."

"So you had brothers and sisters?" Penny's curious about the allusion to 'us kids'.

"My sister Sarah. She's two years younger than me… married a sheep farmer and still lives in deepest Yorkshire, so we hardly see her! Then a younger brother, Robin, sadly he died when he was seven. I was at Boarding school and came back for the funeral. Mum was distraught…

Dad too, of course… so sad."

Penny notices that he seems uncomfortable, or maybe simply trying to hide his feelings… not manly to show any emotion, and he quickly recovers… "Anyway, enough about our genealogy… I believe you're here to discover your history!"

"Making a start on that tomorrow. So an early night I think, if that's alright with everyone." Kay speaks briskly.

It's 10 o'clock when Penny goes up to her room, taking with her the book she's started reading. She's glad of the peace and quiet to mull over the events of the day as she's found it hard work trying to make conversation with James, who, she noticed, has his own opinions about everything.

She's soon engrossed in the book until the pages swim before her eyes and she turns off the light to fall into a deep sleep.

* * *

"I want you so much my love…" a man's body sliding into bed and running his hands down her body. Her body begins to respond… turning towards him… then somehow knowing something is wrong. It's not Davy… he feels different… trying to move away from his embrace… crying out… "No… I'm not Jane!"

* * *

The Sudden realisation wakes her with a start; half out of bed, the bedding in disarray. She's alone. Her heart pounding, she switches on the bedside light. What just happened? She's shaking, going into the en-suite to pee, drink a little water and peer into the mirror. No, she's still the same old body she recognises as her own. Not morphed into someone else.

58

Returning to bed, she wonders if it's possible that James has been doing a little sleepwalking. Then why had she thought he was after Jane? Of course not. Jane was his mother! Had she gone back in time again? She's sleeping in Jane's room after all. Maybe it's haunted? Was this an action replay of what had been going on so many years ago? It's some time before she sleeps again.

Chapter 9

Week 2 : Day 1... Tuesday... Therapy

I t's a dark morning, she sees as she opens the curtains, and pouring with rain, still dazed, remembering the events of the night. *Maybe I really am a Time Traveller*, she wonders, *only now I'm going back into other people's lives*. The thought is ridiculous.

She's relieved that James has already left for work when she goes downstairs, where breakfast is laid out on the kitchen table, Kay busy at the cooker. "Morning Penny... hope you slept well?"

Penny puts on a smile, wondering if she should tell her of the night's encounter. Did she know that her mother-in-law's room was haunted by Uncle Peter? That he'd been having an affair with Jane when James was young. Did James know? Maybe it's the family secret that no-one talks about. How can she tell her that she knows? She can't say anything... it could have simply been her own imagination!

After a light breakfast, Kay suggests they get started on her therapy in her study, another room she's not seen before. She almost expects to see a shadowy figure appearing or disappearing through a wall wherever she goes, like an old movie; *'Blithe Spirit'* ... Rex Harrison haunted by his ex-wife... and that mad old actress acting the part of a medium... what was her name? Margaret Rutherford. Very funny, she recalls. But not this time.

* * *

Kay sits her in a chair she can relax in and sits opposite across a small table, pen and notebook ready for her to take notes. She starts talking about how the mind works; mind, emotions and body all affecting each other. "You feel happy, lift your head and smile... or you feel sad and your mouth turns down, shoulders droop, losing energy. E-motion is simply energy in motion. But when your mind recalls something really good, or someone you love, your emotions feel good and your body is energised. And it happens the other way round. Think of going for a lovely walk... make the effort to get up and go out... you start to feel happy. You can learn how to make yourself feel really good and energised, just with your imagination. Very underrated, imagination!"

"So now... take a few deep breaths and feel your body relax into the chair... every muscle letting go any tension that might still be there... relaxing even more with every breath... and every word you hear... it doesn't matter if you don't hear everything I say... just sinking into the deepest relaxation... deeper and deeper... relaxing even more..."

Kay's pleased to note that Penny seems to be responding to her hypnotic suggestions.

"While you're so relaxed... take yourself now to a very special place... some place you may remember... or somewhere you can imagine... where you feel completely happy... and safe... and relaxed... Good. Are you there? Where are you?"

"On the beach... it's Shell Beach... all tiny shells... not proper sand... "

"What are you doing on the beach?"

"Just sitting... picking out some of the perfect shells to take home... as a keepsake... it's so warm and lovely here...," Penny's voice trails off.

"And you feel happy... and safe... and relaxed...," Kay gently repeats. Penny nods. "Hold on to that Penny... hold those shells in your hand... and whenever you feel distressed... come back to this memory and feel happy and safe. Good. Deep breaths now... and relax..."

Kay stops to write notes before she resumes.

"You're doing really well, Penny... take another deep breath and relax again. That's good... relax even deeper...Now... you're so well relaxed... take yourself back to your earliest memory... and when you're there... let me know."

She waits, watching Penny for any response. A slight movement of her legs. "Are you there, Penny?" Again, a nod from Penny. "Can you tell me where you are?" Kay asks.

"The air raid siren is going... it's so loud and scary... I'm being carried into the shelter in our garden. Wrapped up in a blanket. It's cold and smells funny. Mum's lighting candles. I can smell the matches burning. The next door neighbours are here too and their little girl Barbara... I don't like her. She bit me. I can hear planes overhead... They're all talking... 'Jerries... the bombers...' and loud explosions... they're the bombs dropping. Dad says they're hitting the docks... but we're far enough away from the docks... nothing to worry about. Then a different sound... 'They're ours... after them boys...'

Her voice has changed; sounding more like a child. Kay listens attentively, taking notes.

"How old are you?"

"I don't know."

"How are you feeling, Penny? Are you scared?"

"It's scary... but kind of exciting."

"That's good, Penny... go forward now to another memory..."

"I'm on a bus and I can see children running about in the rubble of houses... they've been bombed. Everything is grey... the children's clothes are grubby and some of them don't have shoes on."

"How do you feel now, Penny?"

"I'm so sorry for them. It's not like that where we live."

"Good Penny... now go on to a happier time."

"Walking with Mum and Dad... down a lane... it's sunny and warm... lovely trees and I'm picking buttercups," she murmurs.

"What are you feeling now?"

"I'm so happy to see Dad... we've not seen him for a long time... he's in the RAF... he's an Observer in a Bomber. He's wearing his uniform... he broke his leg when they had a bad landing so doesn't fly now... he's an instructor... he teaches navigation... like he does with me. I can read maps... so I'll always know where I am. "

"How old are you now?"

"I'm four."

Kay wants to know more about Penny's father.

"So your Dad came home from the war? What happened then?"

"Oh yes... I have a baby sister... she's called Susan. I'm six... I'm going to school down the road."

"Go on to another time now... " Penny nods. "Can you tell me where you are now?"

"We've moved to the seaside... we live in a Guesthouse... it's very big."

"How old are you now?"

"I'm ten."

"Do you like the Guesthouse, Penny?"

"I like going down to the sea... walking along the sands... especially in winter when there's no one there. But I don't like all the strange people who stay in our house."

"What's strange about them, Penny?"

"They're strangers... they just come on holiday and then they go home."

"What do you do in the Guesthouse? Do you have your own room?"

"Oh yes... Susan and me have an attic... it's a long way down to mum and dad's room. That's on the ground floor. Sometimes it's a bit scary at night... I hear noises at night... but daddy says it's just the house settling down... because it's an old house. I think it's ghosts."

"Does anything else scare you? Go on to some time you might have been a bit frightened." Penny sits quietly for a minute or two.

"There are two brothers staying on holiday... we're playing tag in the garden... and they're chasing me... I'm trapped in the side passage... and they won't let me out. I'm feeling scared... they're getting too close... like they're going to do something to me..."

"OK, Penny… take a deep breath and move on… What are you doing now?"

"I'm fighting them off... and they're laughing... like I'm a joke. I'll tell my mum..." She's angry.

"OK… that's good… what happens when you tell your mum?"

"Yes... she says not to worry... they'll all be going home tomorrow. I can keep out of the way until they've left. I don't like boys."

After that Kay decides that's enough for one day. She takes her back to her happy place and lets her relax a bit longer before waking her.

They talk about what had emerged, Kay becoming familiar with Penny's memories. "That was a good start." And Penny agrees, surprised at how vivid these memories were, as if she were really there, although they were all still before 1959.

After lunch, the rain has stopped, the sun comes out and Kay suggests a walk with the dogs. Penny's glad to get out into fresh air and stretch her legs. She doesn't feel as fit as she should be. Everything aches; her hips and legs. Her shoulders click as she rolls them. So this is old age, she reflects.

After tea she's glad to sit in the Drawing room with her book and before she's read a few pages, falls asleep. When she wakes, she's relieved that no more apparitions have appeared.

Later, as she goes up to bed, she hopes there will be no more nightly disturbance.

Chapter 10

Week 2: Day 2 … Wednesday… 'The Beeches'

I t's a lovely morning, the sun slanting through the windows of Kay's spacious kitchen, as Penny gratefully accepts a cup of coffee. She's slept well and feels more hopeful that another session with Kay will uncover more of her memories.

She can't help but reflect on the differences in the lifestyles of Kay and Sylvie. Kay's home is immaculate; with tasteful furnishings and everything in its rightful place, cushions plumped and floors vacuumed at least every other day by Kay or her cleaning lady, Barbara, who comes twice a week. While Sylvie's home is cluttered, to say the least, with books and papers everywhere and bags on the floor… "waiting to go to the Charity shop…," she'd explain.

She's noticed the floors had been cleaned once while she was there, which involved moving a lot of things around the floor. But she loved the cosiness of Sylvie's home; the warm fire and Sylvester purring as he stretched out to her touch. That's what a home should be. Although she did appreciate the comfort and elegance of Kay's home, it seems more impersonal, more showy, to demonstrate the status of the occupants, like a Stately Home.

That morning's session goes well, as Penny relaxes into hypnosis even more deeply. Her memories this time reveal more about her teenage years.

Kay asks her to recall a time when she was happy.

"I'm with Sally... walking her dog on the beach... I love walking the dog... Nicky... a lovely black Labrador. On the beach I can see for miles... the sea's well out. There's another country over there... far away... looks like mountains... I'd love to go there."

"Tell me about Sally..."

"She's my best friend from school. We go cycling together... and horse riding at weekends."

"How old are you now, Penny?"

"Fifteen..."

"What about boys? Do you have any boyfriends?"

"No...we're at a girl's school... we don't know any boys... except for her sister's friends... the boys all go to the boy's school... "

"Tell me about Sally's sister and her friends."

"Dorothy's older than Sally... she has a boyfriend... he comes around to Sally's house with his friends. They all meet up in the garage to smoke and play records. Sometimes we go in there to listen to music. Her mum calls them 'The Gang'... she says 'The Gang's all here... why don't you go and join them."

"Do you like the boys?"

"Not really... they're so loud... showing off... but I like the music... Frankie Laine... "

"Do you spend much time at Sally's?"

"Yes... they have a TV... Sally's mum is nice... always talks to me. They have a car as well... her dad has a business so they're better off than we are."

Kay brings her back to discuss the memories that have surfaced and encourages Penny to enlarge on her teenage life.

She tells how she was rather lonely living in a Guesthouse, with her mother so busy, and couldn't wait to leave home when she'd finished school with O-levels and got a job in a Photography Studio, learning to process film and print photographs in the darkroom. Then her journey to Guernsey to be a beach photographer for the summer, after the long dark winter when she'd hardly seen the sun.

But after the memory of her love affair with Davy, there was still nothing. They're disappointed, but Kay says more will transpire in coming sessions. "It takes time Penny... but we'll get there," she assures her.

Kay has an appointment with a client in the afternoon and is pleased when Penny offers to walk the dogs while she's out. When she's got the dogs home, relieved that they'd behaved well for her, Penny decides to explore the gardens some more while the sun's still out. She walks around the lawn behind the conservatory and through the beds of rose bushes, some still flowering; flowers, Michaelmas daisies and Chrysanthemums; remembering them in the garden where she'd grown up. Around them are shrubs, some flowering in vibrant colours, and Acers with glorious red foliage. She had to ask Kay what they were; Japanese, she'd told her. But following a path into the trees beyond, she realises how much land comes with the house. A grove of Beech trees, recalling that the house was named because of them, their glowing autumn leaves drifting down around her. There's something comforting about the trees. A silver-grey mist is wreathing round the trees and she falls into a sort of daydream, wandering along the path as it winds through the trees, skirting a fence, until she glimpses ahead a glade with an ornamental structure and wrought iron seat and is surprised to see a woman sitting there.

Penny hesitates, noticing that she appears to be crying softly, hugging her arms around her. The woman looks up briefly and appears to look in Penny's direction. She wonders if she's a local who's wandered into the garden by mistake. Penny moves a little as she's right behind a large tree, but as she rounds the thick trunk to see better, the bench is empty… there is no-one there. No… she can't have moved away so quickly! Penny approaches the seat, wondering if that will disappear too. It doesn't, and there's nobody around.

She seats herself where the woman had been, puzzled and intrigued. The mist is cold and damp and she shivers. There's such an aura of sadness, Penny feels a pain in her chest, and wants to cry. Maybe this was another apparition… an action replay of something from the past. Could it be Jane? Then she recalls the little boy she thought she's seen previously. Could it have been a vision of Robin, Jane's son? How had Robin died? She was getting used to seeing dead people… but Jane wasn't dead. Why was she seeing these things? She wasn't even asleep this time! Was someone trying to connect with her? Was it Jane? Maybe it's time to tell Kay what has been happening and see if she can find an explanation.

* * *

There doesn't seem to be an appropriate time to talk about it when Kay comes home, as she's busy preparing dinner and talking about something that had happened at the supermarket, where she'd stopped for some shopping. "You wouldn't believe it… some mothers shouldn't have children… their kids just don't know how to behave!" Penny isn't really listening, still pondering her own experience. Then James is home and after dinner, they all watch television; some programme they both enjoy… University Challenge or something. Penny liked quizzes, but she doesn't understand most of the questions, never mind the answers. She feels quite ignorant.

Please let me have a quiet night! she requests silently, as she makes her way to bed.

Chapter 11

Week 2: Day 3… Thursday… Disclosure

The next day's session takes an unexpected turn.

Penny's in deep hypnosis when she says… *"It's so sad…"*

"What's so sad, Penny?" Kay queries.

"They're quarrelling… a man and a woman… he's shouting at her and she's crying."

"Can you hear what he's shouting?"

"'How could you?' He's very angry." Penny's close to tears herself.

"Move on a little further now. What else is happening, Penny?"

"She can't stop crying… now he's saying 'It's Peter, isn't it? He's the father!'"

"Do you know who they are?"

Kay's expecting her to be reliving a memory of her mother and father. But Penny's too distressed to continue and Kay brings her back to her happy place until she's woken properly.

As she recovers, Kay brings her a glass of water and when she's ready, asks who she thinks they were. Penny takes a deep breath.

"Well, I know this sounds crazy, but I know they were James's parents, Jane and Alexander, I recognise them from the family photographs." Then she feels able to recount her ghostly encounters to the astonished Kay, who is silent for a while.

"I've often wondered about poor little Robin. You know it was a terrible thing... he drowned in the pond."

He drowned! A shock runs through her, as her mind reveals a man lifting the limp little body from the water, laying it on the ground and attempting resuscitation. The woman, Jane, cradling her son in her arms, rocking back and forth, in deathly silence. Penny feels engulfed in grief, as though it were her own child that had died. She stifles a sob and Kay glances at her. "Are you alright Penny?" She nods, though wanting to let it all out, but not able to express all she's feeling.

Kay's still talking, absorbed by what she's heard.

"Seemed he'd hit his head on a rock when he fell in. They filled in the pond after that. James has never talked about him and how he died. I think he knows more than he'll ever admit. He might have known about his Mother and Uncle Peter before he went to Boarding school... or maybe Sarah knew and told him. Kids can be very perceptive. But I wonder why you'd be able to tune into something that's not personal to you...," Kay muses as she sips her tea.

"Maybe you're just psychic and picked up on this tragedy somehow. But hey... Jane is still alive and kicking, so how does that work? I usually go to see her on a Friday afternoon. She's lovely, though it's sad to see her so confused. If you'd like to come with me tomorrow?"

Penny's happy to agree, thinking she'd like to meet Jane, even with dementia.

They talk more about what Kay knows about psychics and mediums, which, although she considers these things most unscientific, has to acknowledge hold a certain fascination for her.

Today's session has given them both something to think about, and after walking the dogs Kay does some research online to show Penny.

Kay and Sylvie often talk on the phone in the evening. She wants to talk to Sylvie about these revelations but has assured Penny that anything that went on in therapy sessions would be confidential. She hesitates to ask for Penny's permission to tell her sister.

"I wonder if Sylvie would be interested in hearing about all this." Penny must have read her thoughts. "I'd like to keep her up to date anyway."

"Thanks Penny... I'm so glad you feel that too. Let's call her now."

Sylvie's amazed at what she hears. She'd known about James's family history and had often wondered what more remained to be revealed. That Penny somehow had psychic abilities doesn't really surprise her. There is more to Penny than seems apparent.

The sisters talk on for a while, while Penny reflects on what she knows of her own history. It seems to her that Kay has been expecting some early traumatic incident that might account for her own memory loss, but Penny knows somehow that whatever it was must have happened more recently, if at all.

In bed, Penny continues reading her book until she falls asleep in the midst of a chapter.

Chapter 12

Week 2: Day 4… Friday… Revelation

The next day, as Penny is deep into hypnosis, Kay asks her to go back to any particular memory that may have been disturbing her. "Is anything coming to you?"

Penny takes some time before nodding.

"Now… put that memory up on a TV screen… you have the control… you can start or pause it whenever you want… and you're in control of the brightness and the colour. Look at it now as if it's a movie and tell me what you see… what you hear… and what you feel or sense."

"There's a kitchen and a woman at the cooker…. and a young girl sitting at the table."

"Do you recognise the woman… or the girl?"

"I'm not sure…"

"Pause the movie for a moment… Can you describe them?"

"They're just chatting… like a mother and daughter… can't see them clearly…"

"Now... run the film... what's happening?"

"A man's come in... shouting at the girl... he's calling her bad names..."

"And the woman at the cooker... what's she doing?"

"She's trying to stop him but he pushes her away." Penny's getting agitated.

"What are you feeling, Penny?"

"I'm fearful he'll hurt her... the girl... he's pulling her arm... I'm afraid he'll hit her..."

"What's happening now?"

"She's pulling away. He's shouting... 'You will never see that boy again... you hear me... you slut!' "

"And now what?"

"She's shouting... 'You're not my father...' He's hitting her... slapping her... he's going mad... dragging her out of the door..." Penny is distressed now, shaking.

"What about the woman Penny? What's she doing?"

"She's trying to reason with him and follow them out of the door... but he's shut it in her face. She's banging on the door... 'Stop it... both of you... stop it!' " She was shouting. Too loudly.

"Move on now Penny..."

"She's just standing there... she looks shocked."

"Alright Penny... let it fade away now... turn off the screen and come back to your safe, happy place... When you wake, you'll feel happy and refreshed... glad that you've retrieved these memories and ready to go further another time. Take a deep breath now..."

Kay talks her back before finally waking her.

Kay questions her more about the memory. Penny thinks they looked familiar but insists she can't identify them. Privately, Kay thinks she's in denial; that she was either the daughter or the mother, though she'd seemed to identify more with the mother. She'd wanted to carry it further, but Penny was so distraught, it would have to wait. It's obvious to her that Penny was disassociating from what must have been a traumatic experience. Undoubtedly there is more to be unravelled.

Penny tries to keep her composure, while in a turmoil of emotions inside; drawn down into a whirlpool of fear, anger, guilt and sadness, confused images flickering round, and around in her head. *Was I that mother?* She twisted the gold band on her finger. *I must be married... who is he? Am I still married? Is he difficult and even violent? And was that my own daughter? Why can't I remember?* She doesn't know if it was her own memory that had surfaced, or someone else's.

While Kay prepares lunch, Penny takes a walk through the garden, finally settling on Jane's bench with the autumn sun trickling through the falling leaves and bare branches of surrounding trees, reflecting on Jane's relationships and heartbreak until she feels calmer.

'What is this Thing... called Love? This Crazy thing... called Love...' The song is haunting her.

* * *

At lunch Kay reminds Penny that they are going to visit Jane, which could be interesting with them both having problems with memory.

It isn't far to the nursing home in Gerards Cross where Jane is living out her old age. A large old house that must have been someone's palatial home in the past and now extended at the back to accommodate more residents. Jane is sitting in an easy chair when they enter her room. It's large enough and feels comfortable, overlooking the spacious gardens. Penny knows the family has the money to provide the best for her.

Kay greets Jane, who turns towards her visitors. "This is Penny. She's staying with us at *The Beeches*...," as Penny approaches, offering her hand.

"Hello... I'm very pleased to meet you..."

Jane smiles at her. "I saw you... in the garden...," as she takes Penny's hand and holds onto it and their eyes meet in recognition.

"Yes... I saw you too... you were very sad... " She knows how deeply she feels her sorrow.

"My poor Robin..."

"You're still grieving... your little boy... do you want to talk about it?"

Jane squeezes her hand. "He was a wonderful child... so clever... and always happy. He'll always be seven now... in my memory... little Robin... my lovely boy..." A tear glistened in her eyes. "And his poor father... Peter had to go away..."

"I know... Peter had to go away...," Penny repeats.

"There was no other way... we couldn't be together... and we needed each other so much. I've waited so long for him to come back. He comes to see me sometimes...," she sighs, "but not as often as he used to... "

"He comes to see you...," Penny doesn't know why she's repeating her words, but wants to comfort this old lady who's retreated into her memories, unable to cope with the realities of life.

"Yes, I know he died... but I know he loves me... I feel it... keeps me going...," she's smiling now, for her lost love.

"He's always here you know... It's your love that never dies...," Penny feels she has to reassure her. Jane relinquishes her hand and relaxes into her chair. "My love...," she murmurs.

Penny glances at Kay, who's been listening, fascinated by this conversation. Jane has never talked like this before. Usually, Kay finds Jane's agitated ramblings confusing. But now she realises it had been mostly about her feelings for Peter and Robin, although she'd known so little of this family tragedy.

At this point a nurse brings them a tray of tea and cakes, which halts the conversation. Jane looks happier than usual, Kay notices as she pours the tea for them. Jane is even asking about James and the children, which surprises Kay even more. It's been a long time since Jane has talked so coherently. It seems that somehow, Penny has calmed her through knowing what she's talking about. She has a lot to digest about second sight, clairvoyance, or whatever it is Penny has tuned into!

As they are about to leave, Jane takes Penny's hand. "I'm so glad you came," she says quietly... "You understand... I know."

On the drive home, Kay comments on how well Penny had done to get through to Jane.

"She only wanted to be heard." Penny considers that's the key and Kay has to agree. "That's an interesting observation. It's the same in therapy... people seem to need to tell their story before we can do anything else. Maybe they just feel they've never been heard before!"

* * *

While Kay prepares supper, Penny goes into the darkening garden and sits on Jane's bench with the sadness still there, though not so desperate, feeling that if she'd had some kind of closure on her tragedy, then she could too. If only she could remember what it was!

James isn't coming home tonight as he'll be away over the weekend to attend a conference, Kay informs her. It isn't unusual for him to stay at the flat at least once a week, especially when the weather's very bad with fog, ice or snow, which could stretch into days. Penny doesn't know why she wonders if this is something else, more personal. She's shocked at her own thoughts, which she quickly dismisses.

They've heard from Sylvie that her acting role is going well and she will be busy working for the next few days. Kay has suggested that Penny will be welcome to stay longer, so they can continue their sessions and hope for more recent memories to surface. Penny's in agreement and is glad that James will be away, as she finds his manner and attitudes quite disagreeable.

After supper, they watch a film that is, funnily enough, about Time Travelling. Though not in the same way as her experiences. She's tired when they go upstairs and is soon asleep.

Driving along a leafy country lane... Coldwater Lane... always thought it was such a chilly address for such a lovely location... although she knows the origin of the name meant that here was a shelter, albeit a cold one... a haven for weary travellers. Heading for home... over the canal bridge... up the rise in the road and turn into the parking area beside the Victorian Villa... Priory Gate. The crumbling remains of what would have been a massive gate forming part of their boundary and any remainder of what had been a Priory carried away by locals to build houses... seeing the children in the garden as she pulls up... Becky and Carrie on the swings and Julian still trying to build his tree house... Davy mowing the lawn... where's young Michael? Struggling to get out of the car... coat caught on the gearstick... calling out... I'm here... Michael... can't get the words out... black clouds overshadowing and blotting out the scene... must get to them... unable to walk... feet dragging in soft boggy ground... dragged down, down, into inky black watery depths.

She wakes in a cold sweat... filled with a sickening dread... crying out... with the realisation that this was her memory... she had been with Davy and they did have children... she was so happy she'd seen the children... they had been happy... she remembered this much... but what had happened? She knows something had happened to Michael. The way she'd connected to Jane's grief over her little boy; now she knew why.

Her head hurts, every part of her hurts. Maybe she can find painkillers somewhere. She's creeping downstairs, trying to avoid the creaking steps, when Kay opens her door, having been awakened by Penny's cry. They go into the kitchen and Kay makes them both a hot chocolate, before bringing out a bottle of whisky, while she hears about Penny's dreaming recollection.

* * *

They'd found Michael in the canal. She remembered how she'd waded into the marshy margins of the unused and overgrown canal that was such a haven for wildlife. They'd loved to take the children down to watch the bird life and dragonflies, dipping jam jars into the water to collect tadpoles. Always telling them never to come down without them.

The little five-year old had found a gap in the hedge that separated the garden from the canal. She remembered how they'd waded into the water where green matted vegetation looked as if it was solid enough to walk on, to lift him out, how Davy had tried to breathe life back into his limp body, but it was too late. Tears coursed down her cheeks. Now she recalled her anger that Davy hadn't fenced it properly as she'd asked. He'd said it was too expensive and there was so much to spend on the house, he couldn't afford it. He'd even implied it was her fault that she'd not been there. He became cold and distant. She couldn't reach him and she had to concentrate on the children.

You lost that loving feeling...' running through her head... *'and its gone, gone, gone.'*

She falls silent. What had happened to his heart? The heart she'd loved so much. Yes, she remembered the recurring dream. Trying to slap him... so angry that he could do this to her... and to his own children.

"That's what broke us...," she's calm now. " He stopped coming home every day, saying he had too much work to be coming so far out of

London. I couldn't talk to him, he was always too busy. Then one day, he told me he was putting the house up for sale and he'd find us somewhere smaller and nearer London. Somewhere he could afford. And he stopped coming home. I didn't know what to do. Mum came to stay and I went into London with a friend. I thought I'd catch him at the studio where he was supposed to be recording to ask him what was going on. That's when I saw him with another woman; just a slip of a girl. Holding hands and laughing together. I had to confront him and she walked away. Right there on the street he told me he wanted a divorce, he couldn't live with me anymore and I'd have to find somewhere else to live. He wasn't even getting us a smaller house. It just broke me."

She sighed... "So much for True Love! Maybe that's what I was doing in Regent Street... trying to recapture that memory of true love." She laughs. "I thought he was the love of my life... my soul mate! How could he do that?" Now her voice is bitter. "How can a man leave the wife and children he's promised to love and care for? I don't understand." She shakes her head.

Another song running through her head... *'Anyone who had a heart... could look at me... And know that I love you'...* Cilla, wasn't it? *'You couldn't really have a heart and hurt me... Like you hurt me and be so untrue... What am I to do?'* She remembers it all.

Kay is sad for her, though her psychological mind notices how calmly, even dispassionately, Penny has recounted this memory, as though it were a story she'd told many times before. A sure sign of disconnection, she thinks. But glad she's retrieved a memory at last.

"What did you do?" she wants to know.

"There wasn't much I could do. Didn't have any money, except for a small allowance the court ordered him to pay to support the children. Then even that stopped and I had to apply for Benefits. We were given a council house in the nearest town, where I made a few friends. He didn't even bother to see the kids, except for a couple of occasions when he took them to visit his mother in Yorkshire. We were happy there; just me and the children. I think that's where I met someone else. But then it gets hazy."

Kay asks if she can recall where the house was or her married name, but names are still lost in the mists of her memory. "But I'd know Priory Gate if I saw it again." Penny muses, "Maybe the people who live there now would have records of previous owners." She brightens up, thinking of her canal friends who might be able to help. She'll contact Dylan tomorrow.

So they are both in better spirits when they retire for a few hours sleep before dawn.

Chapter 13

Week 2: Day 5... Saturday... More Progress

Not surprisingly, they both sleep in late and emerge groggily at about the same time, ready for a revitalising coffee or two before breakfast. Kay is relieved to see her guest looking so relaxed and hopeful to continue recovering more of her memories.

Penny's still getting used to the mobile phone that Sylvie had given her but eventually finds Dylan's number. When she tells him about her most recent memory of the house by the canal, he's enthusiastic about helping her find it. He says that he and Grace have been planning a trip on the Grand Union Canal to visit Grace's parents in Milton Keynes. They want to go as soon as possible while the weather is so lovely and will be delighted to have her aboard. Can she be ready to go mid-week? She can't wait!

* * *

Later in their next session, as Penny slips into a deep hypnotic state, Kay asks her to imagine rising up until she can see her life as a timeline... her whole life stretching back to her birth, as if it were a long journey.

"You can choose to fly or find a vehicle to transport you... just notice the bright spots and when you're ready, let yourself go down to a time and place that attracts your attention."

Penny finds herself in a balloon, floating above the long road she's travelled, through so many varied landscapes and cities. She looks down on the recent past, but it's covered by a swirling mass of dark clouds, except for a tiny flicker of light. She tries to go into the light but the clouds don't part. Kay is asking her to say what she can see, what she can feel or sense.

"I can't see... just a feeling of warmth... and love... a hand reaching out..." She feels a strong body close against her, a man's body... the comforting smell of him... *"I can't see..."* She's back above the clouds, desperate to go back... to connect with this love she can't remember.

"That's alright Penny... go back further now... what do you see?"

Now she's drawn further back... to an earlier time... a small town in a valley... green hills rising on either side.

"I'm in a garden... planting vegetables, I think. The house is in a terrace... a tall Victorian house... the sun is shining... a man's calling me from the back door."

"Do you know who he is? Can you describe him?"

"He's my husband... not Davy. He's very kind... I'm going in to get ready to go out. We're taking the children to see an exhibition... about Space... the kids love that..."

"Go on, Penny... run it on a little... what's happening now?"

"Oh no... he's arguing with Julian again... he can get so angry! Sometimes I'm afraid of his anger. He wants them all to do as they're told... when they're told... and Julian will answer back... I wish he didn't."

"What's he saying... can you hear them?"

" 'I'm the head of this house... and you will respect me.' Julian's walking away... 'Don't walk away from me you insolent boy.' I must break this up before it gets violent... I can't bear it. I have to get Julian to apologise... he's only sixteen... headstrong too... he won't, I know. Now he's gone to his room... looks like we're going out without him." Penny's getting agitated now.

"Ok, Penny... let it fade and come back... "

She's curious to see how much Penny remembers when the session is over.

"Do you recall the name of this man? Your husband?"

His name? Penny's thoughtful for a few minutes. "Gerry... now I remember... rather Victorian in his ways... like my Dad I suppose. He was very strict with me when I was growing up. I think that was what attracted me... I thought the children needed a firm hand growing up in the age of sex, drugs and rock'n'roll. I wanted to keep them safe. I remember now... it was Gerry in that other memory... him and Becky. It was fine when they were younger, but after puberty... he was very strict on morals... too strict... and he seemed to see immorality in everything. I didn't think Becky was immoral... just a young girl feeling the stirrings of attraction. It's only natural. They were all afraid of his temper."

"Were you afraid of him?"

"I think I was... I don't know if it was my fault..."

"How might it be your fault?"

"He always said it was... I was too soft on them... he said I didn't understand the world. You had to learn to be tough. He said I was stupid because I loved art and music and being in nature. He wanted to toughen the boy up... and keep the girls at home. And he wanted obedience... from all of us! Yes, I was scared of him! The girls loved him at first... he was kind and funny... but as they grew up, as teenagers... it all changed... for Becky especially. I asked her a couple of times how she felt about him. The first time, she just looked at me and said... '*I hate him*'... and the second time... she just turned away... the look on her face! I was worried. I began to think of leaving him."

"What did you think was going on?"

"I didn't know what to think. I didn't dare think the worse! I just wanted to get us away, I just didn't know how. How could we manage without him to support us financially? I didn't have any money. I didn't know what to do."

"Do you know how long that relationship lasted?"

"No... nothing more. The harder I try to remember, the further everything seems to slip away."

"Don't be sad Penny... it will all come back in time." Kay's pleased at her progress but wonders what more distress will be uncovered on this voyage of discovery. That's what she loves about her profession; uncovering the root cause of people's problems.

* * *

After a late lunch they walk the dogs through the woods and out onto the common where the late afternoon sun paints a colourful view of the valley. Penny always seems happier out in the fresh air.

That evening Sylvie phones, wanting to know the latest developments of Penny's sessions and Kay are eager to report the successes. But Sylvie has something else on her mind as well.

"Do you know where Angie's got to? I tried her phone but it must be switched off." She's trying to remember the last time she'd spoken to her mother and is feeling guilty. It had occurred to her that if something had happened to her, such as an accident like Penny's, she and Sylvie wouldn't have known to report her missing.

Kay laughs. "Don't you remember? She always goes to her Retreat this time of year, in some remote Welsh valley and isn't in touch with the world for a month. There's no signal, and anyway, they're asked to give up their phones for the duration. I wrote it down in my diary." She rummages in her desk. "Oh, just the dates. A Writers Retreat… Bwlch Farm… that's such a common name in Wales. Not even a proper address. It's been about ten days so far, I think."

Sylvie is relieved of her guilt though she realises she'd not taken enough notice of her mother's comings and goings. It was about time for a visit to Wales; she's not seen her for some time and phone calls are not frequent enough.

Kay tells her about Penny's plan to join Dylan and Grace on a trip up the Canal. "She really thinks she'll find her house, but you know, I've searched the net for the name; Priory Gate, but there's only a couple up in the far North, and according to Penny, her house was not too far from London. I'm thinking of Berkhampstead or somewhere in that area that's on the canal system."

Sylvie agrees. She's glad Penny has recovered this memory and knows she'll enjoy the trip, which is scheduled for Wednesday. They decide that Kay will see Penny onto the train on Monday when Sylvie can pick her up early afternoon, as she won't be working that day. She'll be glad to have Penny back for a couple of days and hear all about her experiences with Kay and her hypnotherapy sessions.

* * *

Meanwhile, Penny's busy writing up her memories in the notebook, not forgetting the songs that keep coming back to her. As she writes, even more seem to emerge and this keeps her busy till bedtime.

She goes to sleep thinking of the love she'd had such a brief glimpse of… the warmth of loving someone else. How could she have forgotten that? Was she really loved again? Or had she lost out once more? No… with a thrill she dares to hope.

Another song ringing in her head. *'You're just too good to be true... I can't take my eyes off you... You'd be like heaven to touch... I want to hold you so much...'* It's too frustrating, but she sleeps anyway.

Chapter 14

Week 2: Day 6… Sunday…

'**M**orning has broken… like the first morning… blackbird has spoken… like the first bird…' Penny's humming to herself as she opens the curtains to a cold bright day, feeling more hopeful than she's felt for some time. There had been no dreams that she could remember, and no nightly visitations. She thinks to herself that this house's ghosts have now been put at rest. Only her own ghosts remain.

Although she rarely eats a big breakfast, today she's ready for what she can smell Kay already cooking; the Full Monty… without meat anyway!

Kay asks her if she's a church-goer and Penny laughs. "I don't think so, though I was very religious when I was young. Always searching for 'The Truth'. But I think I soon realised that 'Truth' is relative. I feel more at home with Buddhists as far as I can recall." Then she wonders how she knows that. Had she known at nineteen?

"Anyway…," Kay continues. "I thought you might enjoy a visit to our local Car Boot. I sometimes pick up lovely antiques there." Penny agrees, though she had no idea what a *Car Boot* might be, except the back end of a car.

As Kay drives them through the gates into the old airfield that houses the Sunday Car Boot Sale, Penny can't believe the extent of cars, vans and campers; row upon row of trestle tables and groundsheets covered in goods for sale. They walk up one row and down another, then another, and another, looking for something to catch the eye. She starts to recognise things, familiar dishes and crockery that could have come from her Grandmother's home, while Kay rummages through boxes of oddments, asking the price of a few things, but buys nothing. "I'm very particular… don't want a lot of junk," she explains.

They've trawled the whole site and start again to see what they might have missed, when Penny spots a small blue and white decorated bowl on a table of knick-knacks. As she picks it up to have a closer look, Kay is at her side. "That's nice. You have a good eye…," she says quietly.

"How much is it?" Penny inquires of the young woman at the stall, who asks for £1.00, which Penny promptly pays. "I do believe you got a bargain there… porcelain and old." Kay nudges Penny as they moved on. "I think it could be quite a find!" Penny just likes it, but intends to give it to Kay as a thank you for all her help and is glad that she rates it so highly. She's so grateful for her help, and the money she's provided her with. How can she ever repay that.

Then Kay finds a rather dilapidated Victorian writing box for £20. "I like the mother of pearl inlay…makes it a bit unusual. I'll show it to my antiques friend. He'll know if it's worth anything and whether it's worth renovating." On the way home, they both agree they've had a good time in the open air and it hasn't rained. Kay accepts the little bowl as a present. "That's so lovely Penny. I'll treasure that. Thank you."

Penny's curious to know more about Kay's family and her relationship with her sister as they both seem so different in their attitudes and lifestyle. She finds the opportunity to ask Kay after they'd watched a television programme about genealogy and lost families in the afternoon and Kay is happy to talk. Penny relaxes into her comfortable armchair to listen, commenting at times, but happy to hear Kay's account of her life for a change.

"We are quite different, Sylvie and I. For a start, I'm older than her by seven years and we have different fathers. Our Mother Angela is a very beautiful woman; dark flowing hair and blue eyes; she's a man magnet. In her sixties now and she still is! She was married to my Father, Henry Wilcox, who's a highly respected Lawyer, until she got involved with her hippie friends, smoking pot and going to Hippie Festivals. She decided she couldn't stand her life with Father anymore and told him so. He gave her an ultimatum; either she stayed and supported him in his career or she could get out. So she did; left with me and a few bags. She must have got money off Father because she bought a decent camper van and that was when we started travelling about with other hippies and travellers. Except I didn't like it, because I wanted to have a proper home and go to school like other children, so I got dumped on Grammy, who didn't mind at all. She came from a strong Catholic family; her grandparents came from Ireland and she inherited their strong moral compass and could never understand her daughter's rebellious streak. In spite of everything, Angie was always welcomed home whenever she was ill or ran out of money or friends. I always suspected she was mentally unstable, but of course, she would never admit it or consult a doctor for anything."

Kay takes a look at Penny for confirmation that she's still interested, as she lays back on the cushions, making appropriate noises to encourage Kay to continue.

"Well, she was soon involved with Carlos, a Spanish student who she met at a Festival, and before long was pregnant. Funnily enough, Carlos was also studying law and was determined to complete his studies, but he was also besotted with Angie, who was very attractive as well as having a strong emotional character that matched his Spanish temperament. So they were together spasmodically and Sylvie, christened Sylvana in church because Carlos was also from a Catholic family, was welcomed into the world with love and celebration with their friends. When Carlos returned to his studies, Angie brought the new baby to stay with us and naturally we fell in love with her. That became a sort of pattern; they would stay with us until Angie's restlessness drove her back on the road, or to meet up with Carlos. Then they'd turn up again and we were always glad to see them."

"So what happened?" Penny's curious to know the rest, which is turning into a monologue. Perhaps Kay had never had the opportunity to be heard either!

"We did meet Carlos eventually, when he was well on his way to becoming a Lawyer. It was Christmas Eve and we were expecting him to arrive by lunchtime. Angie was so restless waiting for him to arrive, she couldn't stop moving about; opening the front door to see if he was there, checking the food for lunch that was ready in the kitchen, then going in the back garden for a smoke. Grammy wouldn't allow smoking in the house or at the front.

Finally, while she was in the bathroom, he knocked on the door and it was me who opened it to him. Angie said he was handsome, but he had real film star looks! Tall and muscular with a light tan and dark wavy hair. He looked down at me with deep brown eyes and said "Hello, young lady, you must be Kathleen", took my hand, kissed it and presented me with a bouquet of flowers. Then he looked beyond me and his smile was full of love for my mother coming down the hall. "My Angel" I heard him murmur as they embraced." Kay looked suddenly a little embarrassed.

"How lovely…," Penny responds.

"He was introduced to Grammy who was as taken with him as I was. Nothing was too much trouble and Grammy seemed to forget they weren't married and made no fuss about them sharing a bed. Well, how could she, when they had a baby? He couldn't wait to see baby Sylvie, who was nearly a year old by now and just waking from her sleep. I could see how much he loved them both, Angela and Sylvana, my mother and sister, and somehow, at that moment, it felt that we were a real family, for the moment at least. With Grammy we always had a proper Christmas with a tree and decorations and presents, but that was the very best Christmas I remember."

"Carlos stayed with us till New Year, but had to get back to Madrid, where he was to take up a new post. He was intending to send for Angie and Sylvie as soon as he was settled. When he was gone, Angie couldn't settle and would pack a bag, take the baby and go off to visit friends, here, there and everywhere. It seemed like ages before Carlos arranged for them to join him in Madrid. Then Angie wrote often that she was enjoying Spain and that while she was learning the language, Sylvie was picking it up too. She sent pictures of them in bright sunshine. Then she wrote that she was staying with friends in the south of Spain, near Granada for a while."

Kay's really into the story now, as though it were a script she'd prepared earlier and Penny is the perfect audience, eager to hear more.

"It must have been a year before we saw them again, because Sylvie was already two years old. A Postcard arrived with a picture of a sunny beach and the message said simply, *'Coming home. See you Friday'*, and they arrived back, suntanned, dishevelled and unhappy.

"How was Spain?" My nineyear old self asked brightly. "Don't ask!" she replied with a grimace. "Fascists!"

"Not married then?" Grammy asked sweetly.

"His high and mighty family wouldn't even meet me!" She was bitter.

I never knew what had happened. Only that Carlos was so busy being a Lawyer that he had no time for family life.

There were other boyfriends, of course. Angie was too beautiful not to attract men. Bees to the blossom. All that pot-smoking wasn't good for her. It shows. But she became interested in other things; Civil Rights, CND, Ban the Bomb, Greenham Common, Women's Refuges; she was there. So Sylvie grew up with all that; Peace and Love etc. And Carlos was always there in the picture somewhere; coming and going. I know he always tried to see Sylvie on her birthday and sometimes she went to visit him in his home in Spain. He became a Civil Rights Lawyer, fighting for Justice. Angie was still travelling, going to all the festivals, though now she has a home in Wales; might be a women's commune sort of thing. I've never been there, though Sylvie has. I know she's spent some time abroad, helping out in third world countries; always the do-gooder. Where Sylvie got it from, obviously!"

Penny shows her obvious curiosity by asking about Kay's own father.

"I've always been in touch with my Father. Visiting him weekends, summer holidays, sometimes on my birthday. He's always been very good to me. Helped me through university and been very generous with money when I needed it. Came to my Graduation when Angie was too busy doing good somewhere. I don't know if they ever got divorced. I think Father still sends her an allowance. I wouldn't know if they ever see each other. I think he still loves her. I do admire his persistence. There's been no sign of other women all these years. Maybe he's a latent homosexual! Never thought of that before, he's just steady, predictable, my rather boring Father."

"So that's why Sylvie is so different to me. While I value the importance of a stable life, secure marriage, working hard at a profession, having a good reputation, Sylvie is the opposite, more like our mum, a bit wild, wants her freedom! I wish she'd settle down with someone steady. But we still have the fierce love for each other that binds family relationships, and that's more important than anything else."

That evening, Kay decides to Skype Sylvie on her laptop, to the amazement of Penny. The wonders of modern science seem to be boundless. This enables them all to be able to see and talk to each other in comfort, and there is plenty to talk about. After Penny's animated account of the Car Boot and what she'd found, she feels ready to disclose her recollection of another, later love interest. She hasn't even talked about this with Kay.

"It was such a strong feeling....," she says, blushing a little, to her own discomfort, "and it came back to me last night. I just feel there is someone I'm close to... and it's driving me nuts trying to remember!"

The sisters are full of questions. Who was he? Can she describe him? Does he have a name? She can only answer 'No' to everything. "It's just a feeling...," she explains..., "warm and... familiar. I think it's love."

After that revelation, conversation turns to the perennial subject of women's concern with Love.

"*What is this thing... called love...,*" Sylvie croons theatrically.

"*This crazy thing... called love...,*" Penny joins in giggling.

"What is love anyway?" Sylvie queries. "Do we really understand it? What makes us fall in love? And out again? Come on sis... you're the Psychologist... you must have some explanation! Is it just chemistry?"

"Well, of course it's chemistry; biological hormones drive us... but very simply, love is a complex mixture of emotions, and as you know, that's energy in motion. Love affects you both mentally and physically. It moves you. Love... that intense craving to be with the particular person who triggers you... but it can be difficult to tell whether it's simply lust, because the chemicals in the brain act like an addiction. It activates a flood of neurotransmitters... dopamine, oxytocin and serotonin... to reward our pleasure centres. We just can't help ourselves."

"That's very scientific Kay, but what about *romance*? What about love for your family? Love of a mother for her children? What about love that transcends sex?" Sylvie wants to know.

"Yes, there are many different kinds of love... the Greeks had seven different names for it... family, erotic, and altruistic love etc. Then think about the great Romantic poets, musicians and artists; all that love poured out into their art." Kay sounds unusually passionate. "But love seems to be a biological drive. Love makes us *feel* something out of the ordinary. It literally gives us an addictive high. But I'd like to think it connects us to a higher plane of existence... that I'd call the 'higher mind'."

"Now you're talking Spirituality. Angels? Spirit Guides? God? Surely that's something else?"

"Maybe... but I believe Love is the most powerful energy in the Universe. Maybe what we call 'God'... 'Allah'... 'Father Sky'... is only a way of describing Love. Christ said it too. God is Love."

"Love is a many splendoured thing...," Sylvie adds.

"Pure Love...," Penny mused. "No strings attached... no ifs, ands or buts. I suppose that's what all the saints, monks and nuns, gurus and holy men are all striving for... pure love."

"All I know is that when I'm in love I lose all my common sense!" Sylvie sighs.

Penny laughs out loud. "You and me both! Whatever happened to romance? All illusion? I reckon it's simply a biological instinct to ensure the human race keeps reproducing! I can imagine the last man and woman on earth falling in love having never met before and speaking different languages. Simple, isn't it?"

"Oh Penny... you're so pragmatic!" and both sisters fall about laughing. Penny's shocked at her own cynicism, yet it's hardly surprising, considering what she's learned about herself.

96

* * *

Penny goes to bed singing to herself… '*Love is the sweetest thing… the oldest, yet the greatest thing… I only hope that fate will bring… Love's story to me.*"

Chapter 15

Week 2: Day 7... Monday. An encounter on the train.

On the train back to London, Penny relaxes into her window seat reading through her notebook, hoping that something more concrete will occur to her. She notices a young teenage girl sat across the aisle, and thinks she looks a bit anxious. She seems to be in school uniform under her coat. Maybe she's playing hooky, going into London when she's supposed to be at school, she thinks. She looks quite young; but then girls these days seem to be confident and capable at an early age. She resigns herself to watching the landscape pass in a blur of colour and light.

"Will you speak to her? She can't hear me... but you can, can't you?" A woman hovering over the girl attracts Penny's attention. The girl is ignoring her. She hadn't been there before, had she?

"I'm sorry... what's that?" Penny says.

"Please tell her not to do it... she's too young to leave home... her name's Molly. Maybe if you tell her... just say, your mother understands... please!"

To her surprise, Penny feels compelled to say something to the girl who is studiously ignoring all around her. "Hello… I'm sorry to bother you, but someone wants to speak to you if you're not too busy…," which she can hardly dispute.

"I don't know what you mean. Who wants to talk to me?" The girl is alarmed, but can't move away. *"Molly… please listen…,"* the woman is distraught. Penny nods at her.

Penny decides to come straight out with it… "Molly… your mother wants you to know that she understands… and don't ask me how I'm able to tell you that, because I don't know why I'm seeing people who aren't really here… but she's right beside to you. Please don't freak out… she says you're too young to leave home." The phantom woman hovers… *"Please tell her I love her… and I'm always with her."*

The girl looks bewildered, turning around to see very few people nearby. "My mother's dead… and how do you know my name?" she demands anxiously. Penny moves across to her. "That's what I thought… your mother told me your name… don't let it worry you… but I keep seeing dead people and it's very disconcerting. She wants you to know that she loves you and will always be with you. If you like, you can tell me all about it."

The girl responds with a sad smile, thinking that this strange woman could be mad; but how on earth did she know her name? She decides to trust her. *"Thank you… thank you…,"* her mother responds.

For the rest of the journey, with frequent interjections from Molly's Mother, Penny learns that she's been looked after by her grandparents since her mother died in an accident two years ago. Her father had not been there for her growing up, but had somehow persuaded her to come and live with him in London, against her grandparents' wishes. Penny wants to know why she would want to do that. "I guess your grandparents, lovely as they are, seem a bit stuffy? Laying down rules about staying out late? Trouble with boyfriends?" The girl nods.

"So what makes you think it will be any different with Dad?" The girl looks back stubbornly... "Well... he's my Dad after all..."

Molly's mother is frantic... "He's no good... he was never a father to her... we didn't see him for years... and now he wants to know her?" Penny relays that to her, hoping it will have the desired effect. Molly is uncertain, but decides to trust that these messages really are from her own dear mother, which seems to encourage her to reply. She turns to Penny...

"I know he never seemed to care about us... Mum had to do everything... going to work every day... I miss her so much." Molly's mum glows and gestures to Penny.

"That's good... she hears you... you can talk to her whenever you want, you know. Tell her all your troubles and she'll answer somehow... you'll know inside you that you're heard. And what are you going to do now, Molly? Will your grandparents have missed you?"

"No, they think I'm at school. I'll go back and tell them. I think they'd like to know I've had a message from Mum. Thank you so much... I wasn't thinking straight... letting Dad talk me into leaving... I knew it wasn't right... being sneaky like that. I've got to finish school first! Then I want to go to Uni... I have so much to do." Now she's flushed with enthusiasm... "Thank you Mum... I know you're watching over me. Thank you for telling me...," she takes Penny's proffered hand. "I don't suppose that was easy! I can feel her here...," and she touches her heart as the spirit of her mother envelopes her in a hug. Then suddenly, she isn't there, and Penny wonders if she'd just imagined her.

She laughs. "Well I could hardly ignore your mother... she's so desperate for you. You should be proud to be her daughter." They hug before parting, having exchanged names and phone numbers. Penny makes her promise to keep in touch.

***

Sylvie meets her at the station and they walk home. She's amazed by Penny's account of yet another ghostly encounter and wants to hear all the details. "Wow... sounds like you were in the right place at the right time for that poor girl. How wonderful that you were able to help her like that! You could make a career out of it...," she laughs. "Come on, let's get home for tea."

Home, she thinks. *Where is home?* She's looking forward to her trip on the canal; surely she'd be able to find the home where she'd once lived: Priory Gate.

It's good to be back in the warm, cluttered kitchen of Sylvie's home, where she prepares a lovely supper. The Chinese vegetables and rice stir-fry is delicious.

That evening talk is all about what had transpired at *The Beeches*. Sylvie is curious to know more of what had happened there and Penny is happy to fill in the details.

"Of course, I knew about the tragedy in James's family, but I never dreamed...," Sylvie shakes her head.

"I thought I'd been dreaming, but it all fit. Kay thinks I have psychic abilities but I don't know... I think that because of my dilemma I'm just more sensitive to the vibrations of other worlds. It feels like Time Travelling! I don't really understand any of it. And I still don't know who I am!"

"Never mind Penny... you're getting there... and let's hope you'll be able to find out more."

She reflects on these supernatural abilities that have come unwittingly into her life. It had been quite a shock to be confronted by a spirit that was so insistent on being heard. She's glad though, that Molly had reacted well to her mother's message. It isn't clear to her whether she was actually seeing these spirits, or whether they come to her in her mind, perhaps in response to what she was feeling. What if the word got around through the spirit world and other spirits start coming through the woodwork, demanding to be heard? It's all so confusing. She sees that Molly had sent a phone text to say she'd arrived home safely, that her grandparents sent their grateful thanks and would like her to visit them in Slough... that would be lovely.

* * *

As she goes up to bed she reviews all of her own memories that have surfaced in the last few days. She's so happy to have seen her children: Julian, he's so clever and helpful... and my lovely girls... Becky and Carrie. At least she now knows their names, but what's happened to them all since they were young? It was sad she'd not recovered the important surname that would identify her. Why hadn't anyone reported her missing? Did anyone care about her? And what was this memory of another love? What was she thinking? Who would want her at her age with her tired old body? Men want younger women, don't they? She drifts off...

'You're just too good to be true... can't take my eyes of you... you'd be like heaven to touch... I want to hold you so much...' A man's voice, deep and throaty. Feeling that warm protective hand in hers.

She's jolted awake. Has she just been dreaming? Or is it simply her wish to be loved again? But the voice... not Andy Williams... this voice was much lower.

Her heart's beating in a most irregular way. She wants to call out... *Who are you?... What's your name?* She tries to open her eyes but all is pitch black... a darkness so deep it feels as though she's suspended over an impenetrable chasm that absorbs all sight, sound, sensation...

can't move… can't speak… like she's paralyzed… panic rising in her throat as she tries to scream… a silent wail of fear and frustration… in the darkness a sudden thought of spirits and demons trying to control her… trying to speak … *Whatever you are… I don't believe in you… go away… leave me alone…*

Finally, she remembers her mantra… *Love and Peace… Go to my safe, happy place… slowly sifting sand through her fingers… picking tiny intricate shells… miniature marvels… fragile memories… for a keepsake…*

She's soon asleep .

Chapter 16

Week 3: Day 1… Tuesday. The Medium.

She wakes in the morning from yet another dream that simply fades away as she opens her eyes. She doesn't recall last night's episode until she hears the song on the radio when she goes down for breakfast. Andy Williams… *You're just too good to be true… can't take my eyes of you… you'd be like heaven to touch… I want to hold you so much…'*

"Gosh, that's an old one," Sylvie laughs… "Bet you know it!"

"You won't believe it…," Penny starts… and tells Sylvie of hearing a man's voice, singing to her, then about her experience of feeling paralysed.

Sylvie is very matter of fact about this as she butters toast and stirs a pan of beans. "I've heard of this… it's not uncommon apparently. *Sleep paralysis* they call it. Nothing to worry about."

"Maybe, but it was very frightening at the time!" Penny's indignant. "I actually thought I was under some kind of psychic attack… you know... demons with pitchforks and stuff!"

"What? Hieronymus Bosch? The stuff of nightmares, indeed!... but you didn't actually see anything? Just a feeling? I'm not sure if this sleep paralysis is something that actually happens to you or whether you only dream that it's happening. How did it feel to you?"

"Oh... it felt real enough... I was convinced I was awake... but then dreams often feel so real at the time. And sometimes I dream that I've woken up out of a dream... but it's still a dream! So hard to tell."

"Anyway... what about this man?" Sylvie inquires as she offers toast and avocado. "Any idea who it might be?"

Penny feels heat spreading round her neck and face. Surely, she's too old to be blushing? She notices Sylvie grinning. "Must be someone I know... or I wouldn't get this feeling!" and laughs... "Ironic isn't it? Nothing to see... just a feeling!"

"It's that old feeling alright!" Sylvie starts singing. *"There's a somebody you're longing to see... I hope that he... turns out to be..."*

"Someone who'll watch over me...," Penny joins in, both giggling like schoolgirls.

* * *

After breakfast, Sylvie has a phone call and she can't wait to tell Penny the surprise she's organised. "I was telling a friend about your situation and she said she knows a woman who might be able to help. She's a Medium and Clairvoyant, and my friend says she's amazing. People go to her for information on anything... a lost will or jewellery... even to solve a crime. So if you feel like giving her a go... we have an appointment in Clapham."

Penny is ready for anything and feeling quite excited at the prospect of hopefully meeting a genuine Psychic Medium who might be able to help unlock her remaining her memories. Taking the tube to Clapham

Common they can't help but speculate on what they might find in the person of Ms Lena Franklyn. Sylvie's certain that she'll be surrounded by crystals, with a cat or two, and shuffling Tarot cards. Penny's more imaginative… "I see a large lady in diaphanous dress and fringed shawl… and maybe a turban." That sets them both off in hysterical giggles. Something is making them very skittish today.

They find the small, ground-floor flat in a leafy side street away from the noise and bustle of the high street. A tall, slim figure of indeterminate age and elegantly dressed, greets them warmly at the door. "Come into my parlour my dears…," she smiles as she ushers them into a comfortable room. No fringed shawls in sight, though several large crystals sit on the window ledge together with flowering plants. "Now make yourselves comfortable and tell me what brought you here."

As they introduce themselves, Ms Franklyn says… "Do call me Lena. We don't stand on ceremony here. And understand that anything we discuss here is absolutely confidential."

Penny warms to her friendly smile, although there is something a little puzzling about Lena that she can't put her finger on. Her voice is unusually deep and if Penny hadn't been looking at her, she might have thought it was a man's voice. She feels a movement at her feet. A cat, almost silvery grey, winding around her legs, rubbing up against her with arching back, as if in welcome. She turns to Lena. "Lovely cat… ," she remarks, but reaching down to stroke it, realises it isn't there. "Where did it go?"

"Aha! So you've met my friend Lucinda! She's my spirit companion. Actually, she isn't really my cat. I think she's always lived in this house. But she's very insightful and she's obviously taken to you! So how can I help?"

Penny starts to explain how she's been seeing ghosts or spirits, not only of her own past, but also of other peoples.

"Ah... so you're a natural clairvoyant! That means clear-sighted. Some people are clairaudient, which means they hear voices. And some are clairsentient; they just sense things. I'm also a Medium, which simply means I can converse with the spirits. But you haven't had any training? It just started to happen?" Lena is curious to hear more, crossing her elegant legs.

Penny explains about her memory loss and how she had just happened to start seeing dead people and how some even speak to her.

"You realise how privileged you are to be able to commune with the spirits of the departed? One doesn't choose to have this ability. You are somehow tuning into another world that ordinary people are blissfully unaware of. How do you feel about that?"

"I couldn't believe it at first, then I began to realise how I could help these souls who I think just want to be heard. They must be so frustrated at not being able to communicate with their loved ones. But I'm also hoping you may be able to help me find out who I am...," she continues.

"Ah yes... your friend mentioned you've lost your memory. Well, we could use the Tarot cards, but in these unusual circumstances I'd like to ask my Spirit Guide and the spirits of your departed to enlighten us if they can. I need to go into trance, so if we can all stay very quiet, I'm going to take your hand and see what comes... while you just relax."

Penny closes her eyes while her hand is being held, suddenly feeling a little self-conscious and apprehensive, but gradually calms herself by concentrating on her breathing, as Kay's taught her to do.

It's a minute or two before Lena speaks again in a different voice. *"My lovely girl... you've done so well... I was hard on you but you've needed to be strong... you were quite the little rebel. I had to teach you discipline and self-reliance... to survive in this world."*

Penny gasps. "Mother?" She's silent for a few moments, then... "Yes, you were hard. Sometimes I thought I'd been adopted and you didn't really love me. I don't remember you being loving and soft and cuddly like Gran. You never felt like that. But you did teach me to be strong… maybe too strong. And I think I was hard on my children too… just like you."

"She really does love you, Penny. She's saying she's sorry you only remember the lessons." Lena's voice is back to normal.

Memories came flooding in like a sudden ray of sunshine through a window. *Mother, dressed up for the evening in her lovely grey crepe dress and best necklace. Sitting by her bed reading a story. Wiping her forehead when she was sick. Wiping her floury hands to take a look at her latest drawing. Those strong capable hands that could wash the bedding in the big copper and put it through the mangle in the washhouse while cooking tasty meals for the family in the kitchen. Hands that lifted her across stiles and streams while walking through woods and across fields, picking wild flowers and leaves. Those careworn hands that were full of love.*

Penny takes a deep breath. "I know… she was a good mother. She always read to me… and taught me to read and write… always showed me interesting things about nature and art. It was Mum who educated me… far more than school ever did. I love you, Mum." Penny was close to tears now, remembering the woman who'd always been there, strong and secure through the wartime fears of her childhood, always teaching her that life is a great adventure.

"I'm sorry, Mum… I don't think I really appreciated all you did for me at the time. I love you so much."

"She knows." Lena is still holding her hand. "How are you feeling, Penny?"

"Just so sad… that I'd never really showed my gratitude for all she did for me."

After a pause, Lena asks "Would you like to see who else might come through?"

Penny nods, and all is quiet for several minutes. Penny's mind begins to wander... wondering if Davy might show up, full of remorse.

"Here's an old soul... a man is calling you, Penny. Does the name John mean anything to you?"

Penny looks puzzled for a moment. "John is such a common name... any other clues?" she queries.

Lena seems to be muttering to herself... "He's saying teacher. Would that make sense?"

"Oh... that John! He was a teacher at the Buddhist centre I used to attend. An old Soul? How lovely... he was so wise and kind when I was going through a bad time... after Michael... and Davy left us... I was in such a bad way. John counselled me to help me get on with life for the sake of the other children. He was quite a bit older than me... lovely man."

"Yes... that's it. He's saying that you had a hard time getting over the loss of your husband... "

"Oh yes... I had to learn that it wasn't Davy's fault he couldn't keep loving me... he could never be faithful to anyone... not even his children... it was just an aberration in his personality that he couldn't form lasting relationships. No-one was good enough and he had to keep moving on to feel loved enough. He wasn't really a bad man... just frustrated and couldn't deal with life like an adult." She's surprised at how she remembers this much.

"John is saying you have very high standards and expect others to behave towards you in the same manner... but you have to allow that other people's conduct may be quite different. To have expectations is to invite disappointment. A Buddhist has no expectations and therefore has inner peace."

"Oh yes... I remember our talks... I had so much to learn."

"He's saying that he was very fond of you... if you hadn't been so emotionally hurt, it might have gone further."

She's getting that feeling again; a lurching in her stomach spreading through her body. She's always been so careful not to give into any emotions that might expose any weakness in her character. Almost as though she's afraid of what might happen if she were to allow the floodgates to open.

"What? Really? I do recall him telling me he wasn't a monk and was free to have relationships. But I never thought of him like that." She's suddenly aware of a hot flush spreading from her chest up to her neck and into her face but decides to pretend it isn't happening and hopes no one will notice. "Can he tell you my name? My married name or whatever?"

"I'm sorry... he's fading... I've often noticed the spirits don't give much practical information. It's more about feeling and emotional information. As if the practical aspects of life aren't even worth bothering about."

Lena's pouring a drink from a carafe of water with lemon and offers it to her.

Penny lets out a long sigh... "Thank you. I'm grateful for anything really. I was wondering about my son Michael who died when he was five. Is it possible he might come through?"

"I'm sorry... I haven't detected any one like that. Sometimes the spirit moves on very quickly... there's no guarantee that any particular individual is still around... it depends on the circumstances... but I'll ask my Guide... if we can be quiet again."

Penny goes into her own relaxation mode, wondering if she could will Michael's spirit to appear, but she can only replay that dreadful memory of the afternoon he died.

Running... rolling down the slope... clawing her way through the hedge onto the canal path... frantically wading through weed-clogged green water towards the bright red jumper half submerged where a rotten plank has collapsed under the weight of Michael's little body... helping lift him towards the bank... that helpless feeling... the world capsizing... turning upside down...

slowly... sickeningly... losing all sense of direction... too late... too late...

Tears now streaming down her face, giving way to a wellspring of repressed emotion, sobs racking her body, Penny wails as she'd never done before with gut-wrenching sorrow.

"That's it, girl... let it all out." Lena's murmurs softly as she offers a box of tissues and waits for her to regain her composure.

She gasps through her tears... "I'm so sorry... I can't help it." Her flood gates are opened. All the pent-up emotion at being lost and recollections from her past that have surfaced in the last two weeks... was it only two weeks? She lets go of any attempt at control and feels carried along in this torrent of emotion... tossed and tumbled in the violent flow. A roaring sound fills her ears as she is sucked down... down... thoughts and memories dissolving in the confusion of feeling. Then she isn't drowning, as she'd feared, but buoyed up in the turbulence of not knowing what will come next and a feeling of almost exhilaration at just riding the wave, which slowly and gently subsides, leaving her finally floating in a stillness that she's not experienced before. Just pure light. She doesn't want to come back, but Lena's deep voice cuts through her trance.

"I sense the spirits of all your loved ones around right now... giving you all the love you need to heal. Just let go all that grief and breathe in the love. They are all so full of love now they've left this earthly dimension. Just let yourself connect with them. None of our earthly cares matter when we've passed over... just a few loose ends to clear up. You only have to acknowledge the hurts and sorrows in order to let them go. Can you do that Penny?"

"I think I'm doing that now..." She's very quiet, observing herself as if from a distance at how calm she feels... so peaceful... feeling so much love... the pain of confusion gone. She is ready to carry on with whatever she has to do next.

She feels a deep purring on her chest and strokes the soft fur of the beautiful grey cat.

* * *

"Are you awake Penny? Ready for a cup of tea?" Lena sits opposite offering her a cup of tea.

Sylvie's sitting next to her on the couch, holding her hand and asking anxiously, "How are you feeling now?"

Penny raises herself up and accepts the tea thankfully. She's quiet for a little while as she recovers her thoughts. Then she looks up and a smile spreads over her face. "Well, apart from feeling as if I've been through the wash, I feel very good. In fact, I'm so grateful for all I've been through, it's almost as if I don't need to know who I am, because I know who I am! If that makes any sense at all."

The sense of release is palpable as they all laugh together.

As they prepare to take their leave, Lena takes Penny's hand and holds her eyes. "Stay mindful Penny. Life is all about living each moment. You know what I mean?" Penny realises she does know what she's saying.

They are both very quiet on the way home. Sylvie feels as though her mind has been blown open, reflecting on all she's heard and witnessed over the past two weeks of her acquaintance with Penny. She can't help but think about all that has happened in her own life; events she's pushed to the back of her mind, emotions that maybe she doesn't want to think about.

Penny feels a strange lightness. She's light-headed... light-hearted... and even her tired old body feels as though a great weight has been lifted from her. The dreadful fear and anguish that had threatened to overwhelm her had gone, to be replaced by a sense of euphoria that fills her as she's never experienced before. *Enlightened*, she thought, *whatever that means!* Her thoughts about life and death have expanded somehow to encompass a bigger picture than personal loss and grief. We live, we die; the cycle of existence. Her lovely son Michael had lived a wonderfully happy five years before he'd died. She knows now that she can let him pass on to whatever lies beyond the veil of death with gratitude for the five years he'd lived. She can remember with love and pleasure that part of her life.

The days of wine and roses... singing to herself now... *laugh and run away... like a child at play... through a meadowland towards a closing door... a door marked 'nevermore' that wasn't there before.*

Nevermore... she'd lived a fantasy of the loving wife and mother with the perfect relationship and happy family in a dream home that she'd thought would last forever. But what is forever? Only memories can preserve those feelings and they too will pass away, but the power of love lasts forever, she knows that now. She's been freed from her heartache, at least for the time being.

After supper, they're watching a programme on the television that catches Penny's attention. Her mind has been wandering, so she doesn't know what it's about, but a person is talking and she sits up. "Why does that woman remind me of Lena?" she muses.

Sylvie looks at her with amusement. "Maybe because they are both transvestites."

Penny looks confused. "What?"

"This programme is about people who are Lesbian, Gay and Transgender. Like Lena. She's a man who prefers to dress as a woman. Didn't you notice? I know a few like that myself."

Penny feels as though she's entered into another universe of which she knows nothing. She's grateful that Sylvie can explain these things to her in detail and goes to bed bemused at this world that she must have been living in all these years, even though she can't remember.

Wandering around some kind of Visitor Centre... signs pointing various ways that seem incomprehensible... taking a path that leads out and through trees... walking in sunshine towards a summit... but can't find it... take another path... coming back to the same place... must find the way back... can't remember where I left the car... where's the car park? Stopping people to ask... pointing in different directions... panic... Where am I? Where am I going? Who am I?

Chapter 17

Week 3: Day 2. Wednesday... The Grand Union Canal.

Penny is awake early and it doesn't take her long to prepare for the trip on Dylan's boat. All she has to do is dress and repack her case to bring downstairs where she finds Sylvie already up and making coffee.

"Morning Penny. All ready?" Sylvie realises she's feeling quite emotional at Penny going away again, almost as though she were the mother seeing her off on a school trip.

Penny is feeling a little apprehensive herself, wondering how she'll get on with Dylan and Grace on the long slow journey by canal, which will probably take two or three days at least.

Over breakfast Penny mentions her dream of last night and Sylvie laughs.

Penny is not amused. "Not funny... I was panicking!"

"Not surprising really. Here you are, going off on a canal boat to look for a house you remember from... what... 40 odd years ago? That may, or may not, be where you think it might be! Of course, you're feeling a bit concerned. Just look on it as a good way to get to know Grace and Dylan a bit more. I'm sure he'll be eager to hear more about your story, if he's the writer he claims to be. There could be a novel in there… maybe a movie! Could make you both rich!"

"I was looking for my car! Didn't even know I could drive!" Now she's laughing. Somehow though, she does know she can drive. She can remember that!

* * *

Dylan and Grace are all ready to go when they arrive at Little Venice. Penny hugs her friend goodbye and boards the boat with her case. Then they are off, with the sun breaking through the morning cloud.

Grace brings her to the forward end of the boat, away from the smell and noise of the engine at the stern where Dylan steers, so they can talk. Penny thinks she's so beautiful, with her long dark hair tied up in a colourful scarf. She's admiring her clothes, which are colourful too and unusual, and can't help remarking on them. Grace explains that she prefers ethnic clothing, usually in thick cotton from Nepal or Peru, or thin cotton from India and Pakistan for Summer wear. "The ethnic clothing industry supports women and girls of the poorer regions and I just prefer to buy these clothes that are so well made, rather than cheap imports from huge garment factories in China." Penny is impressed. She has no idea where her clothes came from, or why she'd bought them.

Grace, of course, wants to know everything Penny can tell her, and Penny obliges by relating the events of the past two weeks, which takes some time, with many questions and debates, until Grace says she'll get them a hot drink. "Herbal tea ok?" Penny nods, and though she might have preferred coffee, she's sure herbal tea must be more healthy.

Penny shows interest in the route of the canal and Grace produces a complete map of the canal system. "Had this for years… it's a bit worse for wear." She spreads it out on the table and points to the London area. "This is where we started… on the Paddington Arm, and here's where we are now, I think. We'll be joining the main Grand Union Canal at Parkway. I think we'll just be getting out of the Greater London area when it gets dark and we'll find somewhere nice to stop for the night… out in the countryside."

Studying the map, Penny sees they've been travelling westward through the great metropolis of crowded houses, Maida Hill, Kensal Town, Ladbroke Grove, Willesden, following the great railway system at times, under road bridges; Ealing Road, Black Horse Bridge. South through Northolt and Southall, then west through Hayes and Drayton, before passing the Slough arm and turning north. Penny realises she doesn't know this side of London at all and is fascinated to be passing by the edge of parks and sports fields, council estates with the backs of houses displaying their gardens right down to the canal, some beautifully planted with trees and flowering plants, others neglected with scrubby grass and overgrown fences, then faceless facades of factories or warehouses, or stretches of trees overhanging the towpath where people run or cycle, push prams or walk hand in hand. Another, hidden side to the conurbation of this city that makes life here so rich and varied.

"I do love maps!" Penny enthuses. "It was my father who taught me all about maps and navigation…," and she launches into her childhood memories of wartime.

After lunch Penny is eager to hear about Grace's life and she's happy to tell her story.

"I'm the youngest of five… two brothers and two sisters… so I suppose I was spoiled rotten. At least that's what the others say," she laughs. "So my parents are quite ancient!"

Penny can't help remarking that they must be as ancient as herself!
Grace smiles… "Yes, they must be! Sorry about that. You don't look
ancient and they're doing alright! I was an unexpected addition to the
family when Ma was in her forties. The others are a lot older than me.
So I never felt I quite fit in somehow. I think I'm the black sheep; the
others are quite respectable, with proper jobs. I just wanted to be free."
Penny thinks she knows how that felt.

"My parents write books… stories from ancient history, myths and
legends that they weave into magical tales… and Ma does the most
wonderful illustrations." Penny is impressed. "Tell me more."

"Da is Irish… he'd been Reading History at Trinity College in Dublin
before he came to Oxford to do his PhD on Medieval History where he
met Ma who was doing Art History. He proposed to her on Magdalene
Bridge on May Day because they both loved the old traditions! Anyway,
they married and settled down and I suppose they just couldn't help
having so many children. Although they were raised Catholic, we
were not, though we were a big, happy family in the Catholic tradition.
Anyway, long before I was born they moved into a house right by the
canal, so I grew up loving the canals. They bought this boat and did
it up… took ages before it was fit to stay in… and we'd spend our
holidays exploring the canal system. Anyway, as they've got older and
I was having troubles of my own, they've passed it on to me."

"So you get on well with your parents?" Penny queries.

"Love them to bits! Though I was a lot of trouble to them when I
was a teenager… a wild child! Going off to Festivals by the time I was
fifteen… disappearing for days on end. They didn't know what to do
with me. Then I fell in love… as you do… and got pregnant. I was
only seventeen. But Michael was lovely… older than me… and he had
money and looked after us. Actually… it's a long story…"

"I don't mind long stories…"

"Well, we have a long journey ahead. But I must tell you we have a beautiful daughter... Orla... means 'Golden Princess'... and she has the golden-red hair of Michael's Grandmother, who left him her money, so she's named after her. So what with my father and his mother being Irish... we were a match made in heaven!"

Watching her, Penny sees a sudden darkness cloud her features. She knows immediately what that means...

as the darkness envelopes her and she's looking at a motorcycle speeding through mist and driving rain... watching as the rider suddenly comes through the fog into a huge truck on the road... skidding through the wash of the wheels into a wall. A tangle of flesh and metal... the wail of Police and Ambulance... the knot of people gathering around the wreckage... rivulets of blood spilling off the side of the road with the pouring rain... and a young man in cycling leathers who seems to be looking down from above the scene...

"Penny... are you alright?" Grace is standing over her holding her hand and she suddenly realises she's fallen to one side and leaning over the side of the seat. Gathering herself together, she sits up. Grace is looking concerned. "You've gone quite pale... here, have a drink... it's only water." Penny gives her a grateful, if wonky, smile. "Thank you... I don't know what came over me." Though of course, she does.

"I think you must be hungry... you stay there and I'll get lunch... it's about time... ," and Grace leaves her to gather her thoughts.

She's soon back with sandwiches and salad, and Penny realises it's been some time since breakfast with Sylvie and they've travelled quite a distance.

"I'm so sorry...," Penny says in a low voice, wondering whether Grace will realise what she means.

"Don't worry about it...," Grace replies, then looks at her quickly. "You don't mean...?"

"You remember I was telling you about having these visions?"

Grace is very quiet as she slowly chews the food in her mouth. "Yes..," she murmurs, her eyes lowered.

"Well… I saw… what happened… to Michael… the motorbike accident. I'm so sorry."

Grace turns her head… "You saw it happen?"

"Like a dream… it just came into my mind."

"Can you tell me? I know what the report said… he died instantly."

"Yes… I saw it all… and then his spirit… hovering… as though he couldn't quite believe it."

Grace is crying now, and laughing through her tears. "Just like him… he was quite mad sometimes. He was on his way home. He always said he couldn't wait to get home. I loved him so much." She's sobbing now. Penny puts her arm around her, feeling her sorrow until it subsides and Grace dried her eyes.

"At least I have Orla… my Golden Princess child."

Penny looks up quizzically.

"She's a young woman now. Twenty last July and flourishing at University. Or so she tells me. What do I know? She's much more sensible than I was at her age."

"So what were you doing at her age? Your daughter must have been what…two?"

"Yes… we lived in a campervan. Michael and me and Orla in nappies. Travelling mostly… round Europe… Italy and Greece… a few months in a Kibbutz in Israel. But we'd come back, usually in the summer. Then further afield… India was amazing… we lived in a Buddhist Ashram for a while. Orla was five when we came back here. It was a great start for her… so much education about the world we live in… other cultures. So we came back and settled in North Wales… my mother's family are Welsh and we camped the van in a field at my cousin's farm in deepest Snowdonia… which was great… for the summer! But with the cold, snow and rain of winter, we couldn't face it… so we bought a house, got jobs, Orla went to school… it was a good time for us… I'm so grateful we had that… and Orla blossomed."

"Is that where Michael died? What did you do then?" Penny wants to know how she'd survived such a tragedy, before realising how it resembles her own experience.

"Yes... Orla was fifteen... so we had to continue our lives... like wading through treacle... day after day... in our own fog of grief."

Penny nods and takes her hand. "I know... it's not easy..."

"But survive we did! Orla came through it all and when she was ready for Uni... I came to live on the boat. The house in Wales is Orla's... she lets it out as a holiday home, so it gives her an income. What Michael wanted."

"So where does Dylan come in?"

"He was already a good friend... we all played together at folk clubs and festivals... Michael on keyboards and Dylan on guitar, Orla too... she plays guitar... me on penny whistle and percussion... and singing. A proper little group. He rescued us both through music... made me practise when I didn't want to... took me to the club... kept me going when all I wanted to do was bury my head in the pillow... Orla thinks the world of him... we both do. We were all grieving Michael... now we make each other happy."

"It's not been very long then? Only five years?"

"As you say... only five years. It's taken this long to come to terms with it. The grief will always be here...." she touches her heart. " But I'm ok with my life now... that was another life... I needed a new beginning... to decide to leave the other life behind and live on the boat with Dylan. I feel safe here... and I can go anywhere... taking my home with me!" She turns her head towards Dylan at the tiller and blows him a kiss. Penny sees his face light up.

* * *

As the afternoon quickly darkens they find a convenient place to moor for the night and cook supper. They've been travelling for nigh on six hours with the constant noise of the engine, and it's a relief to relax now in the cosy cabin, surrounded by dark, peaceful countryside.

After a good supper she's really feeling that these are her kind of people. Dylan wants to hear more of her experiences and Penny is glad she's been writing in her notebook... just to remind her of the sequence of events. They are intrigued by her account of Lena, the psychic, and the memories she's recovered since they'd last talked. But especially of her ghostly encounters. Dylan is taking notes. "You don't mind, do you?" She is grateful for his interest, but begins to feel tired, half dozing in the warmth and comfort of the little cabin.

Dylan reaches for his guitar, which he does automatically without any trace of self-consciousness when he has nothing better to do. Penny notices more musical instruments; a couple of Irish drums... bodhrans, he tells her... hanging from hooks, penny whistles standing in a wooden box and a couple of harmonicas lying on a shelf.

"Do you play anything?" Grace asks as she hands round glasses. "Just fruit juice," she assures Penny, who recalls the effect of Jasmine's elderberry wine.

Penny responds with a laugh... "Thanks... no... I don't think I do, though I tried to learn the piano when I was young and I believe I can read music. My fingers never seemed to get the hang of doing what I wanted them to do. But I do love singing!" That sets the tone for the rest of the evening, as Dylan plays and Grace sings from various songbooks of Irish, Scottish and English folk songs.

Penny finds herself observing the affinity between her hosts; Grace at the centre with Dylan hovering on her periphery, even when he's playing, always ready to hand her a shawl or fetch her a drink. When Grace sings, her voice is hauntingly beautiful; laced with sadness and grief as well as happiness and great joy, emotions that bring tears to her eyes. There is one song that Grace and Dylan sing together in perfect harmony, gazing into each other's eyes, moving Penny to applause. The more she watches Dylan, the more she begins to realise that he isn't as young as she'd first thought. A boy-man, she thinks, recalling his favourite practise spot in Kensington Gardens near the statue of Peter Pan, the boy who never grew up, who wanted Wendy to be mother. Has he found a mother in Grace, she wonders. What's his story?

Penny is introduced to her sleeping arrangement as their seats were folded down and sheets, pillows and duvet brought out to make her bed. "Good night and sweet dreams Penny..." as they both disappear into the other cabin.

Her sleep is untroubled...

Hauntingly beautiful music fills her dreams with radiance, and she is flying, swooping over fields and woods, skimming over water and soaring up like a phoenix into clear blue space.

Chapter 18

Week 3: Day 3. Thursday… Through the locks.

She's awakened the next morning by the sound of a kettle and
the rattle of teacups, to find Grace busy at the stove. "Good
morning… hope you slept well?" Penny assures her she's slept
soundly, as she had. As she quickly folds her bedclothes and helps
Grace put the cushions back into seats again, she mentions her dream
and the sensation of flying… like a phoenix. "I just wonder why it was
a phoenix and not an eagle or something."

"Maybe you noticed…," Grace motions to their surroundings…
"Phoenix… It's the name of the boat!"

Penny's surprised she's not noticed the name on the side of the boat,
but then she must have seen it subconsciously.

"When my parents bought the boat, it needed so much doing up
because there'd been a fire and it took them a couple of years or more
to get it watertight and fit to move, so by the time it was ready for the
first trip, Ma came up with the name as she said it was like the phoenix

rising from the ashes. We all thought it was a great name, and I feel it's true for me too. If you know what I mean." Of course, Penny knows.

Dylan is anxious to make the most of daylight hours and they are soon underway, eating toast and jam for breakfast, with the usual herbal tea. Grace has explained that they don't buy milk and anyway, they don't have a proper fridge.

The day has started with light rain, which continues intermittently till the afternoon, so Grace and Penny stay in the warmth and comfort of the boat's interior, looking at Grace's photographs of previous trips and poring over the map.

"So we're looking for an arm of the canal that was overgrown in the sixties... and I can't see anything obvious on this map. When the canals were being dug, sometimes the local gentry fancied having their own branch... or a local industry needed access. However, it could have been simply blocked off or even filled in since then. Do you have any clues?" she asks Penny, who recounts her memory as fully as possible. "I think the nearest town was Hemel Hempstead. Or was it Berkhampstead?"

"Priory Gate, you say? Nothing on the map. But that area around Abbots Langley and Kings Langley certainly attracted religious communities in the past. You say you were out in the countryside... so maybe more towards Berkhampstead. There is a little arm at Tring that may be worth investigating. Anyway, we'll see when we get there. There are so many locks to go through to get over the Chilterns... the going will be slow. Thankfully, there aren't many boats moving at this time of year. We always wait till the summer melee is over!"

They encounter the first of many locks at Cowley, which is quickly passed, then through the Uxbridge lock, where they begin to leave houses behind and enjoy the open countryside. Soon enough progress is slowed as both Dylan and Grace are kept busy opening or closing the gates at each lock, waiting for water to empty or fill it, which takes some time to get through. As Penny had seen on the map, the way over the Chilterns necessitated so many locks she soon loses count of them.

After lunch, the rain stops and Penny's glad of the opportunity to get off and walk along the towpath while the boat takes it's time to go through the locks. She begins to think that her quest to find one spot that may, or may not, actually be on this canal, or any canal, is a bit like finding a needle in a haystack. Just what had she been thinking? Her memory is so fragmented that the location of her former home could be anywhere… on a small stream perhaps. Why did she think that it was a canal? She begins to wonder why her new friends have encouraged her, as though they also think she'll recognise the spot. Or maybe they are just humouring her, the mad old woman with no memory. But, she comforts herself with the thought that as Grace had said, they were going on the trip anyway and seem glad to have her company. As she walks, she tries to get back to that place in her memory and conjure up the feeling sense of it, to see if that helps, but nothing more comes to her and she's soon glad to return to the warmth of the boat and a cup of tea.

* * *

They moor for the night near an old waterside Pub, 'The Rising Sun', where they plan to eat and meet up with an old friend. Penny sits in the bow, writing in her notebook and watching the fiery glow in the sky as the sun sets. *Red sky at night… sailor's delight…* glad that it portends a fine day tomorrow. She's been trying to ignore the people passing by on the towpath. Too many of them appear to have spirit appendages and she doesn't want to attract any of those attentions. An elderly couple holding hands, although the man is but a shadow and appears to have no contact with the ground. The shade of a man hovering over a teenage boy on a bike, like a guardian angel or a father trying to keep his son safe. A young girl, lost in a haze of first love and insubstantial fantasies, with an aerial protective grandmother fussing over her.

She begins to realise how walking is such an unconscious process that one doesn't have to think too much about it, except to keep on the path and not bump into anyone, leaving the mind open to memories and daydreams. Walking on one's own, it seems to her, is to open a door into the subconscious, attracting any unresolved emotions to rise as ghosts; of lost love, bitter regrets, chronic frustrations, smouldering anger or deep fears. The whole gamut of human emotions, coalesced as wraiths hovering on the periphery of consciousness, waiting to be recognised, clamouring for reconciliation, justice or retribution.

They are the first in when the Pub opens, hungry and ready to eat. It soon becomes obvious that this is a popular place to dine as the tables begin to fill. Their friend joins them as they finish the meal, not to eat, but ready for a pint and they all retire to a lounge area where they can talk. Mark is a charmer, well built, with a deep throated laugh; he's introduced as a fellow musician, a bass player and composer. They joke that he's the only 'real' musician because he plays in an orchestra. The conversation is lively and interesting. They've all been friends for some time and it's obvious how much they enjoy each other's company.

Penny's enjoying her half pint of Bitter, wondering how many years she's been drinking beer, when she notices a couple in the next alcove. She doesn't know what it is about them, but something doesn't feel right. A young girl, probably still in her teens, and an older man, very good looking in a smooth, oily kind of way, draping his arm around her shoulders and gazing down her cleavage. *Demonic...* springs to mind. *Really? A Demon? Oh please... stop imaging things!* He seems to be plying her with drink. *(Where did that expression come from, she wonders.)* But the girl is giggling naively and seems unsteady. She's certainly not noticed them before, but then realises, as several women begin to materialise around them, that this is almost certainly another supernatural situation.

"I wondered when you'd notice!" One of the women is speaking to her urgently. *"For goodness sake, warn the girl! You must get her away from him."*

"What's the problem?" Penny realises they are conversing telepathically.

"Isn't it obvious? He's doing what he always does. What he did to all of us! He's a Vampire... he lives off women's energy and leaves us drained... sick, dying or dead!"

Penny is shocked into silence. How to process such information in an appropriate way? What can she do about it anyway? The wraith woman is talking again...

"He calls himself Dominic... thinks that makes him sophisticated. No one knows who he is. He's the kind of man who gets a girl to love him so much she'll do anything for him. He absorbs it all and gives her nothing. Just leaves when he's ready to move on and find another vulnerable woman. Anyone who'll give him what he needs. And there's always some lonely girl who thinks he's the most romantic man she's ever met!" The nebulous group of women swirl in and out of focus, as though enveloped in a thick fog.

"So what about you? Are you dead?" Penny can hardly breathe.

"I was the first one... he married me... but cancer got me eventually. I was so depleted I was defenceless against illness. He sucks out your essence... I believe he's evil. How can I convince you? The others have similar tales to tell. One had an accident and is still in a coma and another went out of her mind and killed herself. His Mother too... she got Alzheimer's... he put her in a home and sold her house... never went to see her... broke her heart... she died alone. No one who's been with him has escaped unscathed. He sucked the life out of us. Those still alive, live in fear of men, fearful of life, escaping from the world one way or another. Please get her away from him. Please!

And if you get the chance, tell him Marie is watching him!"

What can she do but act on this shocking information. She can't doubt it, not after all she's been experiencing recently.

Penny watches the girl who has started hiccuping. This is her chance. She stands up, walks past their corner and stops as though she'd just noticed the girl's discomfort.

"Oh you poor thing... got the hiccups? Come with me. I know how to cure that!" taking her arm and propelling her towards the Ladies. The girl can't speak, for every time she tries, a *hi'* interrupted her. But she stumbles along with Penny holding her up.

Having regained the privacy of the Ladies, Penny sits her down and gets her to hold her breath, while she tries to talk to her between the *hics.*

"Now you don't know me, but I have it on good authority that you are in danger from that man you're with."

"Hic..."

"Yes, I know you think he's the bee's knees, but you've had a lot to drink and you're not thinking straight."

"Hic..." The girl looks confused. *"Wha? Hic..."*

"You don't know who that man is... do you?"

"Yea...Hic... he's my boyfrien... Hic..."

"And how long has he been your boyfriend? When did you meet him?" Penny's getting exasperated.

"Party... a friend's birthday... Hic...last weekend..." Her hiccups stop, at least temporarily. She's looking worried now.

"So you don't know him!" Penny's determined to ram the message home. "You really don't know who he is. Could be a serial murderer as far as you know!" Keep it simple. Be afraid.

"He's a philanderer... he uses young women. He's not honourable!" Penny isn't sure she's using the right sort of language to get through to her. How do young people speak these days?

"I know Dominic. He's dangerous!" Now the girl is shocked!

"Can you ring someone now... someone you can trust to get you home safely? I can't let you go back in there to him. Are you OK with that?"

The girl is trying to regain her senses. Penny's getting desperate.

"Who can you phone right now? Where is your phone?"

The girl stands there looking dazed."In my bag... on my seat."

Oh god... Penny knows she has to go back and get the girl's bag.

"Stay right there and don't move." She takes a deep breath and leaves her standing there while she goes back.

"I'm so sorry... your lady friend isn't feeling well and needs her bag." But she isn't quick enough to grab the bag off the seat before he has it.

His smile is disconcerting. "That's alright. I'll see she gets home safely. Thank you for your trouble."

"Oh, no trouble. I'm an old friend of her mother. I'll take responsibility for her now. Thank you..." holding out her hand for the bag. The man looked at her as a gamekeeper would look, with a loaded shotgun, at a trespasser.

Stalemate.

"Marie says Hi by the way."

"What the...?" the colour drains from his face and he suddenly looks older.

Penny's aware of her friends coming across to find out what's going on.

"Everything alright Penny?" Dylan enquires casually, eyeing up the man confronting her.

"Oh yes, everything's fine... I'm just getting my friend's bag for her. She's in the Ladies... not feeling very well. I've told Dominic we'll see her home safely." Hoping that Dylan will understand and play along. She notices the man seems to shrink as he registers his own name spoken after the reference to Marie.

With the burly Mark by his side, Dylan acts immediately, holding the man by the arm and swiftly taking the bag. "Thanks Dominic. I'm sure she'll feel better once she's home."

Dominic's attitude changes swiftly to apologetic charm. He's a consummate actor. "I'm so sorry Deirdre's not well. We were having such a lovely time. Tell her I'll be in touch. And thank you so much for your help. I'm sure she appreciates having such good friends." They all watch as he leaves to make sure he really does go. Penny goes to retrieve Deirdre, who's still sitting where she'd been left, confused as to what just happened.

With help and not a little persuasion, Deirdre phones her sister Carol, who agrees to come over and rescue her. Penny actually takes the phone and speaks to her, urging her to come ASAP so they can explain what's happened. The only thing that Penny hasn't explained to anyone is her conversation with the dead women; something she can't really explain. She has to think of a rational version of events that would satisfy even an investigator, while they wait with Deirdre for her sister, sobering her up with coffee.

"I realised that Deirdre was intoxicated, but it was this woman who told me..." No mention of a gaggle of ghostly women. "She was watching Deirdre and Dominic from the bar... and... she started signing to me... yes I know signing... she was telling me he's a well-known seducer... she actually signed rapist... but she obviously didn't want to get involved... so I had to do something." Maybe not the whole truth... but truth is relative and has to be interpreted. She thinks she might tell Dylan and Grace in confidence. Sometime appropriate.

"You're so young Deirdre... you need to know who to trust and who to avoid in this world." She gives the girl's arm a squeeze. "You'll know in future."

The girl is grateful; though still unsure what had happened to spoil her date, but happy with all the attention and glad when her sister arrives to take her home.

Back on the boat they sit around the stove with a nightcap. "Just a wee dram…." Grace says… "A little *spirit* to settle us after all the excitement!" She emphasises the word, both looking at Penny in expectation. "So are you going to tell us?"

Penny blushes. "Yes, alright. Should have known you'd see through me. There were spirits!" And she recounts the whole conversation with Marie, as far as she can remember. Her memory seems to be in fine fettle and she decides to make her own notes tomorrow.

However, the discussion goes on for some time as to why these women's spirits were still with Dominic, when, surely, they would want to be as far away from him as possible. Do they haunt him out of revenge? Or to try to warn other women? Or were they tethered to him by Karma or some kind of energetic connection? So much speculation. Penny thinks they might be there to prick his conscience, like Jiminy Cricket in that old cartoon. Maybe they couldn't leave until he'd redeemed himself in some way.

"How could he do that?" Grace wonders. Penny thinks he'd have to apologise from his heart to each and every one of them. Grace isn't so sure. "If he's not changed by now, how do you think he can ever change?"

"With the greatest difficulty!" Penny responds. "But nothing's impossible!" She can't help bursting into song… *'Nothing's impossible I have found… for when you feel you're on the ground… just lift yourself up… dust yourself off… and start all over again.'*

"Very metaphysical!" Dylan remarks.

She's glad to get to bed, and sleeps soundly.

Chapter 19

Week 3: Day 4. Friday... Discovery

P enny wakes as the sun sends bright rays through the tiny window. She decides to write down the events of the previous night before the memory fades. As she writes, she does wonder if she'd imagined it all... or whether it had been a dream. Or maybe all life is a dream and only the spirit world is real.

A thought crosses her mind... so rapidly, she has to backtrack to catch it... then tease it like a cat with a ball of string... to form it into something comprehensible. And the thought surprises her. It is the realisation that she is glad she is no longer nineteen; knowing that she has loved and lost, but has lived... happily, she hopes ... for the most part. That she is older and possibly even wiser in her old age. Maybe even that she is the one now loved and lost... for the moment. She notes that in her book in case she loses it again. Older and wiser, she muses. She'd certainly felt it last night in dealing with Deirdre and Dominic. She couldn't have acted so decisively at nineteen, she was sure of that. Last night she'd been strong and determined... on a crusade for women... Boudicca on the rampage... she smiles at her own confidence! Not at nineteen though.

Her bed is neatly put away when Grace comes in to put the kettle on. "We should be in Tring by nightfall. Hopefully you'll recognise something along the way today."

Penny feels a thrill at the thought of finding her old home. *Not far now...* she keeps repeating to herself as she scans the way ahead, looking for something she can recognise, some landmark she might remember. It takes some hours to clear all the locks, until they are at the top of the Chilterns on a long stretch which seems interminable. Then, as the sun is going down, an opening became apparent and Dylan swings the boat through a very narrow arm of the canal. Penny's heart is in her mouth as she looks about her at the trees crowding the banks. The canal has clearly been rescued from dereliction over the years, and they move slowly, to give her time to recollect any landmarks.

"It's all so different... all these trees! Look... the canal goes around this hill, where the house should be. The gardens ran right down to the water's edge. Maybe I'll recognise the bridge." And there it is, much like all the other canal bridges, but the angle at which they approach reminds her of walks with the children along the towpath... and surely there... "Let me off... I think we're here."

Dylan pulls into the towpath and she takes off unsteadily... up onto the road and across the canal bridge, up the rise to where her house once stood...

Dylan and Grace catch up with her, standing there with a bewildered look on her face, "I know it was here... but it's gone." And indeed, it has gone. To be replaced by a small estate of modern, upmarket, desirable four-bedroom residences for London commuters or retired business people with money. Named *Priory Close*, they observe.

She's wiping her eyes. "This cold wind," she remarks. "Makes my eyes water." Or possibly a wayward emotion leaking out. She points out a thicket of bushes and trees. "That's where the ruins of the Gatehouse should be, but there's nothing to see now. There are so many trees that weren't here before. It's all so different."

Grace and Dylan on either side give her a hug. "Back to square one then," she laughs through her tears. "But thank you so much for helping me find it. I can't believe we found it!"—

They're glad to be back on the boat and find a mooring for the night. They'd planned to be in this area for the Friday night *Open Mike* session at a local pub and want to eat before they take their instruments along, but there is plenty of time before it kicks off.

The Old Bell Inn is certainly old and the décor, if you could call it that, rustic. No modernising hand had touched it for at least a hundred years, or maybe two. The stone flagged floor worn down by generations of working men's boots; simple to sweep up the dust or swill down with a bucket of water. Oak settles, not unlike church pews, lining the walls that are roughly plastered between the wooden structure; the original whitewash (who knows when that had been painted!) darkened by smoke from a large open fire and pipes of countless smokers. A solid oak bar, the colour of the beer it had absorbed for so long, polished by the greasy arms and coat sleeves of so many drinkers. The ambience is more like someone's cottage than a public place. Locals, looking almost as ancient, ensconced in a side room; the snug, with its own small fire blazing. A small side table holding a wooden board; an old game that Penny recognises from somewhere. *Shove-ha'penny*, she seems to remember. She wonders how many people are able to squeeze into such a small place, for the open mic sessions welcomes all-comers to come and play or sing.

Dylan is apparently quite at home and is welcomed by a couple of players there already. Grace says that he's often out and about to play in various locations, whether she goes with him or not, and knows many musicians up and down the country.

A young man starts off the proceedings at the piano, singing a couple of folk songs that everyone seems to know well. "A local lad," says Dylan... "nice voice... knows all the local folk tunes. His Granddad used to collect them... wrote them down." A fiddler comes next, more inspired by Irish songs... sad and lonely melodies. Then a young girl on guitar singing her own songs, met by much applause from her friends and family members. The audience has grown by the time Dylan and Grace take their turn, bringing some rocking liveliness into the proceedings, and they are very popular, encouraging the crowd to join in with familiar numbers. Penny's enjoying the music, quietly singing along to many of the songs.

During the break Dylan goes to the bar and comes back with a smile on his face. "You'll never guess!" he says, carefully putting down their drinks and looking very pleased with himself. "Talking to this chap at the Bar...," waving his hand towards a burly man who waved back... "I know him as Billy Bodhran... makes those lovely Irish drums... turns out he used to be a reporter for the local paper years ago... in the 70s in fact. Thought I'd mention Penny's story, hoping he might recall the story of a little boy drowned in the canal, and he did! Here... Billy..., " he beckons the man over.

"I'd like you to meet Penny...," as the man brings his pint over to sit with them. He takes Penny's hand.

"Aye... I'm glad to meet you... Penny, is it?" he looked at her quizzically. "It was a long time ago... I was young and handsome then... " They all laugh. He's still holding her hand, warm and comforting. "Such an awful thing to happen. I felt for you and your family, but I don't think we ever met. Didn't want to intrude on such a tragedy. We had more respect in those days."

Penny withdraws her hand, sorry to break the connection that's so full of compassion. She wants to ask more of this man who'd been there, or at least nearby, but can't ask the question. It's Dylan who does ask. "What do you remember about it? Penny is anxious to remember her married name."

"I see. Only that the little boy drowned. I seem to think the family moved away soon after. I'm not sure, but I think the name was Hughes." He looks at Penny, who looks blank. "Tell you what... I'll look up the back issues... let you have a copy. Then you'll find the name of the family. How about that?"

Penny feels her heart flutter at the prospect of finally knowing her married name, which should lead to revealing her family name. The rest of the evening passes in a blur as she recalls as much as she can of her past life, though her thoughts seem to whirl round and round in her head getting nowhere, and her head aches. *Hughes?* Was that her married name? It's strange that she remembers emotional events but not names. Maybe in the end we are only connected by emotions; and names, places and dates don't really matter.

Later that evening she sleeps fitfully.

Driving down a country lane... a narrow road, winding round blind bends alongside a rushing, boulder strewn stream... driving cautiously, until rounding a bend the road widens and straightens out... into a panorama of snow-capped mountains rising into a blue-black sky, touched by the rays of a late afternoon sun... going home... home... home...

Chapter 20

Week 3: Day 5. Saturday... Penny

I wake as morning dawns slowly, dark with rainclouds. Now the canal descends through several locks, which means that Grace has to don waterproofs each time the locks needed to be opened or closed. By afternoon we're cruising into Leighton Buzzard, which looks familiar. Dylan's had a call from Billy Bodhran, who said he'd tracked down the report of Michael's death and would bring a copy of the paper to Leighton Buzzard. They've arranged to tie up near the centre and find a local café, where Billy will be waiting.

I'm feeling a little disorientated, to say the least. Even though I've seen the place where Michael died, along with some memory of the perfect family life, as I'd thought, the name of Hughes still means nothing to me and I'm even more confused. Was this really a memory of my past or have I been tuning into someone else's memories again? Davy Hughes. Was this really my Davy? The love of my life? How can I be sure?

We find the café and sure enough, Billy is waiting for us and produces the account of Michael's drowning. I look at it in a daze, hardly able to read the words on the page. Billy is talking about his time as a novice reporter so long ago. Dylan and Grace are obviously interested to hear about it, but I sit there silently, attempting to follow the conversation, in a confused world of my own. They are saying how it would be possible to find out the date of Davy's birth and my own from a marriage certificate and it can all be done online. However, as they don't have an internet connection on the boat, they'll relay this information to Sylvie to see what she can do. Apparently, everything can be done online these days. I'm mystified by all this modern technology. It's all too much to take in.

What to do next? We talk about how I could take the train back to London and the comfort of Sylvie's home, or go along for the ride to Grace's parents in Milton Keynes. Grace and Dylan encourage me to stay and I have been enjoying their company. It just seems easier to carry on with them to whatever the future holds in store. That will give Sylvie plenty of time to do whatever she has to do to research Marriage and Birth Certificates to find out my birth name, which will identify me at last.

After lunch at the café we're on our way again as the rain has finally stopped, and we're cruising through the countryside. I sit alone in the bow, mesmerised by the flow of water as the prow cleaves the surface, watching trees on the banks approach and recede, ducks flapping out of the way and the occasional plop of a fish. No sound but the constant throb of the engine. The sky is steely grey with no clouds scudding across the horizon. No breath of wind moves the trees, as though the world has stopped, except for our progress. I feel as though I'm in suspended animation, unable to move, like a photograph that freezes the moment and can never change.

After all the excitement of setting off on this journey, all the tension as my expectations mounted, hoping to clarify my memories and longing to see my old home, now it all feels a bit dead; an anti-climax that has left me feeling... like this canal... calm and unruffled on the surface... not knowing what lurks in the murky depths. No, not the right analogy! Somewhere from the mists of memory I recall once seeing a portion of canal that had been blocked off for repairs, revealing the debris strewn bed; the inevitable shopping trolley and various other unwanted objects. The canal is man-made; a shallow basin that a tall man could probably walk across with his head above water. I suspect that my emotions are not so shallow... more like a deep river or lake... or the sea on a calm day. So deep, I can't see further than a few inches and can barely guess what lies beneath.

What am I feeling? Deflated, like my balloon has lost height and plummeted to earth. Did we actually achieve anything? Well, maybe all will be revealed in due time. I'm not holding my breath. Nothing as yet has released any further memories.

This is a rural farming area, with few towns and just the odd village somewhere nearby. I have a vague recollection of walking and cycling in such an area. Now and then we pass a few people on the towpath, walking their dogs or cycling as we glide under road bridges. We're approaching a lock and for some inexplicable reason I start to get an uncomfortable feeling. The view ahead seems to become misty as though the light is swirling in a strange way. I feel as though we're going into a tunnel, though I know it's only a lock, the same as all the other locks we've been through. As we move into the narrow opening, I think I glimpse a man and young woman near the edge, who seem to be arguing. It's only an impression, out of the corner of my eye, as it were, and how I know they're arguing I have no idea, but I'm feeling uneasy. The lock gates close behind us and the boat sinks lower as water rushes out. The lock is deep and it's as if everything goes dark. I hear a sudden cry, a loud splash and instinctively duck my head.

"What's that?" I shout. "Grace! What's happened?" I'm turning to look back, trying to see what fell into the water, hoping it wasn't Grace, but I can see she's at the tiller.

The cry echoing in my head... a woman's cry. A body dragged down in sodden clothing... being hauled out... blood on the head... distant voices saying... 'She's dead... won't bother you now master...'

I look up as Dylan appears with a cup of tea.

"Anything wrong?" he queries.

I'm shaking as I try to explain what I just experienced.

Dylan sits quietly... "Just breathe... now drink your tea. I was wondering how you're getting on... and now you've seen another ghost!"

I do actually feel as though I'm coming out of a tunnel as the light returns and I'm back in the real world again. Now I realise he's right. It had to be an apparition. Some dreadful happening from another time.

"I can't believe it. A woman was murdered here!"

"Yes, you're right. Seems a local lass was seduced by the local Squire's son and was *disposed of* when she expected him to do the decent thing... as was often the way in those days. Sad but true. The coroner's verdict was that she'd hit her head as she fell into the lock, but locals said she'd been attacked and pushed in when the water level was low. It's a deep lock as you may have noticed, so she couldn't get out easily if she was even conscious. She's quite a celebrity round here! There's even a notice board that tells the story."

"I might have known... I was feeling very weird."

"Feeling better now?"

"Thanks, I'm alright. Just a bit shaky still. I seem to have lost track of where we are. What time is it?"

"Tea time, my dear... have a cake...," Dylan produces a plate of little cakes.

"Oh thank you. So Grace has the tiller?" I'm thinking it's unusual for him to relinquish control of the boat.

"Oh yes, Grace can steer for a change. There are no more locks now and we should be at Joe and Mary's by nightfall."

"Joseph and Mary! A match made in heaven...," I laugh, having almost forgotten where we're headed and ashamed that I hadn't even registered the names of Grace's parents, but from what I remember Grace telling me, they sound most interesting, and I say to Dylan that I'm looking forward to meeting them.

"Mary's a witch, you know." Dylan looks at me mysteriously.

"Really? A witch? How do you mean? Bedknobs and Broomsticks witch? Or dance in the woods naked witch?" I can't help giggling.

"Actually, I think it's more nature spirits and old magic, but I don't know if she dances naked in the woods. Wouldn't be surprised though!" he laughs.

"Grace said she's into pagan traditions. Now I'm really looking forward to meeting her."

"Didn't want to scare you, I expect. You'll get on well, I reckon."

"I thought they write books!"

"Oh yes, they do. But that's just a front you know." He's smiling so I know he's joking. Well, half joking anyway. "Can't wait!" I laugh. "Never met a witch. Is he a wizard then?"

"Doesn't look like Gandalf... but you can never tell!"

I've brightened up, as I always do in the company of Dylan. He's so *upbeat*. Is that the word?

"So how are you feeling now?"

"I'm just wondering where I go next. Keep feeling I'm still up against a brick wall. Yes, I know, I should keep positive. I'll get back to myself soon enough." I laugh as I speak... "Whoever myself is that I'll get back to. I wonder if my current self will like the other self when we meet. Now that's an interesting question!"

"Quite the philosopher Penny... I like your style!" Dylan regards me with some amusement and suddenly bursts into song... *"If you knew Penny... like I know Penny... Oh... oh... oh what a girl. There's none so classy... as this fair lassie... da da da-da da-da da-da..."* and goes inside to get his guitar. Just what I need to get me out of these blues.

However, I can't get the thought of that young woman out of my mind. She was pregnant of course... and desperate for the father to do what's right and marry her. How many other young women and even younger girls have expected their lover to *do what's right* and been disappointed... jilted... deserted... abandoned... disposed of... murdered? An age-old predicament. Not so easily solved. No wonder that fathers would *lock up their daughters* in the old days, as one way of curbing the recklessness of youthful lust. Not until the *pill* loosened all limits on licentiousness, with doubtful results. With the lifting of restrictions came the loosening of responsibility, as though no-one wanted to handle the repercussions or accountability. Love now and pay later! Which so many women have done. Women always pay; one way or another.

I'm thinking now of my own mother, deprived of a career in classical music which she could have had, if she hadn't done what was expected of her by her family, married my father and become housewife and mother. I suppose they were happy enough, but I'm sure she was attracted to another man while I was a teenager. Mum hinted as much when I was older... just a wistful look as she recalled her singing days and spoke his name briefly... John. She would have been about forty then and was really attractive, at the peak of life, I suppose. I remember that she'd joined a choir and enjoyed the company of other music lovers. I recall that John was the pianist that accompanied the choir. My Dad had no interest in it at all and usually stayed at home, reading or playing games with me and my sister when she went out. I remember one evening she got a lift home with this man, John, and

Dad went ballistic. I'd never realised before then how jealous he was. They never had much of a social life. It was as though he wanted us to be a nuclear family, in our own bunker! That was the main reason I couldn't wait to leave home and live my own life. Then what do I do but follow the same pattern and marry someone like my dad… who goes off working and socialising while I start producing babies. Such is life!

* * *

Before I know it, we're approaching the outskirts of Milton Keynes. The roads we pass under are bigger and busier, one in particular I remark on. "Looks like we're reaching civilisation," I laugh.

"That's the A5. Much bigger road than it used to be."

Something clicks into place in my mind. "A5? I know that road… I think… it sounds familiar. Roman Road… London to Chester, I think. Or further… leads to Ireland eventually."

"You know your geography! Actually, it leads through North Wales before it reaches the ferry that crosses the Irish sea."

I suddenly recollect the vision I had of driving along a winding road towards the mountains… towards home!

"That's my way home!" Now I'm sure… but I can't believe it. Is it North Wales or Ireland? Maybe I do know where my home is… if I can only remember.

* * *

Daylight is fading fast as we round a bend to see houses ahead and slow down to stop alongside a wooden landing stage. A half hidden house is set back from the canal, surrounded by trees. We step into an enchanting garden, full of flowers, shrubs and unruly vegetation.

Following a winding path through this jungle I begin to notice little figures half hidden by foliage; brightly coloured gnomes peer out and fairies watch our progress from among the branches. It's all so delightful I'm surprised when we suddenly emerge at the house onto a paved patio, surrounded by pots of all shapes and sizes overflowing with plants, and furnished with carved wooden seats and table. The house is larger than it first appears, in an L-shape. An old farmhouse, I think, with attached barn or perhaps a dairy, that must have been incorporated into the house.

A door opens as Grace calls out to her parents. Mary and Joe are effusive in their welcome, as though they've not set eyes on their daughter for so long. Mary takes my hand as I approach, smiling at me with her soft blue-grey eyes.

"You are most welcome in our home, my dear. We've been hearing about you from Grace, and I'm looking forward to getting to know you much better now you're here."

I'm charmed by her welcoming manner and after all the hugs and affectionate greetings we settle down with mugs of tea in the warm and cosy kitchen to exchange all the latest news.

"How was the trip?" Joe wants to know everything that happened along the way, and while Dylan and Grace recount all the events of our journey, I sit near the business end of the kitchen, watching Mary at the cooker that's exuding the most mouth-watering aromas. Before long, she produces not one, but three delicious curries with rice and succulent Nan bread, and the chat defers to expressions of satisfied appreciation.

I notice that Mary is quite short and a little on the plump side, but quietly elegant in a flowing skirt and embroidered blouse that conceal her figure, while Joe is lean and tall, at least six foot, in corduroy trousers and linen shirt; his blue eyes lively with amusement that seem to find the funny side to everything that's said. I imagine that when he proposed, if he'd gone down on one knee, his eyes would have been almost level with hers!

After our meal Mary beckons me to follow her upstairs. "You'll be glad to know that you'll have your own bedroom tonight. A lot more comfortable than on the boat, I'm sure…," as she leads me into a lovely small room. She's right. The bed is wider than the narrow one I've been sleeping on the last few nights and I collapse onto it to feel how comfortable it is. "Oh Mary… thank you so much. This is heaven!"

"Yes, isn't it? I loved our trips on the boat but Tara is my heaven. The older I get the more I appreciate home comforts!"

I like Mary. "Did you say Tara?"

"That's what we named the house. Joe was born not far from the hill of Tara; the place of the great Kings of Ireland. I like that ancient connection. We've been here a long time and it holds all the memories of our family. Anyway, I'm hoping you'll stay with us for a bit. Just relax and make yourself at home. I think you need a bit of space." How did she know? "Now the bathroom's across the landing if you want to freshen up, then come down when you're ready and we can chat downstairs." I notice that my bag has been brought up, so take out my night clothes and toiletries. What luxury!

* * *

We all congregate in the spacious sitting room where a log burning stove is glowing warmly. Everyone is talking about the trip and my experience at the lock and I try to answer their questions as well as I can, but I'm feeling quite tired. "What would you like? Beer or wine?" Joe asks and I gratefully accept a glass of red wine, which soon has the effect of making me feel very relaxed and sleepy as the conversation becomes a murmur.

"Think it's time for bed…," someone says and I'm glad to be ushered upstairs to crawl into the enveloping folds of the duvet.

Chapter 21

Week 3: Day 6. Sunday... Penny - Tara

I wake slowly. I was so cosy in bed I didn't want to wake up. I'd been having a lovely dream, which slipped out of reach as soon as my mind surfaced. Try as I might to return to dreamland, my mind kept swimming to the surface and eventually I give in, suddenly realising I needed the bathroom as quickly as possible.

As I get washed and dressed I become aware of noises downstairs that indicate everyone else is up and probably enjoying breakfast already.

"Good morning... I'm so sorry I'm late up." I'm most apologetic as everyone looks up and cheers.

"Good morning to you... and you're allowed to get up as late as you like! It is Sunday!" Mary is laughing. "I hope you slept well? You weren't kept awake by this lot, were you? Drinking till late, they were!"

"Not that late Mum." Grace protests. "You make us sound like a lot of drunkards!"

"Just enjoying your wonderful hospitality, as always, Mother Mary!"

Dylan chips in.

I have to smile. "Actually, I slept so well I just didn't want to wake up."

I didn't think I was hungry but enjoy the cooked breakfast more than I expected.

* * *

When we've all had out fill and cleared up, Mary asks… "Tea? Coffee? or Herbal?"

"Coffee please." I know Herbal teas are more healthy, but I need the caffeine. She makes two mugs for us.

"How do you like your coffee? Strong and sweet… like me? We can take it into the study, so we can have a good chat…," as she leads the way through the hall and past the sitting room to a small room at the far end. I look around as we sit in comfortable chairs to enjoy our coffee. The walls are lined with books, with more books stacked on the floor around the desk, which is piled with papers around a computer. I think I'd be very happy to have a room like this. It feels very comforting and familiar. "It's lovely!" I say, gazing around. "I believe you write books Mary… I'd love to read them."

"Ah… all in good time my dear. I'll give you the first one, because they're all written in sequence. But I can't wait to hear about your adventures… if you're ok with that, Penny? Dylan tells me he's writing all about it, so I hope you don't mind my curiosity. I do love a good story."

I'm happy to relax into the chair. "So much has happened in the last three weeks… I can't believe it's only been three weeks. I don't know what would have happened to me if Sylvie hadn't come to my rescue when she did. Another bag lady on the streets, she reckons. Or dead in a back alley. And Kay did so much for me, recovering memories. Then

Dylan and Grace… they're such wonderful friends who just want to help me. The kindness of strangers!" I'm suddenly close to tears.

"Sorry… you want to hear the story. Sometimes I just get carried away…" I stop to drink more of my coffee and recover my composure.

"No hurry, Penny… only when you're ready. You seem to be coping with it all very well. You must have been on an emotional roller-coaster! Now you relax while I'll find that book." She moves across the room.

She's right about an emotional rollercoaster! I feel that I'll be ready to talk soon enough, but I'll need my notebook to help recall all the events more clearly.

Mary hands me a book. The cover catches my eye, being a colourful Celtic design of intricate knot work around a beautiful fairytale scene of a woman in a forest. "How lovely! Is that your artwork?" Mary nods. Penny is impressed. "Does this come from history or legends?" I want to know.

"Both really. History is very nebulous, while legends and myths are so enchanting and we like to mix it all up in a good story from our own imagination. Joe is really the historian and I'm into the mythical and spiritual realm. All the old traditions that have lasted through the centuries… they all reveal something about peoples' beliefs, their hopes and fears and how they felt in the old days. Not easy to put ourselves into their mindset from our modern perspective, but we try. The books do quite well and give us an income anyway. I think you'll find that some of our tales reflect what's been happening to you; people lost in the forest, finding themselves in another strange world, befriended by *other folk*, fairies, elves, wizards and even helped by birds and animals."

"But I seem to remember a time when people thought some of those old stories too violent for young children. Witches and wolves who eat small children and monsters waiting to get you. I think that worried me when my children were young."

"Yes... I remember that too! But I read them to my children anyway. I do think they need to know that the world isn't all playful bunnies and airy-fairy happy-clappy playtime. They need to be aware of the dangers of trusting everyone they meet... that not everyone is good at heart. All the old tales correspond to what happens to us in real life. The wolf who tricked Red Riding Hood for example... that's a simple warning to young girls to be aware of predatory men! I think stories have always helped people understand their feelings and emotions, more than anything."

"I know what you mean... their way of understanding the psyche... basic human psychology."

"You got it," Mary smiles, delighted to find a kindred spirit.

I'm flipping through the book, intrigued by the lovely illustrations, reminded of my favourite books from childhood.

"When I was little, I had a lovely book of stories by Hans Christian Anderson. That was my favourite and the illustrations were wonderful. A bit like yours; so detailed and mysterious... they invite me to go into them to explore what they promise. Thank you, I know I'll enjoy this."

"Illustrations by Edmund Dulac?" Mary gets up to look through one of her bookshelves.

"Yes, I think so."

Mary is soon back holding a large book "Like this one?"

"I can't believe it!" I gasp. "That's my book!" taking the old book in my hands reverently. "I suppose we must be about the same age. I think it was a wartime edition. The paper isn't very fine, but the illustrations are great quality. Was it a Christmas or Birthday present? I think mine was."

"Yes... it must have been." We're both laughing with joy at discovering shared memories.

After that, I retrieve my notebook and I'm then happy to relate my story from when I was mugged and lost my memory, and Mary settles back to listen intently to everything that has happened since.

"So you don't have any memory after your second marriage… is that right?"

"Well, I presume it ended, though I still can't recall what happened. Yes, that seems to be it."

"And where next Penny? Any idea?"

"I have a vague idea. I'm sure my home is somewhere up the A5. That came to me while we were passing under it. And I've had a vision of driving towards the mountains. But how on earth I'd find the right place is anybody's guess!"

Sunlight playing on the remaining leaves of a large tree outside the window invites us outside and Mary rises. "Shall we walk round the garden? It looks lovely out…," as she leads the way through the sitting room and out through large French windows onto the Patio area.

I remark that it seems larger than it actually is, as we pass through a stone archway festooned with creepers and wander along narrow winding paths. "There was nothing here but bare ground and patchy grass when we bought the house, so this is all our own work." Mary is obviously proud of their achievement.

Each curve of the path reveals a variety of flowers and bushes, tall grasses and lush undergrowth, now in their autumn colours, interspersed by large moss-covered boulders and occasional rustic seats in alcoves. We cross a Japanese-style wooden bridge over a watery depression, full of leafy hostas and what looks like water lilies.

"Our bog-garden… started as a pond… but turned out like this." Mary explains. "We had big ideas, but it just sort-of developed into this hotchpotch… and that's how we like it." Arriving at the canal we sit on a stone bench, watching the play of sunlight on the surface of the water.

"Quite mesmerising, isn't it? I often sit here to get my ideas when

I'm writing. Puts me in the right mood for going into the past. The sense of flowing water... like the passing of time. Although a canal doesn't really flow like a river... but I can pretend. We couldn't afford a house by a river anyway! When we moved here, the canal was in a right state too.... hardly navigable before they started cleaning it up to use for pleasure craft. Been some changes here, I can tell you."

I sit quietly, lulled by the lapping of the water and a slight breeze that isn't exactly cold, but not very warm either. I have to remind myself that it is October, though what the date is I'm not sure.

Mary must be reading my thoughts. "We're coming up to Halloween. The old name is Samhain... pronounced *Sow-een...* not as it's spelt. I do hope you'll still be with us. I think you'll enjoy our traditional celebrations. It's a time when the veil is thinnest between the worlds. You know what I mean?"

I nod, wondering what spirits would be likely to show up, if at all, at All Hallows Eve or Samhain. Anyway, it would be interesting to experience the rituals. "Can you tell me a bit about it? what happens exactly?"

"Well, we have a bonfire, of course."

"Is that where you all dance around naked?" I can't resist giggling.

"Only if it's not too cold." Mary looks serious before she laughs with me. "I expect that was done in the past... they were hardier than we are! But you can if you like!" That sets us off again. Schoolgirl humour!

"No... seriously... what is it really about?" I want to know.

"We have some friends round who like to follow the old traditions, but it's not necessary for anyone to believe anything in particular. We simply like to honour the spirits of nature as well as the Father Sun God and Mother Moon Goddess, each in our own way. We have many books on the subject and you're welcome to browse in the study. Many of our books are based on Wiccan beliefs, which is really magic!"

I'm surprised, not by what she's saying, but that it all seems so familiar to me. I think I must have read books or studied Wicca at some time.

"But don't most people think Wicca is Satanism... evil magic? And that's why the Church was so against it."

"Yes, you're right. There are still Satanic cults that practise black magic. But the Church itself was based on fear... fear of the Devil and Hell-fire. Just think of the witch hunts... all those women healers and midwives drowned, hanged or burned out of superstitious fear. And the Spanish Inquisition... all that fear... torture and horrible death. That was evil power. The Wicca we practice is based on love. Love for nature and humanity... healing and compassion... Love and Light... that's the real power. Any power based on fear is self-destructive eventually. That's why the Church has been trying to get back to Christ's teachings on love."

"Do you believe the Devil is real?" I ask.

"I think that anything you really believe in can become real to you. There are those who claim to see the Devil... and those who believe they see God or the Christ. The Ancients believed they saw their Gods too. Belief is a very strong energy. Never under-estimate the power of imagination."

She looks at me with a twinkle in her eye. "It's Samhain on Saturday, so you've plenty of time to find out how you feel about joining us on the night. If the weather's too bad, we gather in the conservatory with lighted candles everywhere. Only we don't call it the conservatory... it's my Studio."

"I've not seen the conservatory... I mean your studio." I wonder where it might be.

"Oh, you must... it's on the North side, so that the reflected light, rather than direct sunlight, makes it ideal for painting. Come with me... it's round the other side of the house."

She guides me along a different path that leads towards the trees and I remark the wood is more extensive than I'd thought.

"My dear… that's our forest!" Mary laughs… "Well, that's what we like to call it. I can show you where we usually gather for our rituals. It's very private."

"I'd have thought the local kids would have discovered it by now…"

"I think the locals are scared witless at the thought of coming onto our property. We are known as the *Witches Coven*. We give talks occasionally to local groups, so they know we're legit and not just cranks. So, if any of them are really interested, we can help them get into studying properly. We do get a few now and then. Then there's Peter… he'll be along on Saturday. He got interested when he left Uni and came back to his parents for a while. That was years ago… he's at Oxford now… English Professor, no less… and a great musician. He was married to Maura, she was lovely… but she was an invalid for some years with MS. He was wonderful with her… used to take her on trips round the country in their big Motorhome before she died. He comes to join us as often as he can. He and Joe are thick as thieves when they get together."

As we walk into the wood, I glimpse a view ahead through the trees; a shaft of light illuminating a stone-walled garden full of flowering plants, with a gate leading to an old cottage, reminding me of old Victorian paintings. I have an odd feeling, as though I've stepped into another dimension. It's colder here in the trees where the sun doesn't reach. Then my view is blocked by the twists and turns of the path until we reach the clearing, with no sign of the cottage or garden, as though it was a vision of how it had been once. The clearing is surrounded by thick undergrowth among the remains of old moss-covered walls and the sun is way beyond the trees. We sit for a few moments on one of the wooden benches surrounding a fire-pit in the centre, absorbing the earthy smells, the special ambience and listening to the soughing of wind in the treetops.

"A very special place...," I don't tell her what I'd seen, wondering what she knows about the place.

Mary nods. "I'm glad you feel that too."

I remark on the old ruins.

" Yes, what's left of an old cottage. We've been told that an old woman certainly lived here at the end of the 19th century, probably the local wise woman. Anyway, the locals believed she was a witch and wouldn't dream of coming here, and even the kids seem to avoid it, thankfully! This would have been her garden. I've found some interesting herbs growing around here. She would have been a herbalist and healer, I reckon, and midwife, of course. I did find a very old photograph of the place when the cottage was falling into ruin. It was here in the house, in a drawer. All the old furniture was still here when we bought it."

"I'd love to see it." I say, hoping it would match what I'd seen.

"I think I know where it is. I'll find it for you after lunch." Mary gives me a look and I wonder if she suspects what I've seen.

It's too chilly to sit for long and we rise to rejoin the path that leads to the other side of the house, passing a window on the west side that Mary tells me is the study, where we'd been previously.

* * *

At the front a wide stretch of lawn is bounded by hedges, on the other side of which appears to be a quiet road. A drive leads round to the front door on the far side of a large modern glass Conservatory. The house looks quite different from this side. Mary leads me through the front door and from the hall we pass the stairs then through a glass door into the conservatory. A bright and airy studio, furnished with cupboards, a large table and a couple of artists easels with partly finished paintings.

"Sit down and I'll show you what I'm working on...," Mary indicates a pair of wicker chairs.

She brings over a few paintings, beautifully drawn, but dark and mysterious. "These are illustrations for the new book we're working on. Rather different to what we've done before. Not so much historical as hysterical!" I look puzzled and she laughs. "I mean, it's going into more mystical realms... other worlds... and more humorous. Our wizard is a Magician... Mercury... the trickster. We do like to see the funny side of life. But you should read the other books first, I think. I can't really explain it very well."

One picture in particular draws my attention. A cloaked figure in a misty haze beckons and I feel the hairs on the back of my neck prickle. "Wow!" is all I can say.

"More Tolkien than Merlin...," she explains. "And this is our new heroine...," putting another picture in my hands. This girl is no simpering medieval innocent. She looks ready for anything; as though she could take on any opponent, whether man or monster.

She leads me back to the sitting room and I take the book she's given me to read while she goes into the kitchen to prepare lunch with Grace. The book draws me in, and from the first chapter I'm hooked. The illustrations go with the text and appear at intervals throughout the book. I'm stunned by the next one I come to, because it's exactly my vision of the cottage and garden and I shouldn't be surprised, because in the story, the heroine has just gone to see the Wise Woman for help! I laugh out loud, but Mary is busy in the kitchen, so I'll tell her later.

* * *

I'm surprised when I'm called for lunch. An hour or more has gone by and I'm enthralled by the story of a youth who goes to visit the Wise Woman in her cottage to beg her to save his mother, who has given birth and now lies dying. The old woman tells him...

'In life there is death and in death there is life.'

'But what does it mean?' he wants to know and she replies… 'Your mother has fulfilled her destiny in bringing forth new life… and now it's time for you to find yours. Your father, who is not your real father, will find a new mother for the child and your brothers will stay to work in the smithy because that is their destiny. But you don't belong here… you have another destiny. So now you must go out into the world to discover for yourself what destiny holds in store for you. There's nothing more I can do for you but to tell you to keep your promise.' The boy is puzzled, though he's always known he's different to his brothers with their flaxen hair. 'What promise?' he asks. 'The promise you gave your mother, to always be a gentleman as your father was a gentleman.' 'How can I be a gentleman when I'm naught but a farm boy?' he persists and she tells him… 'Money and fine clothes do not make a gentleman. A real gentleman is gentle and kind. He cares for those in need and protects the weak. He knows what is wrong and what is right. He keeps his integrity, no matter how tempted he may be. Your quest is to fulfil your destiny.'

And that is the start of his journey into the unknown.

I reflect that all life is a journey of sorts… we have to find the meaning in our own lives and I'm still on that journey.

* * *

Lunch is delicious and the conversation lively. Everyone's looking forward to Samhain on Saturday, so it looks like I'll be here for the next week. I wonder if anything else will come into my consciousness to help me on my journey. I'd be grateful for anything!

After lunch, we settle down in the studio, where Mary produces the old photograph of the cottage and I can't wait to tell her of my vision.

"You mean you saw the picture in the book?" she asks.

"Actually, I saw the cottage and garden as we walked into the wood…

just a glimpse… and I couldn't believe it when I came to the picture in your book. It was exactly the same!"

Mary looks at me with amazement. "I painted that picture from this old photograph. You're sure you hadn't seen it before?"

"Well, I hadn't even looked at the book then." I'm afraid she doesn't believe me, but when I look at her she's smiling.

"Well, I never! That's amazing! You really do have the gift…," she paused. "How are you getting on with the book. You seem to have read quite a bit so far."

"I love the way you write. That we're all on a journey of self-discovery… to find our destiny. That resonates with me! Can't wait to get back to the story!"

"We have a Tarot pack that comes with the book…," she rummages in a cupboard and brings out a small pack of cards. "Are you familiar with the Tarot?"

I nod eagerly and take the cards.

"If you like…," she continues "I could give you a reading. That could be interesting at this stage of your journey."

"I'd like that very much… thank you. May I look at them?"

"Please do… you'll recognise the characters by the illustrations in the book. They're all in the cards."

I'm looking through the cards, which seem quite familiar. "I think I had the Rider Waite pack. I was certainly interested in the Tarot. A reading might bring back more of my memory."

"Right… I'll leave you to your book and we can do the reading whenever you feel ready for it. In the meantime, I must get on with this painting."

I'm happy to sit and read, but fall asleep after a while and wake to realise that the daylight has gone. Mary isn't here but I hear voices from the kitchen and smell cooking.

After a delicious supper we move to the sitting room to watch TV; a fascinating programme on ancient routes of Pilgrimage. I reflect that life is all about journeys of one sort or another and wonder where my journey will take me next.

A song running through my mind as I lie down to sleep.

'The shadow of your smile... when you... are gone...Will colour all my dreams... and light the dawn...Look into my eyes, my love... and see... All the lovely things you are to me...'

Who am I singing to? I wonder. Or who might be singing to me?

Chapter 22

Week 3: Day 7. Monday... The Church

Mary is the first one up, and in the kitchen when Penny comes down.

"Coffee?" she asks. Penny nods and sits at the table. "I need a coffee to wake up properly... had the strangest dream. Don't know what to make of it."

Mary brings her mug over to join her. "Really? What do you remember?"

Penny takes a few moments before she begins. "I'm in an old house. The rooms are spacious, but now it's derelict and empty of furniture. It must have been a grand house in the past. Wallpaper is peeling off and the plaster is crumbling off the walls. I go up the wide staircase which must have been beautiful, with a lovely curving wooden balustrade. The bedrooms are empty but through a big bay window I can see a large overgrown garden and beyond that a forest. There's no sign of life. I find another staircase leading up to smaller bedrooms, then through a small door to a narrow staircase and up to an attic that's crammed with furniture and boxes; tea chests overflowing with stuff, and suitcases, all covered in thick dust. I can see another door at the far end, but I can't get through to it. Then I wake up."

"How did you feel as you woke up?"

"Panicky... bewildered... desperate to get to that door." She stops to recover and fishes out a tissue to wipe her eyes. "I didn't know where I was at first when I woke... just bewildered." She looks at Mary who takes her hand.

"You know, usually dreams are the unconscious trying to tell us something... and I think I know what it could be." She pauses and Penny looks at her for an explanation.

"I think the house represents your life and I guess that in your past you lived well. That could be in this life or a past life, if you understand that." Penny nods her head, thinking she understands what she's saying.

"But at least your life was comfortable and spacious." She's trying to use the same words as Penny described it. "But now it's derelict and no-one lives there. That's because you have no memories of the part of your life that really matters. Or maybe you've wiped the memories of who you were and the people who were important to you in that past because it's too painful to remember." She looks at her to assess her reaction. "How does that feel?"

"Yes, I understand. What about the attic?"

"Well, an attic at the top of a house represents your mind. So there are all your memories... packed away and stuffed into boxes... but so disused and neglected they can't be accessed very easily. The door at the other end is the access to your future, but you can't reach it. Now, does that describe your situation? Or have I got it all wrong?"

Penny's shaking her head. "Yes... no... I mean that's it. You got it. That's exactly my situation. How does it help though?" She drains her cup. "Any more coffee? I need it!"

Mary obliges with the coffee pot. "When you go to bed, just ask for a solution and see what dreams come to you. I always record my dreams and they usually respond in some way. Helps me find my stories too."

Penny takes a long breath. "That's really helped me already. That panicky feeling has gone, anyway."

* * *

After breakfast, Mary wants to show her the vegetable garden and leads her through a back door to the other side of the kitchen. Penny remarks on the variety of vegetables and several large orange pumpkins... "Ready for Halloween?" she asks.

"Oh yes... we have to carve the pumpkins. We've always done it with the children and they have a competition between themselves to make the scariest... or the funniest! The girls will be here and Tristan... but Corin can't make it this year. Anyway, we'll be quite a houseful."

Penny wants to know about the other children, wondering where they'll all sleep. "I know Grace told me, but I'm afraid I can't remember who's who!"

Mary laughs... "I'm not surprised... we're quite a tribe! Corin, our eldest, is a Doctor and lives in Scotland with his wife and family. He's just turned 50. My goodness, how time flies. Then Sophie and Freya, who are twins. They're 48. Then Tristan, who's 46, I think. He was the baby till Grace came along, which was a surprise when I thought I'd done with babies. So you'll be meeting Sophie and Freya and Tristan, who's bringing a friend... don't know who. The girls don't usually bring anyone else to these gatherings. Sophie's husband, Ralph, isn't interested in our Wicca Celebrations, but she brings him over to see us when no-one else is here. He's a Scientist... just can't cope with crowds of people... but we get on fine and he enjoys conversation one to one. I'm very fond of him. Freya is divorced and has a very nice job with our Publishers. So we do see rather more of her. Then there are the grandchildren; Corin has two boys and a girl… growing up now. Sophie has a boy and a girl and Freya has two boys. Tristan doesn't have any that we know about! Grace, as you know has her lovely daughter Orla. And that's it… They are all much too busy with University or new jobs to come and see us, unless they're passing, on their way somewhere else, usually. But they do make the effort over Christmas and New Year, and we love to see them. I don't think they really understand what it is we do here… only that we keep ourselves busy writing books!"

Penny thinks she'll have to write this all down in her notebook if she's to remember when they get here.

"I'm taking a walk to the village bakery, if you'd like to come with me. And we have a very fine old church, if you're interested." Mary is putting on her boots. "You'll need a coat. It's quite cold out."

A short, brisk walk takes them to the centre of the old village, where Mary buys bread and cakes. Then a little way further up the road to the church. Mary is talking about how the oldest part of the church is 14th Century as they arrive at the old wooden doors.

"Are you religious?" Mary asks as they enter the church. "If you can remember."

Penny takes some time to search her memory. "I think I was very religious when I was young… and I know I was Catholic. But I feel there's something about old churches… such an atmosphere of reverence… all the effort people made over so many years to express their faith. But I don't feel any need for church services personally. Maybe we do need rituals, but I feel that setting one's belief in stone is no longer relevant. My belief, for what it's worth, is that how we live our lives is far more important than making a show of being holy."

Mary can't help laughing, delighted that Penny feels as she does. "Well said, Penny! Of course, if I'd been practising pagan rituals in those day, I'd have been burned as a witch. I don't know how I dare to enter a church! But they couldn't keep all the old Pagan symbols out… even here!" and Mary points out a carved *Green man* peering down from a corbel where the roof meets the wall. They look at the 15th Century Rood screen with some original paintwork still showing. "It must have been so colourful originally… and the walls would have been covered in painted scenes from the Bible. All that colour was painted over by the Puritans, who took all the fun and joy out of life!"

Mary decides to sit down for a rest, while Penny wanders off to look around at the old stone pillars reaching up to support the carved wooden roof structure, light streaming through the rich colours of stained glass windows to illuminate the high pulpit, stone tablets and effigies commemorating notable people and prominent families of the past. It must have been supported by some wealthy families, she thought, to have built such a beautiful church.

Suddenly feeling light-headed she looks for a way out to get some fresh air and notices a side door, opening into what looks like a courtyard. As she passes through the portal, she's surprised to see people in medieval dress that appear to be enacting a performance. There are jugglers and fire-eaters, acrobats and musicians, while elegant ladies in colourful clothes sit together, laughing and chattering and gentlemen stand in groups to watch. She suddenly recognises the figure of a youth, dancing to the music, The Fool of the Tarot, large as life and twice as handsome, although with something of a shock, she sees in his dark curly hair and swarthy skin that he's at least partly of African descent and notices how some of the onlookers are laughing and ridiculing him, to whom he gives a low, derisive bow. All around the garden are people in peasant dress, some apparently selling food and others with ribbons and trinkets on trays. Thinking this must be a rehearsal for an imminent festival, Penny leans against the stone wall to watch, enjoying the fresh air, only to be accosted by the bowed figure of an old woman, in a dark cloak, holding a wooden bowl.

'Alms… m'lady?' Penny laughs at the authenticity of the performance then is abruptly shocked to see the very picture of the old crone, the wise woman of Mary's Tarot pack peering at her from piercing blue eyes in a gaunt brown wrinkled face. *'I see you…'* as her face softens into a warm smile and her eyes penetrate so deeply Penny feels herself falling as she's drawn down into the dark enveloping folds of the cloaked figure… falling… falling… and everything goes dark.

* * *

"Penny… are you alright?" Mary is looking down at her and she realises she's on the cold stone floor of the church. Mary helps her up and gets her onto a seat.

"What happened?"

Someone brings her a glass of cold water and she drinks thankfully, finding a hanky to wipe cold perspiration from her forehead and calm her trembling body. She can't speak but looks towards the doorway to the courtyard, hoping to discover the meaning of her vision. The old stone archway is plain to see, but the doorway is filled in with stone, obviously a long time ago. "Fresh air,"… she mumbles… looking for the way out into the real world.

By the time they reach the street, Joe is there with the car to take them home where she's grateful to sink into an armchair in the sitting room and accept a cup of tea, ready to tell Mary of her experience. "Why is this happening?" she wonders… "What does it mean? If it means anything!"

"How did it feel to you, Penny?"

"I don't know. I was shocked… then it felt as though she knew me… that she was looking into my very soul… like nothing I've ever experienced before."

"You're obviously a sensitive... clairvoyant... but why you see these things when others don't must have some meaning. I wonder if you've met yourself in a former life... that maybe you were here and you were that wise woman many lives ago. Anything's possible! I often think that when I dream up the characters in my paintings. I see them so clearly and know who they are. I'd like to research the history of the church some more. We have a book on it somewhere... and our friend Peter might be able to throw some light on what you saw. It was probably an annual fair or festival... there were plenty at that time, when people got together for a good time. They knew how to have a good time!"

After a light lunch, Penny's glad to relax and read more of Mary's book, and soon dozes off.

It's nearly five o'clock when she wakes, as Mary brings her tea and cake and some news from Sylvie.

"Good news?" Penny queries.

"She's sent an email with all the details. Your name and date of birth! You were born in Salford in 1940." She knew that. "Your name was Margaret Baxter. Maybe you were called Peggy. Peggy... Penny...?"

She's thinking about that, "Yes... possibly."

"And your parents...," Mary consulted her notes. "Your Father was Samuel Baxter and he died in 1992. Your Mother was Ethel Whitehead, died in 1990." Penny has only a very dim recollection of that.

"You had a brother too...," she looks at Penny for any confirmation.

"Oh... David! I do remember... where is he?"

"I'm afraid he died some time ago. But his family live in Yorkshire. There's an address."

"Thank you... I'm so glad. What about my children?"

"Their names and dates of birth, but no more details yet. You married David Hughes in 1960 and divorced in 1973. That's when you lived in Tring. You have children. Julian, born in 1961. Then Rebecca, in 1963,

167

Carrie in 1965 and Michael in 1966. Divorced in 1973. Then you married Gerald Watson in 1974 and according to the Census Record you lived in Leighton Buzzard. Divorced in 1980. Then you disappear! No more record of Margaret Watson. Strike any memories?"

Penny is thoughtful. "I think I changed my name. A new identity. Not Mrs Watson or Mrs Hughes… or Miss Baxter… a new name… but I don't recall. I think I must have chosen Penny Laine because I loved Cleo Laine, the Jazz singer!"

"I wonder how you'd find that… not so easy to trace a new identity, unless you know where you lived."

"I think I ended up in Wales… North Wales… I've had dreams…"

"But no place names?"

"Not yet!"

* * *

Over supper Dylan and Grace hear all about the day's happenings and Dylan takes more notes to add to his growing compilation. "I will have to call this book *The Mis-Adventures of Penny. A trip down memory lane,* which they all thought very funny and far too cheesy.

"So you saw Jugglers? And Fire-eaters?" Dylan goes to the fruit bowl and selects three apples.

"Didn't know I was a juggler, did you?" as he proceeds to juggle them expertly, until he drops one and puts them back as everyone claps encouragingly.

"Tried fire-eating too. Not very good. Didn't get a taste for it!" he grimaces. "Prefer making music anyway."

"I should hope so too… wouldn't want to be with the joker!" Grace laughs.

Later, Penny phones Sylvie to thank her for the information and they chat for ages; Sylvie anxious to hear how she's getting on and intrigued by the account of Penny's latest experience in the church.

In her sleep Penny dreams of soaring over rugged mountain tops... along rough tracks and rushing streams, sun-jewelled lakes and the wide expanse of beach and sea... like a bird... swooping and diving... vibrantly alive...

Chapter 23

Week 4: Day 1. Tuesday... The Cards

"Interesting visitor we have, Mary." Joe remarks as they're getting dressed. "She's having quite a journey. Reminds me of the Tarot. You know... the Fool... the innocent setting out... meeting all the Archetypes. I think Dylan would be the Magician... and Grace... what would she represent? Strength, do you think?"

"Oh yes. She is that. Quietly confident is our Grace. Very balanced and well adjusted. The Strength to calm animal nature. Good for Dylan anyway."

By now, they're both quite familiar with Penny's story, having discussed it several times together with Penny, Dylan and Grace.

"Who are we then, do you think?"

"Oh... Empress and Emperor, obviously!" Mary says and they both laugh.

"Well, that figures. I wonder who Sylvie might be? And her sister?"

Mary ponders... "From what I gather, Sylvie is very caring... I think she's The Star... ever hopeful... ever helpful."

"Yes, I agree. Kay would seem to be more cerebral. I think I'd cast her as Temperance. The Psychologist... level-headed and clear thinking. Problem solving. Who else has she met so far? What other Archetypes?"

"She was telling me about Lena, the Medium. Sounded interesting... transvestite... psychic. Maybe the Moon?"

"OK... In touch with the other side... the mysteries of the unconscious!"

"And now she's met the Wise Woman... the High Priestess... possibly a memory of a past life. That's very interesting!"

"Amazing... and there's plenty of them left! And she's still on her journey. Looking forward to the weekend. See how she gets on with all the others!"

* * *

Mary is thinking about all the preparations to be done for the coming weekend when the rest of the family and friends will arrive for the Samhain celebration. She'll get Grace and Penny involved in the food preparations anyway.

She notices that Penny seems different this morning. Lighter somehow, as if she's shed some load off her mind, and she mentions it to her as they're clearing up after breakfast.

"Yes... I do feel lighter. I'm sure my home is in Wales... I was dreaming of mountains and the sea. Now, what can I do to help?"

Penny, Grace and Mary spend a busy morning in the kitchen, baking and preparing food to go in the freezer. While they work, the talk is all about the coming festivities, and it seems to Penny that while being a serious occasion, it will also be full of fun with the coming together of family and friends. *Much like Christmas, Easter and Harvest*

Festival... she thinks, recalling her Catholic childhood. *Church first, then the celebratory meal.*

* * *

"I don't know about you, but I'm ready for a coffee." Mary's filling the kettle.

"Yes, please!" Penny and Grace chorus, glad to sit down at the kitchen table.

"How are you feeling now, Penny, after yesterday's adventure?" Grace asks.

"Actually... I feel OK! It was amazing to watch that medieval scene... as though I was really there... so real... I can't believe it was all in my mind... or maybe it wasn't. More like an action replay! And the old woman... she was the Wise Woman of Mary's Tarot... she really was!" Penny sighed. "I'd just like to know why I saw that."

Grace turns to her. "I'm really envious of your visions. It's like you have an inner television screen... what a gift!"

"Yes, I suppose it is a gift... if I only knew what to do with it!"

"How about a card reading Ma?" Grace suggests. "Maybe that would help to clear it up." Penny nods.

"Good idea. I'll get the cards." Mary's soon back with her Tarot pack.

"Let's see... what they say about me..." Penny is relaxed enough in their company to sing out theatrically.

"Don't tell me... I know... Carmen Jones... 1950's movie!" Mary laughs, taking out the cards. *"The nine of Spades!"* she adds, remembering the song.

"De nine... De're he is... dat ole' boy... plain as can be... Death has his hand on me...," they both sing in unison.

"Oh... you too... should be on the stage...," Grace laughs gleefully with them. "We used to watch that film on video... love the music!"

"Would you like to shuffle, or shall I?"

"You'd better do it please, Mary. I'd probably have them all over the floor! Never could shuffle." Penny laughs.

"Right. I think we'll do the five-card spread. Keep in mind what you need to know while you pick the cards. "

Penny picks out five cards and lays them down in order, takes a deep breath and turns over the first one. It shows five young men in a confused group holding staves.

"The Five of Wands. Looks a bit chaotic... like they don't know what they're doing. What's going on?"

Mary takes a moment to consider. "It's showing your difficulties... some conflict between your mind and emotions. Maybe some confusion, but not too serious. If these young men got their act together, they'd make a troupe of Morris Dancers!" Everyone laughs.

"I'd say that you need to know what to focus on. This is what you know but need to look at more closely. How does that feel?"

Penny's laughing. "Spot on! That's exactly how I'm feeling. I have been thinking I've come to a dead end here, but I realise now that this time here with you is going to help in some way. Yes... that's good."

"Right, that's a good start. And the next one?"

Penny turns over the second card. The Six of Swords.

"That looks interesting... A boat journey!"

"Yes, you're right. Journey by water... water symbolising emotions... some kind of transition. There's something you don't know but need to learn."

"Another part of the journey... it's true that my emotions are very confused. I'm so grateful for your hospitality... that you've welcomed me here into your family... and I do feel I'm here to learn something before I can get on with my journey. Yes, that's something to think about." Penny muses.

The third card is turned over.

"Ah... the Magician... and Trickster. Something you need to be careful about."

Penny gasps. "Wow... he was one of the people in my vision of the fair. Dressed as a wizard... surrounded by a crowd... like they were spellbound. Looked like he was doing card tricks or something."

"Interesting... you're seeing my cards come to life!"

"You said he's the Trickster. What did you mean about being careful?"

"Well, he's a wizard... he appears and disappears... distracts you with one thing while he magically makes something else happen. He's also the Shaman... who appears as if by magic when he's needed. Think of Gandalf. You know... in Lord of the Rings?"

Penny looks puzzled, then light dawns and she smiles. "Yes... now I remember. Read the book years ago. Then it was a film, wasn't it?"

"So you must have seen it. Wonderful, magical film! So you get the idea? He can work magic... but he can only assist in your own progression... to find your higher purpose in life. He can't be there all the time... only when you really need him to direct you... to put you on the right path. So you must need him right now. Just be aware that you really understand what he's telling you, or you could be led astray. He often speaks in riddles... that's the Trickster. You have to use your mind to unravel his secrets... follow his clues."

"Maybe I'll find clues in your book. I'm really enjoying the story. The boy's journey seems to echo mine somehow. Fascinating! Ok... what's next?" Penny turns over the fourth card. "Ace of Cups. Looks like the Holy Grail."

"Yes... represents spiritual understanding. In this position it means an opportunity. Perhaps your time here at Samhain will give you the opportunity to understand more about your visions. I do hope so."

"I'm sure it will! I've learned so much. I've been feeling quite apprehensive... but now it's turning into excitement."

"That's very positive." Mary says and Grace nods in agreement.

Penny turns over the last card. "The Moon."

"This card is about water and reflection. Because the Moon has no light of its own but reflects the light from the Sun, we take this to mean it's about the unconscious… imagination and psychic abilities… which we know you have. In this fifth place it's about what action to take… so what do you think? How could you act on this?"

Penny is lost in thought for a few minutes. She smiles. "This is so amazing. I know I've been interested in the Tarot before, but this reading is so pertinent to how I feel… I can't believe it. While I'm here I'd love to learn more about the symbolism. It reminds me a bit of Astrology… I know I've had an interest in that, too… and the Archetypes… myths and legends and all that. I'd love to learn more about the Tarot if you have the time to teach me."

Mary leans towards her. "Well, you've been through psychotherapy… and Lena, your medium, brought back some memories. Then you've had your own psychic visions… talking to the dead… and now you're going deeper into the meaning of it all. Nothing would please me more than to help you find out more while you're here. Anyway, Grace knows as much as I do so she can help."

Grace winces. "I don't know as much as you do Ma… but I'd like to brush up anyway! Any time Penny."

Penny just wants to hug them both, so they have a group hug.

* * *

After their lunch with Joe and Dylan, Penny is glad to relax in the studio with Mary's book. She's beginning to match the characters in the story with the Tarot cards that she keeps at hand, ready to help define the meaning of the plot as the tale unwinds, with its twists and turns that keep her absorbed until gradually her eyes close and she falls asleep. As Mary continues with her painting, she smiles to see

Penny so relaxed.

As Penny's helping Mary prepare supper, Grace comes down from upstairs. "I've been sorting out the old costumes from the attic and they're still in great condition."

"Oh good… you found them…" Mary is stirring a pot on the stove.

"My mother is so meticulous… you wouldn't believe! They've been cleaned and put away in those vacuum bags so they don't get mouldy and musty. We've had them for years, from a Pageant we put on when we were younger. Authentic medieval costumes. I thought we'd all go upstairs and try them on to see what we can wear for Saturday's celebrations. Maybe after supper or before, if we can find the men!"

"I hope something fits me… I've put on some weight since then!" Mary comments wryly.

Penny's impressed. "How marvellous! Can't wait to see them."

"Why don't you come up with me now and we'll find something appropriate? If Ma can spare you."

Mary nods. "Yes… everything's prepared… the stew can simmer for a while. I'll come with you."

In one of the bedrooms Grace has hung the garments on the wardrobe door and others are laid out on the bed. As they hold them up and try them on for size, laughing and making personal comments, Penny is in awe at the beautiful colours and details. However, she finds that most of the dresses were obviously made for younger women with small waists, which wouldn't fit her if she tried. Then she spots a cloak and holds it up. "I think I'd be happy in this…" she says, thinking of her vision. "It might help me understand her."

Mary looks round as she's adjusting a skirt round her middle. "The Wise Woman! Why not? You know… she has a purple dress underneath to indicate her spirituality. That's here somewhere."

Penny finds the purple dress fits perfectly well as it's quite shapeless, and she covers it with the dark cloak and hood.

"How about that! You really look the part, Penny. Could have been made for you…" Grace enthuses. "I think it was made for Aunt Rose, wasn't it?" as she turns to her mother.

"Indeed, it was… she was a wise old woman, too. Used to be a midwife, so that was appropriate for her. How does it feel, Penny? Now you've got it on."

Penny looks at herself in the long mirror. "Quite strange… but somehow familiar. You may be right about a past life. I like the purple dress… "

"*When I'm old I shall wear purple,*" she quotes. "Love that poem. And I like the hood… so I can be hidden." She turns around to get the feel of it.

Mary nods. "Yes… hidden wisdom! That's why people were so fearful of wise women in those days… the midwives and herbalists… because they couldn't understand their powerful *magic*… so they demonised it."

They're silent for a few moments as if to honour the memory of those countless women of old who were put to death for their ancient wisdom.

Mary is wearing a voluminous brown skirt and lacing up a white blouse to wear with a colourful shawl. "I'm a typical Granny… or probably the cook!" she laughs, while Grace shows off a flowing blue gown, edged with silver thread, with long sleeves that come to a point over her hands. "The headdress is gorgeous…," she glows, placing a pearl studded veil on her head.

"Wow… Your Ladyship! It's lovely, Grace." Penny and Mary stand back to admire this vision of loveliness.

"Right… we're sorted. Supper will be ready as soon as the men get in. Don't know what they've been up to. Something mysterious!"

After supper, the men are ushered upstairs to try on their costumes and come down looking very smug in stockings and breeches, with elaborate shirts and jackets and brandishing short swords.

"I can't believe you all made these wonderful clothes!" Penny looks on in astonishment.

"Well, it wasn't all us, to be honest." Mary explains. "We got most of them from a theatre company that was selling them off. So they are beautifully made. We just added some... like the costume you'll be wearing and a couple more very simple dresses to fit the children when they were young."

"We were wondering what you've been up to." Grace remarks to Dylan and Joe, who glance at each other conspiratorially.

"Well, we're not ready yet. It's supposed to be a surprise... so you'll have to wait."

"How mysterious!" Grace says, but she sees Joe wink at her mother, who just smiles.

* * *

Walking a path through a deep dark forest. Treading softly in moccasins, clothed in soft deerskin leggings and tunic and recalling how the women of the tribe would treat the raw hide to make it soft and pliable. Feeling the strength of taut muscles... a young man's body. All around, the incessant hum of insects and an occasional bird call... glimpsing wild rabbits and squirrels scurrying among the trees... aware that there are other creatures in the forest... gentle does with their young and majestic stags... and other wild beasts that could be dangerous... wolves and bears... moving quietly so as not to attract any attention. Coming eventually to a clear stream... and following the increasing sound of rushing water, approaching a high waterfall plunging into a deep, dark pool to sit on a moss-covered boulder... mesmerised by the sound in the green womb of lush foliage and overhanging branches. As daylight fades, a Full Moon rises through the trees, reflected in the pool... feeling drawn in... but is not afraid...

Chapter 24

Week 4: Day 2. Wednesday… Dreams

Waking in the early morning, Penny is anxious to write down her memory of the dream before it evaporates… anxious to capture the special feeling its left her with… a feeling of magical intensity… hope and longing. But she was a young man!

She notes that most wild creatures keep well away from humans, but the bigger animals can kill and maim if they feel threatened… or hungry! But then again, there are other, more dangerous magical creatures to fear… more dangers to be faced. She may have felt safe in the wood, but was that because she was ignorant of the dangers? She realises how this applies to life, too. Has she been so ignorant that she's not appreciated the dangers lurk in unexpected quarters?

As she writes, more details emerge in her thoughts that she records to her notebook, which is filling up steadily with all the notes she's been writing on her journey. As she's so early, she washes quietly and dresses before going downstairs with her book to read in the studio before the others are up. She soon realises that the setting of her dream, even though she was dressed as a native American-, a Red Indian, she'd have said, though realising that's not appropriate these days, resembles the symbolism of the book and also in the cards, which she eagerly examines.

Yes... there is the waterfall in the Ten of Cups. Spiritual over material values and fulfilment of emotional desires... just as she'd experienced it. But what about the dangers? She searches the pictures in the cards. Here's the Bear... number twenty of the Major Arcana... Judgement in the traditional cards, she notices. She reads the explanation... reaping one's Karma. So if one were a hunter, she thinks, the Bear would know and spare no mercy. All about how to tread carefully in the world!

* * *

As Penny's helping Mary to wash up after breakfast, she asks "What do you think the men are getting up to?"

"Something nice, I hope. I just hope the weather holds up."

"So it must be in the wood!"

"Shhh..." Mary cautions, looking round. "Don't go to look. It's supposed to be a surprise!"

"We're going for a walk along the canal." Dylan pops his head around the door. "Anyone interested?"

"What a good idea... we all need a bit of exercise. How about you, Penny?" Mary agrees and Penny nods.

"I'd love to. And the sun's coming out!"

* * *

As they walk, enjoying the fresh air and morning sun, Penny recounts her dream to Mary.

"I was a young man... searching for something... or on a mission, I think. Sort of reflects my journey. But you've mentioned past lives. Do you think this could be a past life memory?"

"Quite possibly. I know I've had dreams like that, which I'm sure were my past lives... but dreams usually tell us about something that's pertinent to our current situation. It will be interesting to see if you have any more dreams like that. There was no-one else around? You didn't meet anyone?"

"No... just aware of all the wildlife around me. Not scared exactly... but aware of the dangers that could be around the next corner." She explains what she found in the cards.

"Well, the Tarot seems to have triggered something in your mind. Some realisation perhaps?"

"Well, probably that I've felt quite scared of all that's been happening to me in the last few weeks. Not knowing who I am... though I do now, I suppose... and not knowing what will happen next. Maybe I'm worried about what more I'll find out about me."

Dylan overhears... "Of course, Penny, you could be a criminal mastermind on the run from the police!" he laughs.

"Well, I feel safe enough here with you... and I'm so grateful for everything you're doing for me. I don't know how I can ever thank you."

"We're all intrigued by your story, Penny... and when my book gets published, you'll be rich and famous! That's all the thanks we need."

"We'll all be rich and famous then!" Penny laughs gleefully.

"If only..." Mary grimaces. "We've been writing books for years and we still need money to do the roof!"

"You just don't write anything sensational enough to become a bestseller..." Grace laughs. "And maybe Penny's story will be!"

"Why? Will it be full of sex and murder?"

"There's still time for that…" Dylan says mysteriously. "How about it, Penny?"

"You never know." Penny replies.

* * *

After lunch, Grace and Dylan are making music in the sitting room, Dylan with his guitar and Grace on her flute. Penny looks in as Grace begins to sing a lovely haunting melody.

"That's beautiful," she remarks as the song ends.

Dylan turns around. "Just practising… we always have music with these gatherings. We're hoping you'd like to sing something, too… or at least join in with us. We've plenty of songs to choose from."

Penny is delighted to be asked. "Yes, I'd love to. Let me see…," and she sits down with them.

A couple of hours later and they've practised several songs, two or three of which Penny is quite familiar with and happy to join in.

"You know quite a lot of traditional songs, Penny. I'll bet you used to go to folk clubs or festivals, if you can remember." Grace remarks.

"Yes, I think so. I do remember country dancing in a big tent… in mud caked boots on rough grass… couldn't keep my balance! I just love music, especially live music, but I don't play any instruments, as far as I know. Wish I did… but it's a bit late now."

"There's always time to learn." Dylan laughs. "If you want to."

Penny pulls a face. "Not sure I have the patience… and if I haven't learnt by now…," she sighs.

Mary brings in a tray of tea and freshly made scones, and wants to know what songs they'll be playing for Samhain. She nods her approval. "That will be wonderful! We always need music in our lives. Where's Joe anyway? Hasn't he got his fiddle out yet?"

Grace nods. "He said he will after supper. You know Da… he'll be ready when he's ready! Anyway, we've got the Bodhran here for you Ma, when you're ready. You don't even have to practise, do you? You know the songs so well."

"I'll join in after supper." Mary assures them.

* * *

That evening is filled with music and laughter as they practise one song after another and Penny is surprised at Joe's prowess with his fiddle, while Mary plays the Bodhran effortlessly. "They met in a Folk Club, you know... and they played in an Irish Band for a while, when we were young. We grew up with all this music... and we all had to play something." Grace tells Penny, who isn't surprised; they're all so talented.

Penny's head is still filled with music and she hums a tune as she gets ready for bed, glad to lie down after a full day's activities. She is soon asleep.

In the darkness of night... following a spiral path in procession to rhythmic incessant drumming... bare feet on stony ground... bare chest painted in patterns of black and white... coming to a central space to sit and drink from a gourd passed around the circle. The Shaman, clothed in the skin of a great Bison... its huge head hanging over his strangely black tattooed face... shaking his rattle over each of them... chanting as they retch and tremble with each draught... naked bodies writhing and convulsing... in pain or ecstasy... under the influence of this concoction that they all must drink to pass through this initiation. Then, as if possessed, they rise... one by one... drawn to the huge bonfire... to stamp and whirl to the beat of the drum and chanting of the elders... until the spirit takes hold... powerful wings soaring into the blue-black sky... skimming over the treetops... wheeling and diving... up and up... dawn breaking over far mountains... elated... ecstatic...

in orgasmic connection with all life...at one with the Great Spirit...

Chapter 25

Week 4: Day 3. Thursday… Carving the Pumpkins

"Better make a start on these pumpkins," Joe says as he places a selection on the kitchen table. "The others will be here later to help, but you'll want the flesh for soup I expect…," he says, while Mary hastily clears the breakfast things out of the way.

"Thanks love… there's plenty of time."

"That's what you always say!" Joe smiles. "But we always end up in a rush, don't we? It would be nice to have Saturday free for everything else we want to do."

"That's all very well for you to say, my dearest husband… but what exactly are you doing with your time, eh?"

"Now that would be telling!" Joe puts a finger to his nose with a conspiratorial look.

"I know… it's a surprise!" Mary laughs. "Go on with you…," as she starts the washing up. "Where is everybody when I need help?"

"I'm here." Penny has just walked in. "Sorry, I just had to go to the loo." She picks up the tea towel.

"You're a guest, Penny… you're not expected to be kitchen maid. I don't know where Grace gets to…"

"She's still working on the music with Dylan and I'm perfectly happy to be of service. Anyway, I want to tell you about the dream I had last night. It was awesome!"

"Wait till we've finished this… then I'll be all ears."

* * *

Over coffee Mary listens to Penny's dream with astonishment. "That really does sound like a past life experience… unless you've made a study of American Indian customs."

"Not that I know of. It was so clear… and I can recall all of it, which is unusual for me. It was powerful… I could feel being a man. And the sense of flying was incredible! I used to have dreams of flying when I was young… loved that!"

"So do you think this was a continuation of your first dream?" Mary asks to clarify.

"I think so… and maybe that time in the forest was something to do with this initiation test."

"You're possibly referring to a *Vision Quest*."

Penny looks curious. "What?"

"It's part of a Shaman's training. You're sent out into the wilds for a day or more to seek your vision. You have to survive without anything to help you… no food or water… no tools or weapons. In fact, just going without food opens you up to connect you with nature… and the Spirits. So you're open to see visions and hear voices. Hallucinations, if you like. That's the rational explanation, of course. But anyone who wants to develop psychic or spiritual knowledge can experience this… even today. There are Shamanic courses that organise such things.

186

I've done it myself and it's very profound... when you get over the fear. Especially during the night. It's the best thing I've ever done." She pauses, watching Penny's reaction.

"Where would you do that? There's not much wilderness in this country, is there?"

"You'd be surprised! I went to Wales. There are high tracts of wild land there... and Scotland... but you're right... not much wilderness left in England, more's the pity. I think people miss that kind of experience in their lives. Young people don't have the opportunity to go through such an initiation these days and I think they suffer from it."

Penny's lost in thought for a few moments. "We used to take the children camping, but it could hardly be called *wild*. We could only find camping sites where everything's laid on... loos and showers... not far from the shops. Not quite the same thing! But I know what you mean. I always wanted to do wild camping but never got round to it, as far as I remember."

"I think we all have this ancestral knowledge somewhere in our subconscious, but it gets dampened down by the conditions of modern life. You can see the results in hyperactive children and young people who can't find any meaning in life and wander aimlessly... trying drink and drugs or sex... or joining gangs... trying to understand where they belong. So sad. We used to take our children's friends with us when we went camping... as wild as we could. We even started a youth club... to get the local kids interested in nature... but that seems to have fizzled out now...," she sighs. "With parents too busy to encourage them or glued to the Telly or the Internet. What can you do?"

Penny's quiet. She can't get the *Vision Quest* out of her mind.

"Why don't you go and relax Penny. I notice you're getting through that book. There are more, you know. But I've got things to do right now...," as she ushers her out.

"Yes, I will. I haven't finished writing down the dream yet, and there's so much to think about it." She's wondering if a Vision Quest in Wales would help in her journey, but surely that would cost money. Money she doesn't have. Or maybe the experience of the dream... in her past life... could provide the answers she needs.

"The girls are on their way," Joe calls from the hallway.

"Good... they'll be in time for lunch," Mary calls back.

* * *

As Penny begins to write it all out, more details emerge. The crowds of people... the tribe she, or he, had belonged to, are all familiar... as though she's always known them... the faces... personalities... but not names. She takes a thoughtful walk round the garden before returning to read the book in the studio and is soon absorbed in the story again, while Mary paints.

When Mary lays down her brush and steps away to survey her work, Penny rises to join her. "May I look?"

"Please do. I'd like to have your opinion."

Penny takes in the large painting of a majestic stag displaying his antlers on a rugged mountain top.

"Wow! The King of the Forest," she exclaims.

"Not too much of The Stag at Bay?"

Penny recalls the famous Victorian painting by Landseer.

"Not at all. I see the dominant male looking out for his herd... maybe sensing trouble?"

"Yes... I'm hoping to convey a sense of vulnerable dominance. He's a shape-shifter in this new story."

"A what?" Penny wonders if she heard right.

"A mythical creature who can appear as a beast or a man."

"Like a werewolf?" she queries.

"Yes... like a werewolf. There are many myths about such things and you know the American Indians have always claimed to do so when they take drugs in their ceremonies to become Shamans. They say they become their totem animal… a beast or a bird… so they can travel anywhere to see things far away… where other tribes are camped, for instance… so they can predict danger coming. In fact, in the sixties, I think, the Americans and Russians got interested in training people to go into trance and see things in other places. *Remote Viewing* they called it. Just like Shamans!" she laughed.

"That's handy," Penny remarks. "I wouldn't mind having that ability. In the dream I felt that I became a bird. I think Kay was trying to teach me something like that that in hypnosis… to look down on my life and zoom into any part I wanted to see more clearly. Only I couldn't see anything more recent because of dense cloud! Something, she said, I could practise."

"Well, that's interesting. Definitely practice… the clouds might suddenly part!"

But why a stag?"

"Well, stags were venerated in the past. They are so magnificent and dangerous when cornered. It's interesting that archaeologists have found many skulls with holes made in them to apparently attach straps to one's head… for Shamans to wear, I'm sure. There are old traditions that still go on in some parts of the country, where a man parades through the town with antlers to his head. I'm sure I have a book on it somewhere. I can find it if you want to know more."

The sound of a car crunching gravel in the drive, then commotion at the front door, interrupts them and they join the others to meet Grace's sisters in the hallway. Penny stands out of the way while they take turns to hug and greet each other.

"How are you doing?"

"Haven't seen you for so long."

"You're looking good!"

"What have you done with your hair?" They chatter, taking off their coats.

"Kettle's on." Mary leads the way into the kitchen. "Come and meet Penny... our unexpected visitor.

"Penny... this is Sophie."

A tall elegant woman with a charming smile extends her hand. "How lovely to meet you." Penny takes her hand, murmuring a greeting, and turns to meet the other daughter.

"Hi Penny... I'm Freya. " She's slightly shorter with a firmer handshake. "Welcome to this crazy family. I hope they're looking after you."

"Thank you... yes... I'm so happy to be here to meet you." Penny's a little overawed.

As they settle down with coffee, talk turns to what's been happening and how the preparations are getting on.

"We'll be carving pumpkins after lunch." Joe reminds them.

"That'll be fun...." Freya turns to him. "Everything under control Da?"

"Pretty well... I think the weather will be with us."

"How's Ralph?" Mary asks Sophie.

"Very busy... hardly see anything of him when he's got a project on."

As they chatter on about their respective families, Penny watches their warm familiarity and thinks about her own family. How could she have lost such precious memories of her children, and her grandchildren?... yes... somehow now she knows she has grandchildren, too.

Grace starts to clear away the coffee mugs. "Out of this kitchen, *dearest ugly sisters*... take Penny into the sitting room," she demands. "We've the lunch to get on with..."

"Yes Cinders..." they rise laughing... "Get on with your work, little sister... you lazy good for nothing!"

Sophie takes Penny's hand. "Come and talk to us, Penny. We've been hearing about your adventures... but we want to hear more!" She leads her into the sitting room where they all sit expectantly.

"I don't know where to begin...," she says.

"Well... why not start at the beginning and go on to the end...!" they chorus, laughing.

Penny has a recollection of the mouse's tale in *Alice in Wonderland*... or was it *Alice through the Looking Glass*? Where the words in her childhood book curled down the page like a long tail.

"Mine is a long, sad tale." she begins. They both cheer. "You got it!"

When they've all stopped laughing, they ply her with questions.

What happened? How did you meet Grace and Dylan? What brought you here? What have you found out? Where do you go next?

She thinks that all her answers are only adding to the confusion. "I think you'll have to read the book!"

"My next bestseller... you'll have to pay for it!" Everyone turns to Dylan who's come in unnoticed.

* * *

As they all clear up after lunch, Joe points to the basket of pumpkins. "Right, you lot. Get yourselves a knife and get carving!"

Mary adds, "Plenty to go around... and save a couple for Tris and his friend. He always likes to do his own. I don't know about his friend. And Peter won't be here till Saturday anyway."

The afternoon seems to fly as they each take a pumpkin to start carving grotesque and fanciful faces, saving the inner flesh to go into a large bowl. "Plenty for a good pot of soup," Mary notes with satisfaction. "With plenty of fresh herbs. If you'd like to help me pick them...," Mary turns to Penny.

"I'd be glad to... any time. When the rain stops...," Penny replies as she peers through the rain-spattered window.

* * *

Eventually the rain stops and they go out to pick large bunches of herbs.

"*Are you going to Scarborough Fair...,*" Penny sings. "*Parsley, Sage, Rosemary and Thyme...,*" Mary joins in. "Love that song. We could sing it together on Saturday, if you like."

"Yes... why not? Learnt it at school... but I'll need to brush up on the lyrics." She's delighted to be asked.

"We'll have it somewhere... and Dylan's sure to know it."

Later on, they take some time to find the lyrics and practise the song with Dylan on the guitar. After this Penny's glad to retire to the studio to resume her book.

The story takes an unexpected turn. From when the young man, Robin, bright spark that he is, finds employment with a merchant, wearing fine clothes and having money in his pocket, is robbed of his master's goods, beaten and left in a ditch, resulting in instant dismissal, and he's turned out into the street where he's mocked for being black and destitute. Taking refuge in the church, he's accosted by the priest who turns him out, calling him a 'black devil'. Then reduced to the most degrading of menial jobs; collecting urine for the tanners from every house and sleeping wherever he can find shelter, he decides to walk to London to find his fortune. On the road he meets a mysterious traveller, who offers to teach him the secrets of the universe if he'll promise to do everything he's asked.

'Ah... the Magician... the Shaman!' she thinks, reading on, but nothing is simple in these stories, as in life, as he's sent on an errand and gets lost in the labyrinth of London.

* * *

The carved pumpkins have been placed on top of the dresser, leering down on them while they are eating supper. "They're giving me the creeps," observes Dylan. "Not very pretty, are they?"

"Not supposed to be...," Joe replies. "They represent the spirits of the underworld or the spirits of the dead... or they're meant to frighten them away... no-one's quite sure... but it's a very old tradition from Ireland."

"We just think they're fun...," says Grace. "Because we've always done it. But I haven't finished mine yet."

Penny agrees with Dylan that they look very spooky.

"Wait till you see them with candles inside!" he laughs.

As she lays down to sleep, Penny can't get those pumpkin heads out of her mind, with their pointed teeth and glaring eyes... she just hopes they don't haunt her dreams tonight.

Chapter 26

Week 4: Day 4. Friday... Preparations

Penny wakes early and goes downstairs to find Mary out on the patio, the early morning sun rising through mist coming off the water. Mary greets her. "Good morning! I like to practise Tai Chi out here when the weather's good. If you'd like to join me... just follow me."

Penny nods and is pleasantly surprised to find her body seems to know the movements without any problem. Of course, she knows how to do Tai Chi... doesn't everyone?

* * *

Helping to prepare breakfast, Penny asks about what she should be doing to get ready for tomorrow's rituals, it being a spiritual festival. "What do you do exactly?" she asks.

"We do treat it with respect... as people have done for longer than we know. This is one of those times when the veil thins between this world and the *other* world... and we need to be ready. So we fast from after supper tonight till our feast tomorrow night. But you don't have to, unless you really want to. And we bathe... bath or shower... not a ritual in the Canal...,"*both laugh.* "So the bathroom may be quite busy before we dress for the occasion in our costumes. We also take time to meditate, which I do anyway, usually in the early morning before anyone's up. It doesn't matter when, but it helps to be somewhere quiet and you're not likely to be disturbed. Meditation just helps me get into the right frame of mind to accept whatever comes to me... whether it's a vision or a message from one of my spirit guides."

Now Penny's intrigued. "I'm sure I know about spirit guides... but my mind needs refreshing. Are they real?"

"Many people believe so. But you might consider them to be a manifestation of your *higher mind*... your spiritual connection... that knows everything."

"This is all so familiar to me, I must have studied it, I'm sure. But how can I connect with my spirit guide?"

"All you have to do is ask... and wait. The request must come from a sincere heart... and it may take some time. But I wonder if you've not already met yours. How about your Native American Shaman? From your description, I'd say that could have been a past life... and he could be your spirit guide in this life! How does that feel?"

"Well, I'd like to think so. Maybe I'll ask and see what happens. He might have the answers I'm seeking."

Mary nods. "All you can do is ask and wait for an answer."

* * *

The girls come downstairs together, ready for breakfast, chattering about their children and the joys of motherhood. "We're going for a walk along the canal if anyone's interested," Freya announces. "I really need some fresh air."

"Not at the moment...I'm finishing my pumpkin," says Grace. "What about you Penny?"

"Not right now, but thanks," she says, not relishing a chattering walk. She doesn't feel comfortable in group walks, preferring the company of one person to talk with, or solitude.

When breakfast has been cleared away, Grace gets her pumpkin head onto the table to finish carving.

"You're making him very comical," Penny observes.

"I don't like the scary ones... so I do my bit to make it funny. Give the spirits a laugh! Haha!"

"Do you take all this seriously, or is it just family tradition... like being Catholic?"

"Well, to be honest... I'm not sure. I've grown up with it so maybe I just take it all for granted. I love the theatricality of it. My school friends used to make fun of me, so I learned not to make a big deal out of it... and now I go along with this family thing... but I do take some things very seriously... like meditating, for instance... I'm more into Buddhist philosophy these days... that's important to me... and Tarot... and crystals."

"I've noticed that lovely pendant you always wear. What is it?"

"Rose quartz... for love. Dylan gave it to me when we made our commitment. Isn't it lovely?"

* * *

Penny's thinking about meditation as she wanders around the garden in the pale sunlight, her coat fastened against a cool breeze. She finds a seat looking across the rippling waters of the canal. *'Yes, of course I meditate...,'* she recalls, sitting upright, her feet firmly planted, hands open on her thighs, mind focussed on asking her spirit guide to make itself known. Sometime later, she feels the cold and finds she's slumped over, having fallen asleep. *'So much for meditation...,'* she sighs, disappointed at herself for falling asleep, and returns to the warmth of the house. Thinking that the cards might have a message for her, she goes into the studio to find them. *'I know the cards aren't magic... and any messages I get are from my higher mind... but I'd be grateful for some more guidance...,'* she thinks as she shuffles as best as she can and cuts the pack, pulling out three cards. *'Right...,'* she says to herself. *'I accept guidance from my higher self...'*

Turning over the first card, she sees number ten of the Major Arcana, *The Wheel of Fortune. The cycle of life...* she reads. *Changing fortunes... Things hidden that will be revealed.* *'Good one! Thanks for that.'*

The second card reveals the seven of Swords and she looks for the explanation. *'Oh... Insecurity... confusion... ungrounded fears. Mistaken confidence. A clever plan that may backfire.* *That's not very helpful! Maybe I'm hoping for too much from the spirits... or my higher self.'*

With a little trepidation, she turns over the third card. *'The Fool... back to square one then.'* She reads the explanation though she knows it already. *Freedom... recklessness... acting on instinct... taking a chance... setting out on a journey.* She sighs *'Tell me about it... still on my journey."* But she considers the cards again, trying to make some sense out the different descriptions.

'Things hidden will be revealed... hopefully this weekend! *Insecurity and confusion...* well that's true enough. Then no doubt, I'll be back on my fool's journey to fulfil my quest... but maybe not so naïve... and leaving my baggage behind...,'* she notices, recalling that Mary's said something about getting rid of baggage, like old worries and outworn beliefs, at Samhain. She wonders what baggage she might be letting go of... maybe fear and old expectations. *'So whatever happens, don't be over-confident. But a new phase of the journey... a leap in the dark... but*

with caution... hopefully!'

'Meditate,' she tells herself, and sits upright in her chair, focussing on her breath. *Breathing in... Love and inspiration... breathing out... all my fears and confusion... in... and out... in... and out...*

She comes to with a jolt. A voice, loud and clear... *'Mother!'...* Julian's voice. "I'm here!" she responds, quickly rising out of her chair... then suddenly aware of a deep ache in her heart... overwhelmed with sadness and despair... and guilt... with a sharp intake of breath. *What's happened to Julian? Why can't I remember?* Trembling as she tries to understand.

"Lunch is served." Grace sings, opening the door. "Hungry, Penny?" Then seeing the look on her face, she comes over and takes her hand. "Whatever is the matter? You look as if you've seen a ghost!"

"Nothing... really," Penny assures her with a wan smile. "Just dreaming. I'll be right in...," she straightens herself to follow Grace into the kitchen. "That's what I need... food!"

She's hungry, but can't eat much, as the others chatter and laugh over lunch. Every mouthful seems to be choking her and she's relieved to help with clearing away and washing up. The habitual chore of kitchen duties help to calm her as she thinks over her dream, wondering if this has always been the way women have dealt with their emotions, through the mundane responsibility of caring for their families.

They hear the phone ring in the hall, then Joe pokes his head through the door. "Tristan and his friend will be here for supper."

"Well, I'll be in the studio...," Mary says. "I want to get one picture finished before tonight."

Penny takes another walk round the garden to breath the fresh air and recover her composure, with Julian's voice still haunting her mind. With her memory stubbornly blocked, she wonders why he'd be calling her and desperately hopes he's alright. He was always a very sensitive boy, and she recalls his love for nature and *artistic temperament*, as everyone called it. She thought he might be gay, though that didn't matter, as long as he was happy.

Back in the studio, Mary is engrossed in another painting and Penny takes a quick peep at the dark canvas; she can make out what she thinks is the shape of a dragon entwined in a lush foliage of twisting branches and leaves. Dark green wings, spines tippet in brilliant red are folded along the spine, while the body shimmers in translucent pinks, green and white. The scaly head seems to be peering out of the frame, its eyes strangely human.

"Wow!" she murmurs, not wanting to disturb Mary's concentration.

"Not any dragon, naturally. A shape-shifting Dragon… in our new story. What do you think?"

"Awesome! But why a dragon?"

"She's an aspect of the fierce mother… the guardian of women and children. As a woman, she's like a snake; quiet and cautious, wary of being stepped on, hiding her emotions… but when she's aroused by cruelty or injustice… she rises up with a vengeance to devour the perpetrator."

Penny wants to tell Mary of her dream, but this isn't an appropriate time, she realises.

"I like it!" she reaches for the book, thinking that continuing the story will settle her.

* * *

She resumes her reading where the hero Robin, lost in London, finds himself at a Blacksmith's forge and having been brought up in a smithy, offers his services.

"Well, young man… you have the face for it… (referring to his dark looks). Let's see what you can do." The good-humoured blacksmith takes him on and is soon happy with his work. Robin turns out quality ironwork and

attracts plenty of work for his master, who appreciates his talent and takes him into his home. However, although Robin enjoys the craft he learned so early on, he's eager to find the strange traveller, 'The Sorcerer' he calls him, who'd promised to teach him the secrets of the universe. Soon enough, the mysterious traveller finds him at the forge, but doesn't reveal their acquaintance to the blacksmith when he orders a new sword. "If this young man can forge a sword to befit a prince, I'll pay you well," he declares, barely glancing at Robin. So the task is set, and although Robin has never made anything more essential than horse-shoes, farming implements and kitchen utensils, he's eager to improve his skills, hoping the blacksmith will teach him what else he needs to learn about swords.

* * *

"Tristan's just arrived with his friend Jake… he's in the kitchen with Ma and Grace. Wait here and I'll send them in." Dylan informs them.

"So looking forward to meeting his friend… Jake, is it?" Freya stands up.

"Do we know anything about him?" Sophie asks.

"No… Tris has been very cagey about this one. Where are they?"

The door opens and a young man bounds in excitedly.

"Darling sisters!" He embraces them both. "I've brought my friend Jake…"

A man steps hesitantly through the doorway, gleaming white teeth in a wide smile.

"Come on in…" Freya moves towards him. "Meet the rest of us."

Penny's not sure if she's imagining a pregnant pause… a very slight hush… before they all take turns to shake his hand and find him a seat.

Penny observes them both. Tristan… medium height, lean body and blond hair to his shoulders… typical Nordic characteristics. While Jake is the opposite… obviously West Indian, with mid-dark skin and dreadlocks, though his speech is refined English. She notices the brief glances they exchange, as though not wanting to appear too close, as she's sure they are. Tristan reminds her of Julian, in his mannerisms more than good looks and the thought sends a sudden sharp pain through her chest... a stab to her heart. *What's happened, Julian?*

Very soon they're all chatting cheerfully as they get to know Jake, who, it turns out, is an ecologist, doing what he can to make the world more *ecologically aware*, he says, which will mitigate his African ancestry, Penny thinks. Though why she's attributing such a racially prejudiced attitude to this very white British family she has no idea... unless they are her own bigoted opinions! Is this the woman she really is? The very thought shocks her and she mentally shakes off all and any preconceived notions as she watches Jake with his beautiful all-encompassing smile skilfully negotiate his way through the nuances of family conversation. Then turning to Tristan who sits beside him... "I love your family Tris... almost as much as mine!" And there are tears in his eyes as they kiss, right there, showing their love. Everyone applauds, patting them on the back as Grace looks round the doorway. "Hope you're ready for Supper... everyone alright in here?" Tristan goes to her and gives her a big brotherly hug. "More than alright sis... Jake is my partner," taking him by the hand as they crowd round in a big group hug and move into the kitchen to make their announcement to Mary and Joe, who show no surprise at all.

* * *

At supper, Mary reminds them there will be no more cooked food for the next twenty-four hours. "But help yourself to anything in the fridge, eggs or cheese or whatever, whenever you feel the need for sustenance. Fasting is not obligatory."

"No problem Ma'am," Jake comments. "I know how to go without food… and I was brought up to respect all religious observances."

"But this is not religious, surely?" Sophie queries.

"I think all ritual has to be religious in some sense. It's to remind us of our connection to something higher than mere human existence."

Mary and Joe are nodding in agreement. "This is our way of connecting to the old religion… the way our ancestors did. I'm so happy you're joining us." Mary says and Joe asks "Are you religious Jake? How were you influenced by your childhood?"

"Actually, I was adopted as a baby when my mother died and brought up by a very Christian English family… and they gave me the very best start in life. But I also knew my West Indian birth family… so I had two families… one white and one black…. and I think I've been very lucky to have a foot in each culture. It makes me appreciate both sides."

After that, the conversation develops into an intense debate on race and culture, which Penny finds absorbing. Watching the two beautiful, young men, she thinks they could be a pair of Greek wrestlers from a classical painting, recalling that the Greeks apparently had no problem with homosexuality.

The talk continues into the night, but when Penny finds herself nodding off in her chair, she excuses herself and goes up to bed early, first recording all that's happened in her notebook before falling into a deep contented sleep.

Chapter 27

Week 4: Day 5. Saturday... Samhain.

She wakes early to join Mary again on the patio in the early morning sun, going through the slow, graceful movements of Tai Chi.

"Aren't we lucky with the weather?" she remarks, stretching her limbs as they finish the sequence.

"Looks like it will last too... the forecast is good. By the way Penny, do get yourself some breakfast if you feel like it. I'm making coffee anyway."

"Oh great... I do need coffee... but I'm good thanks." Penny's actually not so sure she can go without food all day and thinks she's possibly never fasted in her life before.

* * *

Sitting in the kitchen, Penny asks Mary how she feels about Tristan and Jake.

"I'm so glad for him. I always knew he was that way inclined… but he's never announced it before."

"Not shocked then?"

"Not really… just happy for him. I hope it works out and doesn't bring them any problems."

"Jake's very interesting… with his background. I like him."

"Yes… he seems to have a good attitude to life."

They sit in silence, both lost in thought, until Joe appears. "Ah… coffee…," he pours himself a mug and joins them at the table.

"All set for the day?" he asks and they both nod.

"Well, if the weather does change, we've got it sorted." He smiles. "Just wait and see!"

"Can't wait." Mary grins. "I'm going into the Studio to meditate… you can join me if you like, Penny."

"Thanks, I will." Penny rises from her chair and follows her into the Studio to find a suitable chair for meditation. "Won't the others be joining in mediation?" she asks.

"Oh, they'll probably sleep in… it's still quite early … and they'll do what they want to do anyway. I think they mostly like the theatricality of our gatherings… being with family is important to them, I'm glad to say. We'll be having a guided meditation in the ceremony later."

"Should I meditate on anything in particular?" Penny asks.

"Well, I just focus on being in a good state of mind… to honour those that have passed and to connect with higher spiritual energy. Whatever you feel is appropriate. Part of the ceremony is to give up any negative attitudes or beliefs we've become conscious of. Any repressed anger, shame or guilt for instance, that come out as Ego defence mechanisms and prevent us having good relationships. Anything that we recognise as giving a boost to the Ego. We write them on a piece of paper to burn in the fire… a sacrifice of the Ego, if you like. That's something for you to think about."

"Sacrifice? Not a virgin then!"

"No. you're safe there." She's laughing... then looks serious. "But, of course, they did used to sacrifice to their gods... even children and especially young women were sacrificed, because feminine energy has always been highly prized and they thought that nothing could please their gods more than to offer their daughters in what they thought of as marriage to the gods. They would sacrifice their young men to the God of War... but girls were the ultimate offering to their vengeful masculine gods when the crops failed or the rains flooded. Nothing changes really. Why do you think a young bride is dressed in white for purity and festooned with in flowers and veils? She's the virgin sacrifice to the masculine! And her father *gives her away* to another man. From one man to another. We all did it, didn't we?"

"Wow... never really thought about that!" Penny exclaims. "Serious stuff! But what did you mean by *sacrificing the Ego?*"

"When we sacrifice our ideas about who we are... you know... someone's daughter, wife, mother... or what position we hold in society. But you've been there, Penny! You didn't know who you were. How did that feel?"

Penny takes a moment to answer. "Scary... bewildering. Then I seemed to get more comfortable in just being myself."

"So you didn't have any Ego for a while? That's interesting. How do you feel now?"

"Like I'm learning all the time about myself. I just had my emotions to understand. I was sometimes fearful. I don't really know how to explain it."

"Without Ego is to be beyond limiting beliefs and fears about how we should be and how we should behave." Mary laughs. "Anyway, we could be thinking of that in meditation. See if there are any irrational fears or grievances you'd be glad to sacrifice. Or even any high and mighty beliefs about yourself... because we all like to think we're special... and imagine sacrificing them... to lay your soul bare till you know who you really are. OK?" Penny nods. She does know what she means.

"I'll put on some music... I know..." She goes over to her CD collection, selects one and slips the disc into the music centre.

They sit quietly, as the sound of whale song begins and Penny takes long deep breaths as the ethereal singing of the deep seas slowly envelops her senses... as if she's floating on gentle waves of sound.

Waking, she finds herself slumped in the chair, with no recollection of what's happened.

"You were well away there, Penny..." Mary smiles at her from the other chair.

"I'm so sorry... I was just enjoying the whale song so much..."

"No need to apologise... my clients often do the same thing. But I'm glad you enjoyed it. Maybe take a good walk around the garden, if you feel like it."

Penny shakes herself. "I think that would be a good idea... wake myself up!" She goes to find her coat and hears voices in the kitchen, indicating the others are up and about. Taking a quick look in to say 'good morning', she sees Tristan and Jake busy carving their pumpkins, then slips out of the back door, not wanting to become involved in their banter so soon after her meditation, such as it was. The air is fresh and cool and the Autumn sunshine inviting as she strolls slowly along winding paths to the canal, where she sits for a while in contemplation before deciding to explore further afield. Making her way past the wood, where she resists the temptation to look into the clearing, she rounds the house to go down the drive and out onto the road, turning away from the houses that lead to the village. This is still a country lane with little traffic and she's soon surrounded by fields, mostly ploughed, but also meadows with herds of cows or an occasional horse. She's no idea of the time but would like to find a roundabout way of getting back, rather than retracing her steps. Before long, she's back at the canal and crosses a bridge to get onto the footpath and follows it back towards the house.

Stopping at a bench, she's glad to sit for a while as people pass by, some walking dogs, a couple of runners in shorts and an occasional cyclist, but her mind is on the task discovering any negative traits of her Ego that she can sacrifice. She likes this idea and, of course, she's learned a lot about conscious awareness from Kay, who gave her books to read. *Does she have any unconscious anger or resentment?* Yes, probably she does feel righteous indignation, and maybe even seething rage, at the way she was treated by her two husbands. And yes, she does feel herself on the moral high ground in that respect; as a victim she can feel superior, even special perhaps, and, of course, that gives a boost to her Ego. But can she let it go? Ah, that's the question. Kay told her that holding onto anger is like holding onto a red-hot poker and expecting the other person to get burned... or a virus that drains one's energy, so if she could just let it go, maybe that would release her memories. She rises, feeling she may have unlocked something there.

Resuming her walk, she's enjoying the tree lined towpath. As the canal bends in a wide arc, she sees *Tara* on the opposite bank and stops to view it, realising how hidden it is among the trees and bushes. She has to walk quite a bit further before the next bridge where she crosses the canal and finds her way through a Council estate and onto the road that leads her back to where she started, where she's surprised to find a large camper van parked on the drive.

The kitchen's empty, so she helps herself to a glass of water. Then hearing voices in the sitting room, she finds everyone gathered around their visitor.

"Come on in, Penny... we're just catching up with Peter...," as they welcome her in.

A large middle-aged man with a bald head rises to greet her with a smile. "Hello Penny… I'm Peter," he says as they shake hands.

"I like your camper!" she comments.

"My escape pod…," he laughs. "To get away from the constraints of academia."

"How lovely! Where do you go?" Penny sits in the nearest chair.

"Festivals mostly, in the summer."

"Festivals?"

"Music Festivals… Glastonbury… all over the place these days."

"Peter's an old hippie." Mary explains with a smile.

"But I'm really a walker… like to wander in the mountains. On my way to North Wales actually."

"That's where I'm going… only not sure *where*."

"You must tell me about it. Maybe I could help."

Penny smiles. "I will, thank you."

"Good walk?" Mary asks Penny and she tells them where she's been.

"That's a good walk. You've been out some time!"

"Lost all track of time."

"Well, it's coming up to midday. The boys are having their bath. They only have a shower in their place, so a real bath is a luxury for them." Mary explains. "We're all taking turns before we get dressed up! We do have all day."

"It's so strange to have nothing to do, isn't it?" Freya remarks. "I'm usually so busy all day, I'm feeling quite guilty!"

"And no alcohol either… not till tonight anyway!" Sophie laughs.

"I think I'll read my book if you don't mind. I'll be in the Studio, if that's alright." She looks at Mary, who nods her assent. "Whatever you want Penny."

* * *

She's soon engrossed in the story again.

Robin succeeds in forging a magnificent sword, fine and elegant enough for a prince but grows impatient as he awaits the arrival of The Sorcerer to claim it. The blacksmith is impressed by his mastery of the forge, but insists he return to the mundane items people are waiting for. So Robin learns the lesson of patience. The Sorcerer returns at last, full of admiration for the workmanship of the sword. He pays the blacksmith his due, before he turns to Robin. "I said that this sword is for a prince, and you are he! The sword is yours, Robin, and you must wield it with honour and justice."

The blacksmith is astonished... "What are you talking about? This boy is my apprentice and will serve me till his term of employment finishes. Take the sword and go."

"I will pay you for the term of his apprenticeship and he'll come with me." The Sorcerer takes out gold coins. "This will be enough to recompense the loss of an apprentice who has already served you well. Come, Robin... we have work to do." The blacksmith doesn't like the idea at all, but is struck silent by a gesture from The Sorcerer and allows the boy to collect his belongings, which don't amount to anything more than he can carry in a small bundle. Robin is silent as he hurries after the stranger, who leads him to an inn and orders food. "Now you are my apprentice and will serve me in my task."

"I don't understand... why did you call me a prince?" Robin is grateful but bewildered.

"Your father was a prince of his people, but was slain by an accursed fiend who we must find to avenge the dark deed. But be not afraid, for you have your father's heart." So they set off on their quest that involves much searching through books and talking to mysterious strangers.

She puts the book down. Time has flown by and she thinks she ought to be taking her bath if everyone else has finished. Going into the sitting room she finds Tristan and Jake dressed in their colourful medieval costumes. "I do believe the girls are getting dressed. I think you can go up now." Tristan tells her.

Upstairs, Grace, Sophie and Freya are helping each other dress in their finery. "Wow!" Penny exclaims as they twirl and curtsey. "I'd better have my bath!"

"Plenty of time...," they chorus. "Nothing starts till four o'clock."

The bath is deep and luxurious but Penny doesn't linger too long, anxious to be ready with the others. Back in her bedroom she dresses, feeling the soft folds of the purple woollen dress close around her, knowing it will keep her warm in the cold night air together with the long, felted, hooded cloak. She adds her own red silk scarf around her neck, just in case. Finding a piece of paper, she writes... *All my anger and resentment at Davy and Gerry, and anyone else I've forgotten. I forgive them and let them go. Please let me remember.* She feels a tremor in her stomach... *Can I stomach this?* she thinks, as she puts it safely in a pocket of her dress, thankful that it has pockets.

They all congregate in the sitting room showing off their fine clothes. Joe is resplendent in the garb of a lord. "And me a republican!" he says.

"You... a republican? But you love the Queen!" Tristan laughs.

"Ah, a grand woman. She has a great sense of duty, as she sees it... and I respect her for that" Joe declares. "I'd be her champion any day."

"So, my Lord, how do you reconcile the poverty of the lower classes to your elevated status?" Tristan won't leave it alone.

"When will you ever learn that your politics is a game? The sheep don't know they're going to be fleeced or slaughtered because they trust their shepherd and his grinning dog!"

Penny notices Jake giving Tristan a surreptitious kick. *'Don't mess with your Daddy...,'* she thinks

"Oh dear... he's off. He's not usually like this until he's had a few!" Mary whispers to Penny.

"I'm not sure this is the right time...," she directs at Joe.

"Quite right my dear...," and Joe winks at her.

"I think Peter's been dressing in his van. Here he comes." Mary motions to the door as he enters, dressed in clerical garb. "And who might you be, fine Sir?"

"A scholar… naturally! I write the history books you'll be studying in the future."

"Oooh…," they all chorus.

The front door opens to admit five people Penny doesn't know, and Mary welcomes them in. "Some of my students." She introduces them. "Paul and Andrea… Fred… Donald… and Felicity. Dressed for the occasion I see."

"All I could find." Felicity is wearing a plain long dress with a cloak and bonnet, while the others sport a variety of costumes. Fred is definitely Robin Hood and Donald is a Friar. Paul and Andrea look the part as a Lady and her Knight, complete with hose and knickerbockers. "We're in the local theatre group… borrowed their costumes…," they confide.

"Time for some music before our celebrations," Mary announces, as Dylan reaches for his guitar and they go through the repertoire of songs they've all been rehearsing, ending with Mary's and Penny's rendition of *Scarborough Fair* to enthusiastic applause. "That was lovely… Thank you…," as they're congratulated on their performance.

Joe stands up, banging his staff on the floor to command their attention and they all fall silent.

"I know we all love dressing up for the occasion, but I'd like us all now to consider the sacredness of this celebration. We're about to mark the turning of the year, not only with thanks for a bounteous harvest, which will sustain us through the coming winter, but also to honour the spirits of the land and our dear departed with meditation, ritual and music. This is also a good time to sacrifice any emotional baggage and Ego attachments we've accumulated, which you've written on a piece of paper to be burned." He looks around as they all nod. "So, if we're all ready?"

They all stand and he lifts his hands in blessing as they bow their heads.

"May the Great Spirit, that gives us life, be with us through this night."

Small lanterns containing tea lights are ready on the kitchen table and they each take one and light it before leaving the house. Penny is surprised at how quickly the mood has changed from gay banter to solemn ritual, as Joe, dressed as a great lord, but now the High Priest, leads them in silent procession out of the house, across the patio and along the path to the wood.

The clear sky is darkening and Penny wraps the cloak around her against a cool air, as they process slowly into the clearing that has been transformed with a large structure of wooden posts with walls on three sides made of wickerwork and it seemed to have a thatched roof. All the pumpkins are hung on branches, the light of their candles casting eerie shadows as they circle around a huge unlit bonfire in the centre. They stand while The High Priest Joe utters some incantation that she doesn't understand, raising his staff to point in each direction, then speaks in a loud voice… "We purify this Sacred Space and all participants…," and lights the bonfire ceremonially. Then as it catches and roars into life, he continues chanting something she can't catch. Maybe some ancient tongue, she wonders. *Magical words of the Sorcerer casting spells*, thinking of the story. That's who he is, of course! She shivers, thinking of virgin sacrifice. *What has she got herself into?* But no, she reminds herself… nowadays, we sacrifice the Ego.

Grace is at her side whispering "He's casting the circle and calling on the elemental forces of earth to protect us…," and Penny nods her thanks for the explanation.

They now file into the wicker shelter where they take their seats on the wooden benches that line the walls. Joe and Dylan have been busy, she thinks, to do all this in the last few days. This shelter is brilliant, keeping us out of the wind and rain, just in case. Joe, as The High Priest, stands at a kind of altar, doing something with a knife and a chalice, as far as she can see.

Mary now stands and invites them all to meditate. "Let us start with the *OM…*" Penny closes her eyes as Mary intones *Ommmm* and they all join in, at first hesitantly, then gaining momentum, as the discordant cacophony becomes a resonant chord with every breath… a harmonious melding of voices in the still night continues for several minutes, and gradually fades away as Mary lowers her hands. Then in the silence she begins to speak softly… asking them to go inside and ask their spirit guide or guardian angel to be with them… and to reveal whatever they need to know at this time. Her voice continues, low and mesmerising. Penny can hear her, but can't catch all the words, so tries to focus on seeing her Spirit Guide, whoever that may be. She's glad to feel the heat from the bonfire and the shelter of the wall behind her and begins to feel drowsy. She pulls herself up. *Don't fall asleep…* she admonishes herself… *Spirit Guide… where are you? What do I need to know?*

Falling… falling… down the Rabbit hole… not again… I'm not Alice… am I? Is that the White Rabbit up ahead? No… it's Fluffy… the little dog we had when the children were young… what's he doing here? Or was he a cuddly toy? 'Life is just an illusion'… Who said that? 'Life… is just a bowl of cherries… cherries… cherries…' sings a chorus of voices… What's going on? Will someone please tell me? A white figure emerging from the mist… Gandalf? 'If you like'… You look like my grandfather… 'Probably'… What's going on? 'If you really want to know…' Yes… I want to know. 'You are all in your mind. Everything you've ever seen or heard or touched… every story you've heard and every book you've held in your hand and read… every sound of music… every conversation and everyone you've looked in the eye and cared for… every kind and unkind deed and every thought… everything you've ever said and felt and done have made you who you are... the illusion of who you are... only when you're put to the test... then you'll know who you really are... your true Soul... then you'll know everything. Out of chaos, comes order.' But how?... fading into enveloping mist... distant figures that appear and disappear through swirling white mist...

∗ ∗ ∗

"Are you alright, Penny?" She finds she's leaning heavily on Grace, who looks at her anxiously.

"I'm so sorry...," sitting up, to see everyone moving round the fire.

"Take your time." Grace looks bemused at Penny as she shakes herself.

"I hope that was a good experience. No... don't tell me. Would you like to join in? Hold my hand if you like...," and she leads her towards the bonfire, where the others are beginning to cast their papers into the fire with happy smiles, and Grace follows suit. Penny finds the paper in her pocket and holds it for a few moments, recalling what she's written... *All my anger and resentment at Davy and Gerry and anyone else I've forgotten. I forgive and let them go. Please let me remember...* then casts it into the fire, watching it blaze up. She's not sure what she's feeling... relieved? Perhaps. *Out of chaos, comes order...* she remembers. Something in her has changed... but... *When will I get some real information?* she wonders.

The smell of food soon attracts their attention as baskets are opened and unloaded onto a trestle table. Large plates of sandwiches, pies and quiches, baked potatoes, sausages, hot roast chicken and other meat, bowls of salad and crisps and a huge pot of steaming soup. "Help yourselves," Mary calls out as they crowd around. *Where did all this come from?* Penny wonders. The girls are helping unload cans and bottles of beer, unwrapping plastic cups and opening wine boxes. This is a feast and Penny's thankful to take a bowl of the pumpkin soup, which is hot, spicy and delicious. She's resisted the urge to eat all day and is soon back to fill her plate, returning to sample further dishes more than once.

Sitting in the shelter or standing around the fire, they eat their fill and drink heartily until all are satisfied. After a while Dylan takes up the Bodhran, beating out complicated rhythms until, surrendering it to Mary, he takes up his guitar and Grace joins him on the penny whistle, Joe brings his fiddle and Peter takes out a harmonica... to play lively Irish and traditional tunes.

Who could resist such foot-tapping, blood-quickening music? One by one they rise to dance around the fire, slowly at first, then fortified by the food, not to mention copious amounts of drink that inevitably loosens their inhibitions, and exhilarated by the beat... they stamp and twirl... spin and turn to the rhythm... like whirling dervishes in trance... round and round the bonfire... in this time-honoured celebration of life... as their ancestors did for generations past... before music was banned or tamed into submission... and Penny is reminded of her vision of being a Native American Indian, without the chanting, except for occasional whoops of pleasure. Then, throwing herself into the dance around the fiercely burning flames, she surrenders to a pure feeling of happiness... to be here now, among friends... in an ecstasy of joy under the starlit sky.

* * *

Penny eventually stumbles up to bed, exhausted and exhilarated by a day filled with surprises.

Chapter 28

Week 4: Day 6. Sunday… Dowsing

P enny wakes groggily, wondering how much alcohol she'd actually imbibed the night before. She's not the only one to emerge late morning for breakfast that becomes brunch, with eggs and bacon together with plenty of leftover food from the night before.

Peter comes in from where he's spent the night in his campervan. "Good morning all… I smell food!"

"Oh… not enough for you…," Joe winks. "Well, don't just stand there man… come on in."

"Where on earth did all that food come from last night?" Penny asks of no-one in particular. "It just seemed to materialise!"

"Magic!" says Joe with a smile.

Mary laughs. "Some from here… and a lot more from the local restaurant. Had it delivered, so it would still be hot in their containers. They're very good."

"I should say…," Tristan agrees. "Great food."

"It was a marvellous evening. Haven't enjoyed myself so much for a long time." Jake's helping himself.

"Worth coming then?" Tristan nudges him.

"Without a doubt. Wouldn't have missed it for the world. I feel so blessed." They look at each other contentedly.

Everyone is busy putting food on their plates and sitting wherever they can find a place in the crowded kitchen. Mary puts down her plate as she surveys the scene.

"I don't think I can remember such a lovely time. I do thank each and every one of you for being here."

"Hear, hear…," someone says, which sentiment they all echo through mouths full of food.

"And we're so happy for Tristan and Jake…," Joe turns to Jake. "You, young man, are now an official member of the family. If that's not too presumptuous of me."

"I'm honoured, Sir." Jake takes a bow with his sunny smile, and everyone cheers.

When the debris is being cleared away, Mary tells them to take anything that's leftover.

"Thanks Ma, but there'll be food waiting for us at home." Sophie and Tara laugh, and Tristan joins in.

"I think we'll be having a takeaway… but thanks, Ma. We're not starving these days."

"When will you be leaving?" Joe asks them. "Not that we want to see the back of you!"

"Just joking, Da?" Sophie says and they all laugh.

"In about an hour, I think." Freya replies. "As I'm taking Sophie back, I'd like to catch up with them for a while before I go home."

"We're easy." Tristan comments.

They begin to wander out to the patio with mugs of coffee, to make the most of what midday sun there is.

"What about you, Peter?" Penny asks as they sit next to each other. "You said you're on your way to Wales."

"Yes… I'd like to start in the morning, so I'll have plenty of time to get to my friend's place before dark, with a break for refreshment. I don't like to be in a rush. But how about you? Do you know where you're going next?"

Penny drinks her coffee. "Hard to say, when I can't remember any names or anything."

"Maybe you could try dowsing." Peter suggests and Joe hears.

"Why didn't I think of that?" he says leaning towards Penny. "Peter's a Master Dowser. If he can't help, nobody can."

"*Dowser?*" Penny wonders what they're talking about.

"We can do it over a map if you like. Come with me and I'll show you how." Peter rises. "Have you finished your coffee? No time like the present. I have a very good map in my van and we won't be disturbed. Follow me." So she does.

Peter's van is immaculate. He sits her at the small table and takes something from a cupboard, giving her a small pouch and taking a similar one from his pocket. "This is the Pendulum," he says, drawing out a small object and dangling it between his fingers. Penny opens her pouch to reveal a beautiful pointed crystal on a short chain. "Hold it like this…" he commands, holding it in front of him. "You can use your pendulum to reveal the answer to practically any question you have in mind."

"How does that work?" she asks, holding her pendulum as he does.

"The answer is usually there in your subconscious mind, and especially in your case, in your lost memory. You have to ask the question in such a way as to elicit a simple *Yes* or *No* and the pendulum will respond."

She's intrigued. "I'm not sure how…"

"We'll start by determining how your pendulum responds. I'll start by asking something simple. Is my name Peter Watson?"

She watches as his pendulum starts to move, slowly at first, then gaining momentum in a circular swinging motion.

"Notice how it's moving in a clockwise direction? That's how it indicates *Yes* for me." Penny nods.

"Now I'll ask another question that I know is incorrect. Was I born in 1920?"

She's amazed as the pendulum changes direction and starts moving in the other direction.

"The anti-clockwise direction indicates *No* for me, but yours may not be exactly the same. Let's see how you do it. Can you ask about your name? Just your birth name. You do know that now, don't you?"

Penny nods and takes a deep breath, holding the crystal as he's done.

"Is my birth name Margaret Baxter?" she says and watches as it starts to move erratically.

"Try not to influence it, Penny. Just focus on the question as if you don't know."

The pendulum swings wildly then gradually settles into a circular clockwise motion.

"Wow!" is all she can she say.

"That's good. Now let's see your *No* response. What can you ask that's *not* true?"

Penny thinks for a moment before asking… "Am I nineteen years old?" and laughs as the pendulum swings in a wide arc in the opposite direction.

"Well done, Penny. Now we can start asking more important questions. So what do you really want to know?"

"Where my home is, I suppose. How can I ask that?"

"You said you think your home is in North Wales. So just ask that."

Penny adjusts her position and takes another deep breath, hoping this amazing pendulum will do its work.

"Is my home in North Wales?" she asks, concentrating on the crystal's movement while trying not to influence it, as Peter's told her. The initial erratic swing begins to form an arc and she breathes a sigh of relief as she sees it settle into a clockwise direction.

"Amazing! Is that enough?" she turns to Peter.

"That seems to be a definite answer. Now we just have to find out where in North Wales. You don't have any more clues? No place names you remember?"

"No... nothing at all so far." Penny wonders what else the pendulum can do.

"Right. Now we need the map. It's rather big and there's not much room in here to spread it out, so we'd better go indoors and carry on there."

The kitchen's empty as the others are still out on the patio, and they open out the map of North Wales on the large kitchen table.

"What now?" Penny asks, studying the map, noticing names of towns and villages that all seem so familiar.

"Now we dowse in earnest." Peter replies. "Hold your pendulum close to the map, and move it slowly across while you ask the question."

Penny does as he says, starting at the top-left over Anglesey as she asks the question. "Is my home here?"

The pendulum swings slightly as she moves it slowly to the right across the map, then coming to the edge she moves it down a little and brings it back across to the left, then back again and again. "Not Anglesey," she mutters, until coming to the mountainous area of Snowdonia... "I know these mountains," she says. "Snowdon, Moel Siabod. Is my home here?" she repeats over and over as the pendulum moves from side to side as though making up its mind which way to go. Her arm is getting tired and she's about to stop when she notices a change of movement as the pendulum begins to swing around. "Is my home here?" and she holds her breath as it finally settles into a clockwise direction over a name on the map. "Blaenau Ffestiniog," she cries out in amazement. "Yes... I know Blaenau! Is this my home?" she asks again as the pendulum swings wider and wider.

"Now move the pendulum over another area and ask again... as a double check," he instructs her.

She does as he suggests and waits while the pendulum begins to swing in the opposite direction. Then she returns to Blaenau and asks again. The pendulum immediately swings in a clockwise arc again.

"Well, that's a definite *Yes!*" Peter pats her on the back. "Well done, Penny!"

She lowers her arm gratefully and peers again at the map.

"The town isn't very big and you should be able to locate your home on a more detailed map." Peter's saying.

"I can't believe it!" Penny exclaims. "I just can't believe it! Thank you so much!" She kisses her pendulum but refrains from kissing him.

Mary and Joe come in to see Penny laughing and almost dancing with delight, Peter standing there grinning like the Cheshire cat.

"What's this?" Mary asks.

"You'll never guess!" Penny can hardly speak for laughing.

"The pendulum!" Peter holds up his own. "Took to it like a natural born dowser."

"Never occurred to me..." Mary's dumbfounded, while Joe smiles.

"Peter's better at it than we are. You've found it then?" Joe exclaims.

"Seems so," Peter affirms as Penny nods, still exuberant.

"The name of the town, anyway." Penny adds. "But I reckon I'd find my way home if I could get there. The locals must know me... Post Office and local shops. I might even know the way automatically." A sudden flash of memory reveals a little terraced cottage; Number 3 on the door and now she knows she'll find it.

"Come down quick… Penny's had a breakthrough," Mary calls out to the others. The girls are upstairs getting ready to leave.

Tristan, Jake and Dylan come through from the sitting room. "What's happening here?"

"My home!" Penny hugs Dylan.

"You've found where your home is?" He's incredulous.

"Almost. The name of the town anyway."

"It's magic!" Penny's still breathless. "I'd no idea what we were doing… *Dowsing!*"

"Took to it like a duck to water!" Peter's still amazed at how quickly Penny's found her answer.

The girls come running downstairs to hear what all the fuss is about, and are suitably impressed.

"Always knew you were a magician, Peter. You've shown us dowsing before!" Sophie says excitedly.

"I think a toast is in order…" Joe opens a cupboard and brings out a wine box.

"Is that all you can find? Where's the hard stuff? We all deserve it," Mary responds, taking glasses from a shelf.

"Congratulations, Penny!" Sophie goes to hug her, and Freya does likewise, which surprises her more than anyone else. She's not known for being so demonstrative.

Joe's handing round small glasses of amber liquid. "To Penny!" he says, raising his glass and everyone does the same.

"May the road rise up beneath your feet and the wind be always at your back."

With calls of *'To Penny'* they all drink to her, and she's quite taken aback.

"So what next?" Dylan comes to sit beside her.

"North Wales… when I can get there." Penny's relishing the prospect, though how she'll manage it, she's no idea.

"I'm going to North Wales tomorrow." Peter says quietly and they all look at him. "I can take you all the way to, what is it? Blaenau...?"

"Blaenau Ffestiniog." Penny knows the name well, but hesitates to continue.

"You'd take her with you?" Mary queries... "Tomorrow?"

"Why not? I've no particular schedule and when I'm in the mountains I just go where the spirit takes me. Now, Penny's spirit is telling me to take her home." No-one knows what to say.

"I'll look after her... and I can help with any further dowsing if she needs it. I'll be calling at my friends' on the way and they'll be glad to give her a bed for the night. I'll let them know in plenty of time. How about it, Penny?"

Penny realises she has to make a momentous decision. "I'd be so grateful...," her face lights up.

"It will be my privilege, dear lady." He bows ceremonially. "To get you safely home."

Dylan notices that everyone seems to think Penny will find her home quickly and easily. "Have you thought about the possibility that it might be another dead end?" He looks around at the puzzled faces.

"Yes, there's always a possibility that it may not be her current home." Peter has to agree.

"Hadn't thought of that..." Mary looks worried.

"I could go with you... if that's alright with Peter." Dylan looks to Penny and Peter for affirmation and she nods quickly. "Yes, if you could?"

"No problem." Peter agrees.

"And if it doesn't work out, we can always come back by train." Dylan reassures her with a smile.

"We can make enquiries anyway. Someone there may know her." Peter continues... "and when we do some more dowsing I'm sure more answers will surface."

Penny looks at them cheerfully. "I'm ready for it," she announces with determination, thinking that now must be the time to move on in her quest.

"If you're sure…," Mary queries.

"It just feels as if things are falling into place. I'm sure this is the right thing to do." Penny assures them and they all nod in agreement.

"We must get off…" Freya seems anxious to be on her way. "Are you ready Sophie?"

"I'll bring down our things…" she affirms as she and Grace rise to go upstairs.

The girls pack their bags into the car and say their goodbyes.

"All the best, Penny… It's been so lovely to meet you…" Freya gives her a big hug. "I really hope everything works out for you…" and she gets into the driver's seat.

"Take good care of yourself… we'll be keeping in touch. Can't wait to hear when you're home." Sophie hugs her again before getting into the car beside Freya.

"Love to all the family…" Mary calls after them as the car starts down the drive. "See you soon."

"Well…," Tristan remarks as they troop back into the kitchen. "Never a dull moment! I don't think we've ever had such an interesting Samhain."

"Except for that time a new student of Mary's had hysterics!" Grace reminds him.

"That *was* hysterical…," and everyone laughs.

"I've seen dowsing before… but never really took it seriously." Jake says in wonder. "I'd love to learn properly."

"It's easy to learn," Peter assures him. "I'll be glad to show you."

"Tea…" Mary's filling the kettle. "I think there's some cake left."

"Oh good." Tristan and Jake take their seats, ready for more sustenance.

Grace looks at Penny. "I think you're in shock! I am anyway."

Penny smiles. "Yes… I never know what's going to happen next."

The conversation over tea and cake ranges from anticipation to practical suggestions.

"What about you, Grace? Will you wait here for Dylan to get back?" Penny asks her.

"Oh yes. I was planning to spend some time here anyway. We don't see each other often enough. Whenever we're here, Dylan usually busks in Milton Keynes and we play in some of the clubs and pubs. It's a change from London anyway. But this will always be home to me." She looks at her parents wistfully… "and they're not getting any younger."

"What's that, young lady? I'll have you know, we're getting younger every day!" Joe retorts. "You'll not be inheriting this just yet…," and they all laugh.

"We'll have to be going soon…," Tristan announces. "But we've had such a good time, it's hard to leave."

"I'd like to thank you for accepting me into your home." Jake looks around the room. "You've all made me feel so welcome."

"Our pleasure," says Joe and they all agree that he's been excellent company.

* * *

Penny wanders into the garden, thinking about what's transpired today. *This may be the last time I stand here,* she thinks, *at least for a while, if I really do find my way home.* She's still stunned at the chain of events that have resulted in this new plan of action. *After tonight, I only have to pack and be taken all the way home!* She's forgotten her coat, and feeling the cold. She pulls her cardigan around her as the waning sun disappears behind dark clouds.

As she returns to the house, Tristan and Jake are ready to take their leave with hugs all round.

"Penny... we think you're so courageous to be taking this journey." Tristan hugs her first, then Jake.

"Take care, *live long and prosper*..." Jake raises his palm in a salute with the fingers in strange positions and everyone roars with laughter. "Mr Spock!" they have to explain to Penny. "Star Trek." She's still mystified.

"That's something you'll have to catch up with."

"Just a minute... I think my kids used to watch it on TV..." A distant memory dawning on her.

"Yes, they would. How come you've missed it?" Tristan wants to know.

"Too busy I expect," Penny replies. "With life!"

* * *

When they've gone, Penny's relieved to be quiet again. She can't wait to phone Sylvie to tell her about the latest development, but only gets her answering message. Of course, she remembers, she'll be at the Tea Dance. *I'll phone her later.* And after supper she eventually speaks to Sylvie who's delighted to hear the news.

"Dowsing? I've heard of people dowsing for water and oil... stuff like that.... but I didn't know it could be so simple!"

"I was gob-smacked! Seemed to get the knack of it straight away. Who knew you could just ask for a *Yes* or *No*? Peter said I'm a natural. I don't know! Then I started to recognise names on the map... mountains I've climbed... towns and villages... and there it was... Blaenau... I know it's my home."

"Amazing! So your journey continues... I do hope all goes according to plan."

"I can actually see the front door of my house in my mind. I keep trying to envision going through the door, but that's eluded me so far." She pauses as something crosses her mind. "I don't have the key, do I?"

"Oh no! A neighbour might have one… or you'll find one under the mat. There may be someone there! You'll have to cross that bridge when you come to it."

"Always something else to work out. I'm sure it will."

"It sounds as if you're getting to the end of your journey, Penny. You must be excited…"

"I daren't get too excited or I'll burst. Who knows what I'll find?"

"Good luck dear, Penny. You're having such an interesting journey."

"Sure am! I'm so glad I came here. Grace's family have been so marvellous. They've helped me so much. Mary's amazing… and I've learned so much… in just one week!"

"In what way?" Sylvie asks.

"Learning about myself… through the Tarot… and dreams… Samhain. You wouldn't believe!"

"Tell me all about it when we meet up again. I'll be coming to visit you when everything's worked out. Keep in touch… can't wait to hear how you get on."

"Can you tell Kay for me, please? I'm talked out!"

"I always keep her up to date. When you get to Wales, let's Skype… OK?"

* * *

Saying goodnight to Mary and Joe, Grace and Dylan, her heart is bursting.

"I can't thank you all enough for all you've done for me. I'll never forget you."

"We won't let you!"

227

"Goodnight Penny"

"Sweet dreams"

"Don't let the bedbugs bite." They're all smiles.

Lying in bed, Penny reflects on her disappointment that she's had no more messages about Julian since she heard his voice. She falls asleep with disturbing thoughts of what might have happened to him, mixed with the anticipation of going home and wondering what she'll find there that she still can't remember.

Chapter 29

Week 4: Day 7. Monday… The Journey Home

She's up early, showered, dressed and packing her things, ready for the journey. Downstairs, she finds Mary ready to begin Tai Chi in the hall. The weather's turned and the rain that's been pouring down through the night has become a light drizzle.

"Good morning to you… I'm glad you're joining me again."

Penny relishes the movements of her body as she stretches and relaxes through the gentle sequence, taking deep breaths.

When they've finished and are ready for coffee in the kitchen, she mentions to Mary that she's not yet finished reading the book.

"It's yours… and the pack of cards. And when you're ready for the next one, I'll send it to you."

"Thank you so much! I'm really enjoying the story… and the cards are fascinating."

"I'm very glad. Always happy to know our efforts are appreciated…," as she pours coffee.

"How are you feeling? Ready for the next chapter of your journey?"

"Yes… excited… and nervous, I suppose. I'm all packed up and ready to go anyway!"

"Well, Peter will be happy. He wants to get off early. I think this is early enough! But you must have some breakfast. Scrambled eggs?"

"Oh… that would be lovely thanks."

"I think that's Peter." Mary looks into the hall. "Ready for breakfast Peter? How was your night?"

"Good, thanks. Is that scrambled eggs?" as he sits at the table. "Many thanks Mary… just the ticket. How are you feeling, Penny? Ready for a new adventure?"

Penny grins. "Ready for anything. Can't wait!"

By the time they've finished breakfast the others are coming downstairs, and Penny takes herself up to her room to finish preparations for her departure.

"I'll bring your bag down when you're ready," Dylan calls from the hall.

"Any minute now… thanks…" She takes a last look round to make sure she hasn't missed anything before she's ready to take leave of this family who've made her so welcome in their home.

They all congregate in the hall as Dylan takes her bag to Peter's campervan.

"Dear Penny… you've come a long way and we wish you all the very best for the next leg of your journey." Mary gives her a long affectionate hug before Joe takes her hand.

"You know, whatever happens, you're always welcome here, my dear…" and gives her a big bear hug.

Grace hugs her more gently. "All best wishes, Penny… can't wait to hear how you get on! And Dylan will take care of you."

Then she's sat in the front seat between Dylan and Peter who is in the driver's seat. She turns to see them waving from the front door as they turn a corner, onto the road leading home.

As they join the traffic on the A5 Dylan remarks to Peter "Not taking the motorway then?"

"No... I like the back roads better... don't like driving too fast."

"Oh good," Penny agrees. "I prefer to take the back roads when I have plenty of time."

"Where would you have been coming from?" Dylan wonders if her memory might suddenly kick in.

"I don't know... London, perhaps. I must have some connection there or why would I have been there?"

"Good point! But no memories, Penny?"

"Not yet. Only this road... I know it so well. I'm recognising it as we go along, but I couldn't tell you what's coming." She sighs. "It's like watching an old film that I've not seen for a very long time. I know I've seen it as it unfolds, but couldn't tell you what's coming next."

Their progress is slow and steady along the old A road, passing the odd village, but mostly out in the country with little traffic.

"The stagecoach would have travelled this road." Penny muses. "But it wouldn't have been such smooth riding in those days, until Thomas Telford improved it all the way to Holyhead as a route to Ireland."

"You're interested in history?" Peter asks.

"Oh yes... I think it's my passion!" She's surprised herself. "That's another memory!"

"Well done...tell us about it." Dylan encourages her. "What do you know about history?"

"Oh, the usual stuff... Ancient Britons... When the Romans came... Battle of Hastings. I used to tell those stories to my grandchildren...," she stops, suddenly aware of what she just said, holding her breath for fear the memory will just as easily disappear.

"I don't believe it!" Peter laughs. "What's coming back to you?"

"I had no idea what I was saying then... but now I remember how

I'd write out simple history stories for Neil and Lisa to read when I wasn't there… and I drew funny pictures to go with them. Neil and Lisa… they're Becky's children. Oh my… I do remember!" Reliving the memory to secure it in her mind although she's a little disappointed that she can recall no more.

She's elated at having recalled Becky's children. Neil and Lisa… in this memory, Neil would be about 7 or 8 and Lisa probably 9 to 10… but she thinks that this memory is probably not up to date. They're most likely adults by now. And what about Carrie? Does she have children too? It's so frustrating… like putting a jigsaw together without a picture… and so many pieces missing! She gasps… a sudden memory of Jigsaws with Frankie… Carrie's son. All he wanted to do when he was very young was do Jigsaws!

"I remember…," she says wonderingly, and tells them what she's just recalled.

"All coming back to you then? Brilliant!" Dylan's happy for her, wondering what it will take to recover all of her lost memories.

* * *

Peter stays on the A5, resolutely avoiding the motorway, until they stop for a lunch break at a Garden centre near Shrewsbury where there's a café. Penny's just grateful there are toilets where she doesn't have to queue. The café is busy but the service brisk and they order soup and sandwiches, which appear almost immediately.

Back on the road, the sun breaks through the clouds as they reach the Welsh border, and they all cheer. "Nearly there." Peter grins. "Except it's still a way to go. We'll be stopping at my friend's near Llangollen tonight. They have a B&B so everything's laid on. I'll cover that and no arguing…," he announces, to expressions of grateful thanks from both of them. "He's a mate."

The journey through the Welsh countryside is glorious; the sun shining through trees still clothed in brilliant autumn colours. They pass through Llangollen, after which Peter turns off down a narrow road for what seems like a long way, though he does have to slow or stop now and then to allow oncoming cars to pass, before finally turning up a track to an isolated farmhouse. The sun has been slowly descending and the air is cool as they make their way to the front door, where a middle-aged couple appear to welcome them.

"Sue and Rob... I've brought friends...," as he introduces them.

"Welcome to our humble abode... come in... come in!" and they're shown into a large, warm kitchen where a little old lady sits in a rocking chair by the wood stove.

"My Nan...," Sue says. "That's her name too. Nan, we have visitors..," as she turns to see them.

"Are they all back yet?" she asks anxiously. "Yes, dear... all back safe and sound." Sue assures her.

Tea and cake are offered round as Sue and Rob ply them with questions.

Penny tries to answer through a mouthful of delicious cake and nearly chokes.

"It's alright... we'll talk later." Sue laughs. "Are you alright?" Penny recovers gradually and nods as she wipes her eyes, leaving Peter and Dylan to explain the sequence of events leading up to helping her find her home.

"Not too far to Blaenau from here. I hope you find your home alright." Rob smiles at Penny.

Sue takes Penny up to a small bedroom. "Make yourself comfortable, dear. Supper won't be long. I expect you'd like to freshen up after travelling all day."

* * *

Penny goes to the small window to see a rolling landscape bathed in the rosy glow of the setting sun. "Red sky at night...," she observes. *Should be a nice day tomorrow.* Then having made use of the bathroom, she goes down to find the others in the sitting room.

"Red or white?" Rob's offering her a choice of wines.

"Red for me... thank you. Are we celebrating?"

"We always celebrate with visitors... especially when Peter brings friends."

Before long, Sue calls them into the kitchen for supper; a large casserole of beans and vegetables with baked potatoes. Sue helps Nan to sit at the table, where she looks around and smiles.

"Are they all back?" she murmurs.

Penny looks enquiringly at Sue.

"She always asks that... don't know why... she's not quite with it these days. I only have to reassure her. She's getting on... ninety-five next birthday."

Penny smiles at Nan, who's tucking into her small portion with tiny spoonfuls. As she starts to eat, she thinks she hears a low drone, which slowly increases in volume... and unexpectedly her heart lurches... *as the sound rapidly becomes the throbbing deafening roar of an engine filling her mind... and she watches the huge bulk of an aircraft descend through low cloud towards her... a Wellington Bomber coming in to land.* Then just as quickly the sound and vision fade and she's still sat at the table with everyone else enjoying supper.

She resumes eating determinedly, willing herself to stay present and glad that no-one has noticed anything untoward. They're all too busy savouring their food with exclamations of appreciation to the cook. Finishing with deliciously flaky apple pie and custard, they're instructed to retire to the sitting room while Rob clears away and Sue helps Nan to her bedroom, which is on the ground floor.

Rob and Sue soon join them, ready for another glass of wine. "Nan's been here longer than we have...," Sue explains. "I inherited this place from my mother who ran the B&B for some years. She'd been looking after Nan, her mother, since she was in her eighties, when she wasn't coping very well. She's a marvellous woman... just a bit of dementia, that's all. No trouble."

"She's not Welsh though?" Penny's curious.

"Oh no... comes from a little village near Lincoln originally. A real country girl. She was very intelligent... got a good job after the war in London before she married and had my Mam. When my Mam married they moved to Birmingham, where I was born, long before they retired here. Then when my Dad died, Mam brought Nan here to look after her."

"Do you know what she did in the War?"

"Nan? She was in the WAAF... there are pictures of her in uniform. She used to tell us she was a plane plotter... in the OPS room at a big bomber airfield not far from her home. Scampton, it was, where the Dambusters took off from. I expect you saw the film?" Penny nods. She knows the story well.

Penny remembers. "Funnily enough, my Dad was at Scampton for a while... not in the Dambusters, I'm glad to say. The Blitz was hitting the cities and we lived in Salford, so Mum took us to stay anywhere near where Dad was stationed; always in the countryside. I loved it. That was a big part of my childhood. We got digs in a little village... very rural... I was only about three, I think... but the name is there somewhere... " She pauses for a moment. "Saxilby."

"No? That's Nan's village... well, it's a small world. You could have been staying with a relation! It was a very small village."

The others are listening to their conversation in amazement.

"Where did that come from?" Dylan asks Penny.

"My childhood memories are so vivid. I think it must have been the heightened emotions of wartime that imprinted them on my mind."

Penny wonders if she should tell them about her brief vision. She continues.

"You know why she asks '*Are they all back yet?*'"

Sue's hand flies to her mouth as she holds her breath… "You mean..? Waiting for all the planes to come back?" Penny nods.

"I'll bet there was someone she was especially anxious to see come back… or I could be imagining that."

"Like an old movie!" Rob laughs.

"Right, Penny… are you going to tell us how you know?" Dylan asks knowingly.

"Yes… I did see a vision… very briefly… just a bomber coming in to land. I had to stop it before it got too emotional… and we'd just started eating."

"Yes, of course… Mam and Dad met at that time… he was in the RAF… in bombers. Well, I never… I mean… it never occurred to me!"

"Does this happen often?" Rob wants to know looking at Penny.

"It's been happening quite often… I found it very confusing to begin with. Don't know if it's something to do with my loss of memory… these psychic impressions… they're always very emotional. I seem to tune into an emotional connection that's already there between someone who's here and one who's in the spirit world. I don't even know if it's a new thing or something I've always had."

"Nan does become quite emotional at times… asking me over and over… sometimes it's '*Who's missing?*' and I have to pacify her with a cake or something. Is there anything else I could do, Penny?"

Penny thinks for a few moments. "From what I've experienced, I think her memories are so insistent they just need to be acknowledged. Perhaps ask her '*Who do you want to come back*' or '*Who are you waiting for?*' Then let her talk. And whatever she says, repeat back to her, word for word, in the same tone of voice so she'll know she's been heard. That's important. I think maybe she's never been able to talk about it before. You know, after the war people wanted to get on with their lives and not live in the past, so generally it was never talked about. I'd love to hear how you get on anyway. These psychological issues are so fascinating."

Sue's quick to agree. "I'll do that... and you know you're always welcome to come back. Now we've made that connection... friends for life...," as she takes Penny's hand and gives it a squeeze.

They all want to hear more and the conversation becomes quite metaphysical though Penny can't stop herself yawning, not that the talk is exhausting her, but she's getting really sleepy and is glad to make her excuses to go to bed.

Chapter 30

⚜

Week 5: Day 1. Tuesday… Blaenau

The pale sun slowly rises through mist and the fields shimmer in a gossamer haze as far as Penny can see when looking through her window. *Something to do with spiders' webs*, she seems to recall. Before going downstairs, she takes the Tarot pack from her bag and asking… *What do I need to know today?* selects one card; the Nine of Pentacles. She reads… Success, completion of a task. *Lovely… thank you very much…* she murmurs and goes down happily to find Sue busy in the kitchen.

"Good morning, Penny. Looks like it's going to be a lovely day. Did you sleep well?"

"Great, thank you… slept like a log… I was so comfortable." She moves towards the back door. "I'll see what it's like…," and goes out onto the paved terrace to stretch her limbs and take deep breaths in the cool morning air. *I love Wales*, she thinks to herself… *so fresh, and it doesn't always rain!*

Sue has prepared a hearty breakfast and before long they're ready to depart.

"How's Nan this morning?" Penny enquires of Sue, who smiles.

"She's very slow in the morning... not awake yet. I've been thinking about what you said and I'll do what you suggest when she starts asking. I'd love to set her mind at rest. She deserves it."

Penny nods. "I'll put your phone number on my phone, so we can talk if that's alright."

"Yes... let's do that. I'll get my phone. We must keep in touch." They busy themselves exchanging phone numbers.

"I think you're amazing, Penny. I don't know what I'd have done in your situation!"

"What me? I'm just an ordinary woman... and if it hadn't been for the kindness of strangers... well, I don't know where I'd be now. I've made so many good friends... and I'm so grateful." She feels the warm affection in Sue's lengthy hug.

"All set... bags in the van... let's go!" Peter's waiting at the front door.

* * *

As they drive away down the hill Penny looks back at the old stone house, Sue and Rob waving them goodbye. "The kindness of strangers...," she muses.

"What's that?" Peter asks.

"I've been relying on the kindness of strangers ever since I lost my memory. But I don't feel that any of you are strangers... more like meeting old friends." She laughs. "You've not been having me on, have you?"

"You got it, Penny! We've just been humouring you... haven't we, Peter?" Dylan grins. "But I know what you mean... as if we recognise each other from previous lives..." He continues... "like we got on so well after just meeting in the park. I've read somewhere that we go through incarnations with the same souls... and we recognise our clan whenever we meet. I like that idea."

"I'd like to believe that." Peter joins in. "It would explain things that have happened to me too. I knew I'd marry Deirdre as soon as we met. I just knew we had to be together... and she felt the same."

"What happened?" Penny asks, though Mary had told her a little.

"We'd only been married a couple of years when she began to be ill... then she was diagnosed with MS... not too bad to manage at first, but it went on for another twelve years before she died. She was only forty-one." Peter sighs. "But some of our happiest times were then. Eventually I gave up work, except for writing, so I could take care of her... and we'd go exploring in the camper. She loved that. I have the very best memories of that time."

"How could you bear it?" Dylan asks.

"Love! That's all... that's everything." They fall silent, trying to imagine the kind of love that could endure such a tragedy.

"Maybe when people talk about meeting again in the afterlife, it's really about reincarnation," Dylan suggests and they all agree, as if they know.

"But is there any real proof of past lives?" Penny wonders.

"I've read about past life memories...," Dylan replies. "And accounts of young children who apparently remember their past life. Some of them are really dramatic... they talk about their *other mummy and daddy*... and some recall names and places. One boy I read about had a strange birthmark on his head, which he told them was where he'd been shot and killed and he named the village... so they went to visit and found it was true... allegedly."

"Stranger than fiction." Penny murmured.

"Could have been made up by his family of course." Peter's sceptical.

"Don't spoil the story... I like it," Dylan retorts laughing.

By now they've reached the A5 again; the stagecoach road built in the early 19th Century in the race to reach the coast and secure a route to Ireland, running straight across North Wales after diverting from the old Roman Watling Street leading to Chester.

Eventually, a rise reveals a distant vista of mountains. "Snowdonia!" Peter points out. This road is as familiar to Penny as the lines on her hand. She knows she's travelled it many times before and her excitement mounts as it doesn't maintain its straight course, but narrows into twists and bends between banks of trees and tumbling river. The vision she'd seen in her dream of going home… towards the mountains.

An impressive view across trees and hills brings them to a stop in a convenient lay-by. "That's the valley we turn up to get to Blaenau," Peter points out. "Very soon now."

Going home… she tells herself. *Whatever that will hold.*

The road through the Lledr valley rises slowly through verdant landscape dotted by an occasional house, following a winding river to a small village, after which, it starts to rise more steeply into the hills. The campervan slows on the long hill up to the Crimea Pass, unable to move out of low gear as more high-powered cars pass them by.

"Snowdon to our right…," Peter points out. Penny knows that, hardly able to contain her emotions.

"This is where the *wild men of Gwynedd* used to lay in wait to rob unwary travellers…," she informs them. "There used to be an Inn here I believe…," she points to a lay-by as they pass, gaining speed at last before cresting the Pass and slowly descending the steep hill between slate hills gleaming in the sunlight. Memories come flooding back; of moving to this town that roofed the world, she recalls, a place known as the wettest place in Wales, due to its high mountain location. The place where she'd found peace and security after years of upheaval. *How could I forget?* she wonders.

As they approach the town Peter asks if she'll recognise the way to her house.

"I think so… still a bit hazy. Turn right here… we need to follow the railway." Sure enough, they soon cross railway lines and proceed along a small road with rows of terraced cottages along one side opposite a steep hillside.

"This is it!" Penny exclaims… "Right here…," and Peter pulls into a parking space.

Penny leads the way through a small gate up a shared path between two long front gardens. She opens another gate to arrive at the front door… number 3… as she'd remembered. *Home at last,* she breathes.

"I don't think I ever left a key under the mat," Penny says, but they begin a search for the key anyway; under the mat, plant pots, or anywhere they can think of, but with no success.

"I'll try next door… Sian…," she remembers. "I'll see if she's in." She goes to the house next to hers, but there's no answer to her knocking. There are no people about as far as they can see.

"Can we get round the back?" Peter asks.

"Yes… but I always leave the back gate securely bolted." Penny's memory is rapidly returning.

"Worth a try…," Dylan says.

They have to walk to the far end of the terrace to access a rough back road where most of the houses have a garage door and back gate set into a high wall all the way along. They find the back of her house where bins outside have a large number 3 painted on them. The solid gate doesn't budge.

"I can climb over." Dylan volunteers. "No problem." It looks impossible to Penny but he's soon shinning up the wall and over the top, where he unbolts the gate to let them into a small back yard. The back door is half glazed and she peers into her kitchen, which looks just as she'd left it. Dylan and Peter, who've been searching unsuccessfully for a key, join her at the door which is securely locked.

"We could break the glass…," Dylan suggests.

"But we still couldn't open the door. I think we need a locksmith," Peter replies.

"There's a hardware shop in town…," Penny recalls. "They'd know one, I'm sure." She thinks that maybe in town she'll see someone who knows her, though she's not sure how she might just bump into someone.

They drive onto the high street where Penny points out a shop near parking spaces on the road then they enter the hardware store, where Peter explains their need for a locksmith.

Penny vaguely recognises the woman at the counter, who replies. "I'm so sorry… Eifion's not here at the moment but there is someone in Porthmadog. I'll get you his number." She hands them a small business card.

"Many thanks." Peter's ringing the number as they leave the shop. "No answer," he says as he leaves a message.

As they walk into the centre of town, Penny leads them to a small Café.

"I could do with a coffee anyway…," she remarks as they go to the counter, but the man who takes their order doesn't look familiar and shows no sign of recognising her either. As they sit and look around, she searches her mind for the name of the woman she knows who runs the place, so when their coffee is brought to the table she enquires… "Who is it that's usually here? I can't remember her name."

"You mean Gaynor? She's away for a few days. Sorry."

There are a few other customers sitting at tables, but no-one she recognises. "Of course… this is where people come from the train…," she says, and sure enough, they soon gather up their coats and bags to return to the station and their return trip to Porthmadog.

Penny's disappointed, but thinks there must be other places where she'll recognise someone, surely! They leave the Café, hoping to find someone who'll know her and decide to try all the shops, but leave them frustrated.

After nearly an hour of walking all the way up one side of the high street and back along the other, Penny's wondering what to do next, when a woman passing by stops. "Hi Peggy… haven't seen you for a while. Thought you might have moved without saying anything!" Penny gazes at her in confusion. This woman knows her… she searches her mind for a name… *how can she not remember?*

"I'm so sorry… I had an accident and my memory's not so good."

As Peter and Dylan catch up, she introduces them."These are friends who're helping me get back home."

"Oh, you poor thing. I'm Diana… with the dogs… remember?"

"Yes, you do look familiar now… I feel so stupid. What did you call me? Peggy?" So Sylvie had been right about that.

"Yes… Peggy Vaughan! We used to be in the Art class together."

Peggy Vaughan… yes… that's her name! Memories of a room full of budding artists come flooding back now… and recognition dawns.

"Yes, of course. Diana… do you know anyone who knows me well? I can't get home as I don't have a key. My bag was stolen… with my phone and everything!"

"Oh dear… I'm not sure. Maybe Isabelle? I might have her number… " She rummages in her bag, looking for her phone. "I thought you were best mates! Don't you remember where she lives?"

Isabelle, she thinks… that rings a bell. She's shocked that after all she has recalled, she doesn't remember any friends. *What kind of person am I… she wonders… to not remember my friends?*

She shakes her head. "Some things I remember… but not others. It's a miracle that I've found my way back here… it's only taken a month!"

"Oh goodness… you really have lost your memory! Sorry, I can't find her number. How can I help? Stay here… I'm just going to the

Co-op... be back in a jiffy. Then come home with me and we'll get you sorted. Don't move! Or go into the bookshop. I'm sure you'll remember Eirian. She'll know you."

They take her advice, where Peter and Dylan wander happily among corridors of dusty bookshelves, crammed with old books. The woman at the counter is busy on the phone, and when she's finished she looks up. "How are you Peggy? Haven't seen you in a while."

A sudden flash of recognition confirms a blurred memory. This is where she would find books to add to her library. "Eirian...," she responds, though she wonders if she'd have recalled her name if Diana hadn't reminded her. "I have a problem...," and she goes on to explain her predicament.

"Oh Peggy... what a thing to happen!" she commiserates in her lilting Welsh voice. "I don't know how I can help. Does Isabelle know? I'm sure she can help if anyone can." *Isabelle again...*

"I don't even remember where she lives..."

"Oh my dear! Hang on... I'll give her a ring."

Penny... or Peggy, as she now knows is her actual name, finds she's holding her breath... and breathes out again as Eirian speaks into the phone. "Isabelle... Eirian here at the bookshop. I have Peggy here and she needs help. Would you by any chance have a key to her house, or know where to find one? Hope you're back soon. Bye."

"She must be out somewhere, there's no signal... or her battery's dead." She looks at the deflated Penny. "Come and sit down. What are we going to do with you now?"

"Well, I just saw Diana and she's going to take us back to her house while we sort this out. She'll be back from the Co-op shortly."

"Have you tried your neighbours?" Eirian asks. "One of them might have a key."

"Yes, I've been there... but nobody's in at the moment. The trouble is, I'm not remembering names and my phone's gone, along with all my contacts." She's feeling sorry for herself again... desperately trying to unlock some memory... anything at all... but her mind is in a worse fog than ever.

Ask the spirits... a thought comes to her, or is it a voice? *Yes... I'm asking the spirits... my guide... or anyone who loves me... please help!* She's trying too hard and nothing comes to help in her hour of need. *Where are my spirits when I need them?*

Diana enters with a bag of shopping. "Hello Eirian... has Peggy been telling you?"

"Yes... I've tried to phone Isabelle, but she's not answering. Can't think of anyone else... can you?" Eirian turns to Penny. "Can't you get hold of your daughter?"

Penny sighs. "That's another thing I can't remember without my phone. No numbers... nothing!"

"But you remember where she lives? It's not too far away. Betws-y-Coed, I seem to remember."

Penny shakes her head. "It's all gone... all the pieces of memory that could help. I just don't know what to do next."

Peter joins them. "We could go back to your house and wait for some neighbour to come back for lunch. There must be someone around by now." Penny nods.

"Yes... we'll just have to wait." Dylan's torn himself away from the bookshelves.

"Can you give me Isabelle's number please, so I can put it in my phone. This is a new one." Her hands are shaking as she keys the number into her phone under *Isabelle*.

"Where does she live?"

"Up at the top of town... you really don't remember?"

Eirian shakes her head in disbelief. "I'll have to draw you a map then." She takes a piece of paper to draw a simple diagram of the high street leading up towards the slate mines and places a cross on one side of the road. "The house is called *Meirionfa*."

She gives it to Penny who thanks her gratefully. "I'd better take your number too if that's alright."

"Of course." She tells her the number and Penny enters it under '*Eirian Bookshop*'.

"Do let me know how you get on, won't you? Or I shan't sleep tonight for worrying!"

"I'm sure everything will fall into place soon... please don't worry." Penny manages a weak smile.

"I hope you're soon back in your own home... I can't imagine being in such a predicament. What will you do if you can't get in?"

"We'll find somewhere for the night." Peter assures her. "There must be a B&B somewhere nearby and I'll sleep in my van with Dylan, if you like?" He turns to Dylan, who nods.

"Well, I can help you there. There's a lovely B&B and café right by the station. They'll have plenty of rooms now the season's over. Beth Thomas runs it... I'm sure you know her Peggy! Just call in. Something else you don't remember?"

Penny shakes her head. "Not yet! But memories are coming back... very slowly."

Diana touches Penny arm. "You're welcome to come back with me for a bit of lunch."

"Thank you so much... but I'm not sure. We can get a sandwich to eat in the camper while we watch the house, I think." Peter and Dylan agree. "We do need to find a neighbour."

"If there's anything else I can do... take my phone number too." Diana makes sure she gets it into Penny's contacts.

"You're both so kind..." Penny smiles at them, happy she's beginning to remember. *The kindness of strangers... who are also forgotten friends...* she thinks to herself.

"Take care," Diana tells her as they begin to leave.

"Come in tomorrow… let me know what's happening," Eirian calls after them.

* * *

Before they get back in the Camper, they buy freshly made sandwiches from a little shop near the station. Penny tells them about the narrow-gauge railway and steam trains that run down to the coast, a lovely journey through the hills that's a popular tourist attraction. "Of course, it was originally the way to get slate down to ships that took it all over the world… a huge operation." There's no problem with her memory as far as that's concerned.

Peter nods. He knows North Wales very well, but Dylan hasn't been here before and is very interested.

They park again in the space opposite the cottage, that Penny calls home. Seated in the main part of the van they eat their sandwiches. Peter puts a kettle on to boil. "Coffee, Herbal or ordinary tea?" he asks. "Don't have any milk though."

"Herbal, please." Penny's decided she doesn't like tea much anyway, unless it's brewed properly in a teapot from tea leaves and served in a china teacup.

They're constantly on the watch for any cars pulling up or people walking by, but there's been no sign of any neighbours. Penny notices the time is coming up to two o'clock and decides to start knocking on doors again, in case she'd not been heard before. This time she decides to start at one end of the terrace and systematically work her way to the other end. At Number 1 there's no answer and she remembers it belongs to an old lady who she's never seen, but who has regular visits from the district nurse. She waits again at Number 2, but there's no sound from inside. Now she remembers that Sian has family in Australia and had talked about going to visit. Maybe that's where she is. Number 4 has a *For Sale* notice outside and is obviously empty, but Number 5 is smart and the garden immaculate. She has a brief recollection of a middle-aged couple, but can't remember any names, though she's sure she knows them and thinks they're probably out at work.

At Number 6 the young woman who comes to the door greets her. "Hello Peggy... people have been looking for you!"

"Really? Do you know who?" Penny's getting excited.

"Your daughter came yesterday... and a man was asking if I know where you are. He seemed quite anxious to find you. He was going to put a note through your door. Didn't you find it?"

Penny wonders who the man might be, and her heart skips a beat. But Carrie's been looking for her.

"Well, the trouble is, I can't get in. I don't have the key... and I'm trying to find someone who might have one. I don't suppose you have a contact number for my daughter? My phone was stolen with all my contact numbers... and I have no memory for numbers. We're trying to get a locksmith... but there's no answer yet."

"Can't help you there I'm afraid. Poor you... what will you do?"

"Good question! I wonder if the police might help. Maybe they could break in for me. But I don't have any identification with me."

"I'll bet Gary could... he used to be in the Police...but he won't be home till at least 5 o'clock."

Penny laughs with excitement. "Really? I'd be so grateful. It looks like I'll be staying at a B&B tonight unless I can get in... please ask him for me. I'll be back later when he's got home."

She climbs into the relative warmth of the camper, where Peter's still trying the number for the locksmith. "Probably on holiday or something. So you think Gary could break in? Is he a burglar?"

"Used to be in the Police apparently. I don't really know him except to say *hello.*"

249

"My daughter lives in Betws, but she'll be at work right now." *Of course, Carrie lives in Betws! And Becky lives in Llandudno!* How could she forget? Her memory is still clouded, though information is slowly coming to her out of the fog of her mind. "I'm sure I could find her house if I went there."

Actually, she's not so sure and nothing further is coming to her. "Maybe we could try that if Gary can't open the door?" she suggests and Peter agrees.

"Yes... we'll do that if Gary can't help."

"Right...," says Dylan. "If there's nothing more we can do, is there a nice local walk Penny? I think we need a bit of exercise."

She leads them up the road a little way to a lane and they cross the railway over an old iron bridge into an area where crushed slate paths lead through a small woodland. "This used to be where slate was loaded onto wagons on railway tracks... where these paths are now... ready to be taken down to the coast." Peggy explains.

"You know your history, Penny! Or should we call you *Peggy* now?" Dylan looks at her.

"I don't know... I'm still trying to get used to Peggy, though it sounds more familiar the more I think of it. But I suppose I'll always be Penny to you and everyone I've got to know since I lost my memory... and that's alright."

"Oh good... I was hoping you'd say that. Name changes are so confusing!" Dylan laughs.

They hear footsteps coming up from behind and turn to see a tall figure walking briskly towards them. Peggy realises it's a woman as she draws nearer. She looks familiar.

"Isabelle?" she cries out. The woman stops to look at them before she comes nearer. Peggy moves towards her. Of course, she knows Isabelle... her very good friend... poet and author... met at a writer's workshop.

"Oh Peggy... there you are... I've been wondering where you'd got to...," and they hug. "Home at last... did you have a good time?"

"You wouldn't believe! Am I glad to see you! I got your number from Eirian at the bookshop, but you weren't answering. But first... do you have a key to my house?" Penny asks anxiously, though she doesn't think she's ever been in the habit of giving other people her keys.

"No, I don't. Why?"

"Had my bag stolen... keys... phone... everything. I can't get in. Waiting for a locksmith to break in, hopefully." She's getting tired of having to explain to everyone. She introduces Peter and Dylan.

"My new friends... they've been helping me get home... because I lost my memory."

"What? Lost your memory? How on earth?" Isabelle is full of questions.

"It's a long story, which will have to wait. Do you have Carrie's phone number? Or Becky's?" She thinks it's a long shot but asks anyway.

"I doubt it. What about the gift shop? Where Carrie works?" She looks at her quizzically.

"What?" A vague image of a shop full of beautiful things appears through the mist of her mind. "In Betws?" she queries.

Isabelle nods. "You really lost your memory? Come back with me and tell me all about it my dear and we'll phone the gift shop. I left it charging when I came out. All of you... tea and cake?"

"Thank you... that would be lovely." They all accept the invitation and Isabelle leads the way.

"Have you seen Sam yet? He'll be worried about you." Penny's heart lurches. Is this the man who's been looking for her? She doesn't want to admit she doesn't remember him, though maybe she does. *What about that loving feeling? The touch of a man's hand on hers?*

"My neighbour says a man's been round looking for me."

"That'll be him! I don't have his number though. You haven't introduced me yet!"

"You probably know more about me than I do at the moment. I've been trying to bring back the last fifty years and it's crazy!"

"Sounds like the plot of a novel. Can't wait to hear all about it!"

"I'm worried about Julian… do you know my son?"

"No… but I've heard all about him from you. In Vietnam teaching English, I believe."

"Oh yes… it's coming back to me now. It's funny how I don't remember anything until it's being revealed… then it all comes flooding back." She decides not to go into hearing his voice… it's all too complicated and she'll have to tell Isabelle the whole story from the beginning to make any sense.

"It's like starting to read a book before realising I've read it before… but I have to go on reading to remember what happens… if you know what I mean!" she explains.

"Yes I do… I'm the same… with films too!" They both laugh at the capriciousness of memory.

They've reached the main road and a little way along Isabelle indicates a stone cottage set back from the road. Penny stands and stares at it. "I couldn't remember where you live… but I do now… of course!"

Isabelle puts the kettle on before ringing the gift shop, waiting for someone to reply. "Is that Carrie? Isabelle. I have your mother here… yes, she's just turned up. Hang on…" She gives the phone to Penny, who's waiting nervously.

"Darling… I'm fine… really… I couldn't contact you. I can't get into the house… lost my key… I'll explain later… I've so much to tell you… you won't believe what's been happening. Can you? When you've closed the shop… that's fine. At Isabelle's. See you in an hour… love you Carrie. Don't forget the key…"

"She can't leave the shop until 4.30 pm then she'll come straight here."

She sits down. Suddenly overcome with relief, she accepts a cup of tea. Earl Grey brewed in a pot and served in a china cup and saucer, she notices, drinking it appreciatively. Isabelle's black cat winds around her feet then jumps onto her lap, almost causing her to spill her tea.

"So you know me, don't you, Midnight."

She addresses her friend... "Would you know why I was in London?"

"Yes... you were going to see your Editor before you came back for your Retreat." Now Penny's even more confused. "My Editor?" she queries.

"You write books Peggy. *'All you need to know about...'* History books for youngsters." Isabelle regards her thoughtfully.

"I used to write those for my grandchildren... but are they published?" Penny can't believe it.

"Yes... and they're very successful. I expect it will all come back to you when you see them." She lays her hand on Penny's arm. "Don't worry, my dear... don't rush it. I expect you're in shock. In fact, I think you need something a little stronger than tea." She goes to a cupboard for a bottle and pours a small glass of amber liquid to hand to Penny. "I think I'll join you... though it is a little early! Anyone else?"

"I think a small libation would be in order," Peter acquiesces. "Considering the occasion!"

Isabelle obliges and they all raise their glasses to Penny who bows from her chair and takes a sip, savouring the strong fiery liquid sliding down her throat. "Thank you so much... but I think I need a little water."

Isabelle brings a small jug of water from the kitchen.

Penny gently pushes Midnight off her lap to stand and raise her glass to them. "To my very good friends who've brought me back from oblivion!" They all cheer and drink up.

"I have so much to be thankful for...," she continues. "I was lost and now I'm found... and it's all due to you..." She nods to Peter and Dylan.

"And all the friends I've made along the way... Sylvie and Kay... Dylan and Grace... Mary and Joe... and now Peter..."

He bows to her. "My pleasure, dear lady. You've made my trip to North Wales so very exciting. Not at all what I'd planned... but so much better!"

"It sounds as if you've been having quite an adventure," Isabelle remarks. " Can't wait to hear the whole story. Sounds like it would make a good book!"

"Sorry... you'll have to wait till Carrie's here. Anyway, Dylan's a writer...," Penny explains. "He's been writing about everything as it happened... so he has the copyright!"

"*Penny's Adventures in Wonderland...*" Dylan laughs. "She has been down the rabbit hole!"

"Penny?" Isabelle queries.

"Oh... that's the only name she could come up with... so she'll always be Penny to us."

"You actually forgot your name?" she asks Penny.

"That's right... along with fifty years of memory."

"Oh my god... worse than I realised. How? What happened exactly? How on earth did you find your way home?"

"Only due to the *kindness* of strangers. Trust me... people can be so kind and generous. I can never thank them all enough."

Isabelle raises what's left in her glass, which isn't much. "To the kindness of strangers... who've brought Peggy back home." She drains her glass. "I think I need some more of that! Anyone else?"

"Not me, thanks. I may have to drive." Peter declines.

"I won't say *no*... this is a very special occasion after all." Dylan has no qualms in accepting another small glass and Penny offers hers for a refill.

"I'm feeling better already." She's enjoying the feeling of mild intoxication. *Pleasantly pissed...* she thinks.

Dylan is soon in deep conversation with Isabelle on the topic of writing, while Penny listens, relaxed and half dozing in the warmth of Isabelle's home and her friends' company. Peter's looking through the bookshelves, pulling out an old map of North Wales, which he spreads out on the table to study.

Before long the doorbell rings and Isabelle jumps up to answer it.

"Carrie... come in... come in... Peggy's in here..." She brings Penny's daughter into the room.

"Oh Mum... I was getting worried when you weren't back from your Retreat! How are you? What's been happening to you?" She hugs her mother as she's still sitting there.

"I'm so happy to see you my dear girl... How's Becky? and Julian? I heard him in my dream... is he alright?"

"Yes, he's fine... but he was in an accident, on his motorbike... broke his leg and was in hospital for a few days... but he says he's getting on alright, with his friend to look after him."

"Oh... dear boy... I do worry about him out there. What about Becky?"

"Busy as usual. Gone down to Bristol to discuss a new production. I'll message her that you're home. But what have you been up to? I expected you back last week... but you weren't here!"

Penny can't contain herself... now it all comes flooding back. Becky in the Theatre and Julian in Vietnam!

"Oh Carrie... there's so much to tell you... but that will have to wait. I'd really like to go home... if you have the key?"

"As soon as you're ready." She notices Dylan and Peter. "Hello!"

"Great to meet you at last... I'm Dylan...," as he shakes her hand warmly.

"I'm Peter... ditto...," Peter greets her. "All will be revealed...," he adds, seeing her baffled expression.

"And to think I never knew my mother picks up strange men." Carrie grins. "Are we ready then?"

Penny gets to her feet unsteadily.

"All ready… all three of us…," she indicates the men. "The camper's parked outside the house. But there's nothing in to eat and I'm getting hungry."

"We'll get a takeaway." Peter suggests.

Isabelle nods. "There's a new Indian near the station. I hear they're very good. Anyway, I want to come with you and hear all about it. I'll take Peggy in my car."

"Oh great… love a good Indian." Carrie says as Dylan and Peter get into her car.

Peter takes charge at the Indian Restaurant, ordering lots of dishes and assuring them they do need that much. "My treat…," he insists.

They pull up outside Penny's house and Carrie goes ahead to open the door.

"Home again…," Penny murmurs as she steps into the hallway, deliriously happy to be back. They all follow her into the kitchen where the big bag of food is deposited on the counter and plates found ready to dish up.

"I'll light the fire if that's ok, Penny… " Dylan opens the door of the wood stove.

Penny nods to him. "Thank you… yes, please. It's feeling quite chilly though I did leave the storage heaters on minimum."

"It is almost winter, after all." Carrie agrees.

"Oh… Gary…I must go and tell him he's not needed." Penny rushes to the door. "Won't be a mo."

She's glad she's still wearing her coat as she hurries down the path and up to Number 6 to ring the bell.

Gary comes to the door. "Hi… I believe you're the lady who needs a burglar!"

"No… thank you… my daughter's brought a key and she's just let us in. I do hope your services are not required too often!"

"Any time... but a key is much better. You'd have needed a new lock." He smiles and shuts the door as she retreats down the path. She's almost at her gate when she notices a tall dark figure coming towards her from a parked car, and she hesitates.

"Not so fast young lady..." She knows that husky brown voice as he comes towards her with open arms to embrace her. "Where have you been? I've missed you."

Her heart's pounding as recognition dawns. "Oh Sam...," as she melts gratefully into the warm comfort of his arms... breathing in the familiar smoky smell of his clothes. "I'm home now."

He holds her away from him. "I've been so worried about you. Your phone was dead! Never mind... all in good time."

"I can't tell you now." She indicates the brightly lit window of her house.

"I know... you've got visitors... saw you all come back. I'll not come in now, but I'll be back tomorrow... never fear." He lets her go to return to his car and waves as she watches him drive off. She breathes deeply, as her heightened emotions slowly subside, then approaching her front door notices the small bright glow of a cigarette; Carrie smoking outside as she usually does.

"Happy Mum?" she inquires with a grin. "Didn't know you have a fancy man!"

"So happy... you have no idea! I've never been happier to be home again."

"So am I, Mum... so am I."

They're going inside when she remembers to phone Eirian and Diana to let them know she's safely back home, then joins the others in their Indian feast.

They're all settling down before the roaring fire, waiting expectantly for Penny to be ready.

"Well?" says Carrie… "We can't wait any longer…"

And they listen as she begins, with occasional help from Dylan, the long tale of her journey back home.

She's home and finally all the pieces of the jigsaw fit together and she knows who she is.

* * *

Meanwhile, in London, Sylvie's on the phone to Kay to tell her that Dylan's left a message that Penny's safely home and now knows her name and has met her daughter.

"Oh… Good news!" Kay replies. "And you'll be glad to know I've heard from Mum that she's back from her Writers Retreat."

"Did she say how it went?"

"Only that she was concerned about her friend who didn't turn up and she's worried because her phone's dead…. Her name? Peggy Vaughan. They've been friends for years."

"Peggy Vaughan?" Sylvie's incredulous. "Mum's friend is Peggy Vaughan?"

"Yes, that's right. Why?"

"Only that's our Penny! That's her name… Peggy Vaughan! I'm looking at it now on Dylan's message."

* * *

Epilogue

Week 5: Day 2. Wednesday... Penny - Home

Nestling into the strong warm body beside me, I'm blissfully content. Then drowsily waking to the sound of rain on the window I turn over to find I'm alone in my bed and it takes a few moments to reorient my senses. The clock beside the bed indicates 8.50am. *I'm home again... thank god...* I take a deep breath. A trip to the bathroom clears my head as I recall the events of last night. Oh yes... Carrie and Isabelle left to go to their respective homes... Dylan's slept in the other bedroom and Peter will be in his camper. And Sam... my senses race as memories return.

Yes... I'm in love! Yes... I'm loved! Yes! Yes! Yes! How could I have forgotten Sam?

Going down in my dressing gown I find Dylan and Peter in the kitchen.

"Penny... we didn't want to wake you... you were so tired last night." Dylan greets me.

"Good morning… it was a long day. Yes… I was exhausted," I agree, brewing myself a herbal tea. "What a day! What a night!"

"We'll be off soon." Peter says "Now our mission is accomplished."

"You're not going so soon?" I'm suddenly overcome with sadness at the thought.

"Now you're home, I'm going with Peter to do some exploring," Dylan explains. "Then I can go back with him at the end of the week. You'll be alright now. How's your memory?"

"It's all coming back now… thanks to you! How can I ever repay your help? I'll be so sorry to say goodbye."

"Don't forget we have a book to write. I'll be sending you drafts to check over very soon."

I'm so happy to hear that. I'd almost forgotten about the book.

"You'll be seeing me again, *dear lady*…" Peter always calls me that. "Now I have another excuse to come to North Wales."

"And you must come down to visit us all in the *deep South*," Dylan chuckles. "Anyway, I'll be back with Grace to visit her family on the Lleyn… and my Grandmother's family on their farm… when the weather's better anyway. You've not seen the back of us yet!"

They rise to get their coats and I follow them into the hall.

"Please give all my love to Mary and Joe… and your lovely Grace. They'll always be here in my heart… and you too, dear Dylan." I give him a long affectionate hug. "I was so lucky to meet you. Gosh, that seems so long ago… after all that's happened since."

"Such a great adventure! I'm really looking forward to writing your story… which I will be getting on with as soon as I get back to *Tara*."

I stand at the door to wave them off as they depart in the campervan, sad to see them go.

And now… I'm smiling… my heart overflowing… I hurry upstairs to get ready.

Sam will be here before I know it.

Author's Note

They say that one's first book is usually autobiographical. Well, I can't dispute that, as so many of my experiences have been put to use here. I have to say that I have never been mugged or lost my memory, but the thought did occur to me when I was travelling around the world about twelve years ago as an older woman, what would happen to me if such a thing occurred and the idea developed from there.

I always wanted to be a writer but never did anything I thought would be worth publishing until now. However, it was Covid that gave me the time to take all the ideas I'd been putting down for some time and rewrite from the beginning. From then on, the story began to take on a life of its own and all I had to do was keep up with it. I just loved the journey and couldn't stop writing, so I offer it in the hope that you enjoy it as much as I have.

Patricia Wynne

WITH A LOVE FOR BOOKS

With a large range of imprints, from herbalism, self-sufficiency, physical and mental wellbeing, food, memoirs and many more, Herbary Books is shaped by the passion for writing and bringing innovative ideas close to our readers.

All our authors put their hearts into their books and as publishers we just lend a helping hand to bring their creation to life.

Thank you to our authors and to you, dear reader.

Discover and purchase all our books on
WWW.HERBARYBOOKS.COM

HERBARY BOOKS

Printed in Great Britain
by Amazon

17178509R00155